Tom took me in his arms as the band began playing a slow song and we danced. Laying my head against his chest, listening to his heart beat, I hid my triumphant smile. Finally, something familiar. I was remembering. It turned out to be as simple as being in an accustomed situation, meeting people similar to those I'd interacted with in the past. I knew now that there had been many men in my life, not lovers, but donors. And that Max had often arranged for me to meet them. Here in this club.

With each step of the dance, I inhaled the smell of the man pressed up against me, remembering the sweet touch of blood on my lips, on my tongue, the tingling of my gums with the growth of my fangs.

Soon, I would take this man by the hand and lead him to a quiet room. I would slowly unbutton his shirt and welcome the warmth of his hands on my body. My eyes would meet his and hold him there; slowly and sensuously, my mouth would whisper the words of seduction, then come down on his neck and I would drink my fill . . .

Books in the Vampire Legacy Series by
Karen E. Taylor

BLOOD SECRETS

BITTER BLOOD

BLOOD TIES

BLOOD OF MY BLOOD

THE VAMPIRE VIVIENNE

RESURRECTION

BLOOD RED DAWN

Published by Pinnacle Books

BLOOD RED DAWN

KAREN E. TAYLOR

PINNACLE BOOKS
Kensington Publishing Corp.
http://www.kensingtonbooks.com

PINNACLE BOOKS are published by

Kensington Publishing Corp.
850 Third Avenue
New York, NY 10022

All Kensington Titles, Imprints, and Distributed Lines are
available at special quantity discounts for bulk purchases for
sales promotions, premiums, fund-raising, and educational
or institutional use. Special book excerpts or customized print-
ings can also be created to fit specific needs. For details, write
or phone the office of the Kensington special sales manager:
Kensington Publishing Corp., 850 Third Avenue, New York,
NY 10022, attn: Special Sales Department, Phone: 1-800-221-
2647.

Pinnacle and the P logo Reg. U.S. Pat. & TM Off.

First Pinnacle Books Printing: October 2004

10 9 8 7 6 5 4 3 2 1

Printed in the United States of America

PROLOGUE

Deirdre Griffin: New York City

The surface upon which I lay was smooth and soothingly cool. I rubbed a hand against it; it was leather. My hand dropped further and my eyes began to focus. Black leather, I saw, and supported by chrome.

And I was dressed in different clothes. Instead of the jeans I had been wearing, I had on a black silk nightgown with a plunging neckline and a billowing skirt. Oddly enough, this garment seemed as familiar as the jeans, shirt, and hiking boots. *Perhaps that was the dream,* I thought.

The room was dark but even as that thought crossed my mind, the shadows retreated somewhat, giving me limited vision. A large room, it smelled of new leather and fresh paint.

I sat up on the couch and looked around me at this new place. *It must be a dream,* I thought, *since it seems familiar. And now only dreams are real.*

Feeling more comfortable in that assessment, I relaxed. No matter how terrible the dreams were, I knew they never hurt me upon awakening. I studied the room again. A bar stood in one corner of the room, black and chrome and sparkling. On the bar top, stood a bottle of opened red wine and two clean glasses of delicate crystal.

"Why not?" I said with a quiet laugh. "I am very thirsty."

I rose from the couch on unsteady legs; once standing I discovered that I felt dizzy and slightly nauseous. *Odd*, I thought, *I normally feel well in the dreams*. However, I managed to cross to the bar and pour myself a glass of wine.

The first sip brought tears to my eyes. It was not that the wine tasted bad; on the contrary it was wonderful, sharp and rich. No, the tears had nothing to do with the wine's quality. I cried because I knew I'd drunk this vintage before, in happier times, perhaps, although I could not remember.

Glancing at the empty glass, I wondered for whom it was meant. My head ached and I sighed, turning around with the wine in my hand and leaning my back against the bar. I faced a different view of the room now and saw across from me that there was one door, a heavy wooden one. And deeper in the shadows, back in a dark corner, there was a massive desk, so black it might have been carved of onyx. On the wall next to the desk, seeming horribly out of place in this sea of modern furniture, stood a huge ornate and antique armoire. And behind the desk sat a man, so completely engulfed in shadows that had it not been for the glitter of the eyes that watched me, I might never have seen him.

"So," I said unsteadily, trying to peer through

the shadows to see the face of the man sitting at the desk, "you are Steven DeRouchard."

Attaching the name did me little good. I knew the name, recognized it the same way I knew the difference between my foot and my hand, but the recognition was academic. Cold and emotionless. The name represented a man, no more and no less. He meant nothing to me. Like all the rest of them, he meant nothing.

The voice laughed. "Truly, little one, you have named me. Or have you? The name DeRouchard is, perhaps, unimportant. I like to think of it and the body it represents, as a vessel, or," and he paused, searching, I thought, for a word or perhaps only for dramatic effect, "a bottle, if you will. Its importance, its value does not lie in external trappings. Its true worth can only be determined by that which it holds. The essence of the vessel is all."

"Then I am nothing," I said, following his logic, "since I have no essence."

"Not necessarily, my dear. You have potential. A bottle that is empty can easily be filled."

Suddenly the peaceful feeling I had been enjoying exploded into anger.

"If I am empty, you bastard, it is your doing." I picked up the wine bottle and with all my strength threw it at his head. It came up short and struck the edge of the desk, splashing him with bits of broken glass and wine.

I opened my mouth to speak again, but stopped, dead in the water and drifting. For one second, one very short second, I had a flash of memory. Something about the violence, the tinkling sound of shattered glass, and my anger all blended into the vision of this man and he was . . .

No. The memory vanished, washed away in his laughter. The moment disappeared and was gone.

"There," I said, moving forward a step, "why don't you see if you can fill *that* bottle? Bastard."

He brushed the slivers of glass from his coat. "See? You are not empty, little one, you still have your anger."

"I have held onto my anger. And I have saved it for you. I am glad you are pleased."

"More than pleased, actually." He got up from behind the desk and began to move toward me.

Although I did not want to show my weakness to him, I could not help my reaction. I shrank back into the bar, fearing his approach.

"Why have you done this to me?" I whispered the words as he came closer to me. "What have I done to make you hate me, hate us, so much?"

"Hate?" He stopped about five feet away from me. "This has nothing to do with hate and everything to do with love. I saved your life, Deirdre."

At the mention of that name, I shivered. I had heard his voice say that name, my name I now knew, in dreams and in life.

"How did you save me?"

"If you could remember, you would know. I stopped the attacks on you. I brought you here. And you are alive."

I shook my head. "I do not think I am alive, not here, not in this time and place. I am dreaming, all of this. You have been in my dreams, since . . ."

"Always. I have always been in your dreams. That is where I belong." He moved toward me again and I saw him, clearly, and as if for the first time. His face with its finely sculpted lines, his mouth, his hair, the way he walked—all of it was real. This was no dream. Something deep inside me knew this man.

Only one thing was different, only one detail seemed strange.

He stood in front of me now. Close enough so that I could reach out with a trembling hand and touch the scar that spread from one side of his neck to the other. "DeRouchard," I whispered. "It is the mark."

"Yet still, you've missed my true name. Try again, little one. The memory is there and you must find it if you are to survive. And once you do, I can save you. I alone hold the key; only I can fill you again and make you whole."

He gently grasped my chin in his hand and lifted my head to meet his gaze. I knew his touch. I knew his eyes. Straining for the memory, I stood on the tip of my toes and stared deeply at him.

And then I began to cry.

His arms pulled me into him. "It's been a long road, Deirdre, but now you are back home where you belong. The rest of it is much better forgotten. Now, say my name."

"Steven DeRouchard?"

"No, that is wrong." His mouth came down on mine and he kissed me, causing a thousand memories of him and him alone to stir and rush to the surface.

Oh, dear God. Somewhere deep inside I heard the roar of a caged animal. Somewhere deep inside me a woman was weeping over a lost love, a perfect love. And from somewhere far away I heard a voice, a well-loved voice, say, "Remember me . . ."

Gone. All gone. *I must get them back,* I thought, *the anger and the woman and the memories.*

But all I had left was here and now.

And I said his name.

"Max."

CHAPTER ONE

Mitch Greer: Whitby

"Gone? What the hell do you mean she's gone?"

Maggie looked up at me from where she sat at the kitchen table, her normally pretty eyes reddened and puffy from crying. I hated to see women cry, especially knowing that my next questions would undoubtedly add to her sorrow, but that hatred did nothing to keep me from wanting to strangle her. I sympathized to a degree, knowing that she certainly had enough to weep about without my reaching out and throttling her, so I restrained my instincts and made an effort to lower and soften my voice a bit.

"Where did she go, Maggie?"

She sniffed and shrugged. "Out," she said, "but the dogs went with her. She seemed like she wanted to be alone and said she'd be back in a bit. It's safe now, right?"

"Safe?" I thought for a minute. "Yeah, I suppose

it is, if one can trust that bastard Steven DeRouchard." As soon as I spoke, I realized it was the
wrong thing to say. With the mention of her eldest
son, tears began to stream from her eyes again.
Damn it, I thought, *Deirdre had better be back soon or I
really will strangle this woman.* "How did she seem to
you? Was she acting normally?"

With a visible effort, Maggie pulled herself together. She wiped away her tears and combed back
her black curly hair with her fingers, sitting up
straighter in the kitchen chair. "She seemed as normal as she ever has." Her voice wavered a bit, but she
had finished crying. Throwing me a small smile,
she stood up and stretched, turning on her charm
in a split second as easily and as measurably as throwing a switch. The temperature in the kitchen seemed
to rise a degree or two. "I'm not exactly an expert
on vampires, Mitch. Frankly, you all seem a bit queer
to me." Her voice quivered again, but this time with
repressed laughter. "All of you seem strange—you
and Dot and all the rest." She reached over and laid
her hand on my arm in what I'm sure she meant to
be a comforting gesture. "I'm quite sure she'll be
fine. Give her some time and she'll be back soon."

I relaxed in spite of myself, in spite of the feeling I had in my gut that there was something horribly wrong. Even though normally I would trust
my gut more than I'd trust this woman standing
before me, Maggie had this aura about her, making her irresistible to vampires. Her hand felt warm
against my arm. Something in the scent of her, in
her blood, in her flawless skin and the glow of her
eyes made me want to hold her close to me, protect her from harm. The feeling made no sense. I
knew she wasn't my friend. Not our friend. And I

knew that she'd been instrumental in robbing
Deirdre of her memories. Hadn't she admitted as
much last night? It should have been an easy thing
to reach out and hurt her, make her tell me what I
wanted to know.

I pulled away from her; my hands, clenching and
unclenching, hung useless at my sides. I feared to
touch her, either in anger or in lust. She was a
Breeder, she was poison, and I bloody well knew it.

Maggie flashed me one of her angelic smiles;
she'd won this round. "We'd better open the pub
tonight, don't you think, Mitch?" Her voice sounded
sweet and reasonable. "People will begin to wonder what's going on if we don't."

I nodded. "Sure, we might as well open up." I
started to move out of the kitchen as if on command. I clenched my teeth and forced myself to
turn back to face her. "I'll give her an hour," I said
glancing at the clock, "and then I'm going out
after her."

"An hour." Maggie nodded. "I'm sure that will
be all the time that's needed."

"Needed? For what?"

She laughed. "Why for Dot to get herself together.
Really, Mitch," and she laid that hand on my arm
again. I pulled away. "There's no need to worry."
Again she smiled that angelic smile that made her
seem the most desirable woman alive. Funny that I
could feel that way, but still want to strangle her.
"I'm quite sure she'll be home soon."

At that moment the door to the small bedroom
off the kitchen opened and Chris walked out. *And
here,* I thought, *is another good reason for me not to kill
this woman.* By some bizarre chance or coincidence,
my son was back, reborn through her sexual union

with the DeRouchard bastard who started this whole damned business. Chris's soul had transferred from his dead body into the body of the newborn child through some strange and arcane rite. Even Victor had no idea how that was done.

When I first met Deirdre, I used to say I didn't believe in coincidences, but now I didn't know what to believe. Apparently, when I opened the window to the admission that creatures such as vampires exist, because, yeah, I was one, I also opened the door wide to all sorts of other strange beings, none of whom made any sense whatsoever.

Nevertheless I smiled at my son, for he was my son, there could be no doubt of that fact. And he was Maggie's son as well. It all made for a strange little incestuous-seeming relationship that didn't bear thinking on. My head ached, my heart ached, and the warning in my gut screamed out to be heeded.

"Dad?" Chris nodded in my direction, then in hers. "Mum? I hope everyone slept as well as I did."

Maggie jumped at the sound of his voice and started crying again.

Chris looked over at me. "What's wrong?"

I shook my head and brushed back my hair. "Nothing. And everything. Deirdre's out for a walk, Maggie's crying again, and I'm going out to open the goddamned pub."

Turning my back on the both of them, I stalked into the bar area, flipped on the lights, unlocked the door, and began to clear the glassware from the previous night's celebration. It was hard for me to believe that gathering had taken place less than twelve hours ago. I broke the seal on a new bottle of scotch, put ice into a glass, and filled it to the top.

Calm down, I said to myself, sipping the scotch. *She'll be back soon and everything will be fine.* In spite of the tension from the scene in the kitchen, in spite of the whole situation, I smiled. Stubborn though she was, I loved that woman, more than she'd ever know. *Especially now that most of her memories had been burned away by the poison running in her veins.* My mouth tightened with that thought; I drained my glass and poured another.

The bell on the door clanged and I looked up and nodded at a few of our regulars. They came inside, sat at the bar, and I poured their drinks. One of them glanced around, drained his glass, and pushed it over to me with a nod. "Old Pete back yet?" he asked, "I'd been hopin' after a game of darts."

I smiled and refilled his glass. "I'll play you, Thomas."

The man gave a rough laugh. "Not on your life. Perhaps I should've said that I'd been hopin' after a game of darts I can win. You're too good, man. Dead-Eye Greer, they should call you." He took another long swallow of his stout. "So where's your fine Dot tonight, eh?"

"Out walking, I think. She should be back soon."

One of his friends nodded. "Yeah, I saw her up in t'ruins, I think, now that you mention it. Looking over t'ocean. She's a fearless one, I've always said. There've been some strange sights up there lately. Wolves, they say. To say nothing of the ghosts. I'd not like my woman walking there on her own, there's naught good will come of it. No tellin' who she might meet up there."

I wanted to hit him, but another of the men beat me to it, punching him not too gently on the arm. "Get off it, Jim, what would you know of women?"

"That's true, man."

The bell on the door jangled again and more people entered, tourists this time from the look of them. By the time I'd gotten them settled, more had arrived. It was going to be a busy evening by the look of it so far. As I started washing glasses in the bar sink, I hoped Deirdre would be back soon or that Maggie would get over her tears and come help me out.

As if my thought drew her, Maggie appeared and joined me behind the bar, all traces of sorrow wiped away. She gave me that bloody smile of hers. The tension in my stomach intensified. "Phoenix," she said with a small wink, "isn't feeling well so he won't be out tonight." She moved over next to me and took over the washing of the glasses. Over the sound of the water she whispered, "He thought it might be a good idea to stay hidden for a while, since people are bound to notice his change."

I nodded. The need to keep him hidden hadn't actually occurred to me. I was glad the two of them were thinking. But a thought crossed my mind and I stepped away from the bar and back into the kitchen area.

"Chris," I said, leaning in the door, "since you can't help out at the bar tonight, could you do me a favor?"

"Sure, Dad. What's up?"

"Walk up to the abbey ruins, find Deirdre, and bring her back. I'm still not convinced that it's safe for any of us to be out wandering alone, especially her. She's not in the best of shape these days and neither am I."

He nodded, gave me a small salute that made me smile in remembrance of the boy he was. As I was heading back into the bar, he opened the door to the outside and I heard his sharp intake of breath.

"Dad?" His voice cracked; he sounded frightened and young once again.

"What's wrong?"

"One of the dogs. Curly. Or Larry. I never could tell the two of them apart. He's hurt, I think." Chris bent down and picked up the whimpering dog, carried it into the kitchen and laid it down on the floor. The room flooded with the scent of warm blood and triggered an involuntary hunger response. As I bent over the dog, my fangs grew and Chris drew back from me.

"It's Larry," I said, ignoring Chris's reaction. "Poor little guy. But"—and I gave the dog an encouraging pat—"he's not that bad. It looks worse than it really is. Get me some clean towels and a basin of warm water and we'll see if he'll let me clean him up a bit."

Fortunately the animal trusted me, so I could tend his wounds without fear of him biting me. I'd never asked and had no idea if an animal could become vampiric with a taste of our blood. I didn't think I wanted to find out. The injuries did prove to be minor, shallow gouges on his back and hindquarters. "Keep him quiet," I said to Chris when I'd finished, "and try to keep him from licking at the cuts. Chances are Sam and Viv will be stopping by a little bit later, we'll have him take a look."

"How did this happen?"

I shook my head. "No idea. He may have gotten caught in barbed wire somewhere or maybe another animal attacked him. Could even have been Curly, I guess. Any sign of him?"

"No." Chris knelt next to the dog. "Do you still want me to go out looking for Deirdre?"

"No, you stay here. I'll go. Just let me tell Maggie where I'm going."

I stopped as I got to the door and turned back to him. The love of animals he'd developed when growing up as Phoenix had carried over, readily apparent in the care and regard he gave to the dog. And yet even as my heart twisted with gratitude at the sight of my still-too-young son back with me again, the details of another dog's death nagged at my mind, feeding my natural wariness. Phoenix had been close to that animal too. In my years on the police force and the more recent years living as a vampire, all the brutal deaths I'd witnessed haunted me, but somehow the senseless cruelty of the beheading of an innocent and trusting creature had felt more obscene and depraved than most of them. Pointless and evil. And now, as had happened then, doubts entered my mind. How well did I know this boy? Was he his mother's child after all? Maybe he wasn't what he appeared to be on the surface, the innocent victim of the plots of an evil man. Did something more sinister and diabolical lurk under his skin, in his heart and mind?

I cleared my throat. "Chris," I said, "do you remember how Moe died? More importantly, have you been able to remember who did it?"

His eyes glassed over a bit and his face seemed to grow blurred and vague. "No," he said dragging the word out slowly, making it into a drawl. "I've really tried hard to remember, but it's like there's this wall in my mind."

I nodded, feeling my mouth tighten. Sooner or later we would know the real story. I only hoped there would be no more deaths before that happened. It seemed to me that he was deliberately evading the questions I asked. But I'd already had his mother in tears tonight. One of them was enough.

Without another word, I went into the pub.

CHAPTER TWO

"Everything okay, Mitch?" Maggie smiled at me as she wiped the bar.

"One of the dogs is hurt. But he'll be fine with a little rest. I fixed him up and Phoenix is keeping an eye on him."

She nodded. Her total lack of interest or concern aroused my suspicions again, at least until I remembered that Maggie had never been much of a dog lover. She'd even driven Moe out of the bar her first night armed only with a broom. I chuckled in spite of myself; Moe had been the size of a bear with the personality of a lion and still our little Maggie had beaten him at the intimidation game. She wasn't our friend, that should have been apparent from the minute she walked into The Black Rose, but I couldn't help admiring her courage. She would have made one hell of a vampire.

As if sensing my thought she looked up at me and winked. "Thomas is hoping after a game of darts, Mitch. It would help all of us ever so much if you obliged him, then he can spend the rest of the night whining about how he lost, instead of how much he wants a game."

The men at the bar laughed and I glanced at the clock. Deirdre would be back soon. To be honest, I wasn't too thrilled with going to find her, not because I didn't want her here, safe and sound, but because she'd accuse me of being her jailor again, accuse me of being overprotective. We'd fought too much recently about my desire to keep her safe by my side. And after all she'd been through, maybe she needed some time to herself. The Others were no longer hunting us and she should be fine. I shrugged and ignored the feeling in my gut, reassuring myself that she was more than capable of taking care of herself. After all, she'd been doing exactly that for more than a century before I'd met her.

"One game then, Thomas?" I said through clenched teeth as Maggie handed me the darts and a fresh drink. "Friendly game or are we wagering?"

"Not on your life, Mitch, I know better than to waste my money betting you'll lose."

We moved over to the dart board, but once there Thomas did not seem so eager to play. Instead he looked over his shoulder at his friends still sitting at the bar. I followed his gaze and saw that they were deep in conversation with Maggie. "I wanted a bit of a private talk with you, Mitch," Thomas said in a low voice. "It ain't all that easy to get you alone since that Maggie girl showed up. I wonder that old Pete ever recommended her for the position here. She just don't seem right to me, not right at all."

"How so, Thomas?" I tossed my round of darts,

two ended up dead center, the other fairly close to the first two.

"See," he said in a loud voice as he gathered the darts for his turn, "that's why none of us will play you for money." He dropped his voice again. "Jim told you he saw your Dot up at the abbey, but he didn't tell you the whole story. He seems to have saved that for Maggie and I don't like it, not one bit. She's after you, you know. Set her cap for you, as it were. I can see it in her eyes. And she'd be more than happy to get Dot out of the way."

"Dot's not going anywhere."

Thomas took his turn, making a half-whistling hiss through his teeth as he did so. Shaking his head slightly, he gave an exaggerated sigh. "Good enough to beat anyone else, but not you, Dead-Eye Greer." He clapped me on the shoulder and went back to his conspiratorial half-whisper, "That's not what Jim says. He says she was with someone up at the abbey, another man."

"And?" My voice sounded edgier than I'd intended. What Thomas said may have been true, but not for the reason that was implied. Deirdre probably met someone and fed from them. It didn't have to be anything more sinister than that. But if that were so, why did the sinking feeling in my gut continue?

"Well," Thomas looked over his shoulder again, "you know how Jim is. A great teller of tales, our Jim is. Anyway, he told Maggie that one second he saw Dot, in the arms of another man. And then the next second they weren't there."

"That's ridiculous, Thomas. People don't just disappear."

"And that's what we said. And Jim agreed that it

was odd, but he said all of a sudden there was this shining light around the two of them, like an egg or a cocoon. He blinked and then they were gone." Thomas shrugged. "Some of the men here think Jim had too much to drink, some of the others think he's seen too many television shows. I think he's just trying to make trouble."

I didn't know what to say, instead I nodded to keep him talking. The knot in my stomach felt like it would never untie. I'd witnessed that sort of display before from Eduard DeRouchard. I didn't like it happening again. Not here, and not with Deirdre.

"And then Maggie laughed. Like it was a good story she'd heard before. Then 'Good riddance to bad rubbish,' she said and laughed again. That's why I don't like her. She's just not right and I don't trust her. If I were you, Mitch, I'd speak with her as soon as possible. Fire her if you have to. Pete thinks the sun rises and sets with you. He won't mind."

I clapped Thomas on the shoulder. "I will talk with her, Thomas, and thanks for the game."

"Thanks for nothing, you mean." His laughing complaint followed me to the bar. "Just one time I'd think you could let the old bloke win."

"I'm going out," I said to Maggie as I hurried past her. "I don't think I'll be too long."

"But, Mitch, we're busy here. Don't you think you could stay a little bit longer? I know you're worried about Dottie, but I'm sure she'll be fine."

Glaring at her, I held my tongue and went into the kitchen. To my surprise, Vivienne and Sam were there, Sam examining the dog as Chris knelt by with a worried expression.

Viv came over and stood on her tiptoes to give me a kiss on the cheek. "Mitch, *mon cher*, we are here." She gave Chris a glance and lowered her voice to a whisper. "We came in the back door so as to avoid the Breeder. I do not know how you stand having that woman close to you. She gives me fits."

"Me too, Viv." I ruffled her hair. "You didn't happen to see Deirdre on the way over here, did you?"

Sam stood up. "She's not here? I need to speak with her and you as soon as possible. I've been testing the blood samples she gave me the other day and, well"—he gave Chris a concerned look—"let's go upstairs."

"I was just about to go out looking for her, Sam. Can't it wait?"

"No. I'm afraid not. Chris?" He smiled his best doctor smile at the boy, "Why don't you take the dog into your room if you can carry him? He should sleep for a while and he'll be more comfortable there."

Chris carefully picked up the sedated dog and went into the small bedroom off the kitchen.

"Shall we go upstairs then, Mitch?" Viv crooked her hand into my arm and hugged me to her briefly, resting her head lightly on my shoulder. From that, if nothing else, I knew. And my heart fell.

"Damn. Is the news that bad, Sam?"

He looked at me and shook his head. "Let's talk about it upstairs. There are things I need to say that can't be done with"—and he cocked his head in the direction of the bar—"her listening."

Holding the door open, I gestured for them to precede me, then followed the two of them up the stairs and, ignoring Maggie's curious look, unlocked the door to our apartment and closed it behind us. The flat was small, with a tiny bathroom and kitchen, a seating area of couch and chairs around the fireplace, and our bed on the other side of the room. The steel door and shutters had been Deirdre's and my addition to the decor, sure as hell not pretty but they served their purpose. With them shut, we could sleep in safety, knowing that not one ray of sun would ever penetrate our nest. The steel also served as a deterrent to Others armed with crossbows and guns with wooden bullets.

I looked over to where Sam and Vivienne stood hesitating right in front of the closed door. "So what is it?"

Sam cleared his throat. "Sit down, this may take a while. And afterward we'll all go out and help you find Deirdre."

"Fine."

I settled down on the couch and Sam on one of the chairs, but Vivienne did not join us in the seating area. Instead she seemed uncharacteristically nervous and paced around before walking into our tiny kitchen. "Have you any wine, Mitch?" she called. "I could use a drink, we probably all could."

"You'll find a few bottles in there. Open what you like. I'll have a scotch, thanks. And if you're hungry, there are still some bags of blood left in the fridge."

Sam looked uncomfortable. "Probably best if you throw those out, Mitch. It's part of what I have to tell you. But first I want to say that it's not all bad news."

"Are we playing the doctor's good news/bad news game now? Just tell me, damn it. It's not like you to sugarcoat the medicine, Sam. Get to it."

Vivienne walked back into the room, carrying a tray with drinks, scotch for me and wine for her and Sam. She put it on the coffee table, picked up the two wineglasses and sat on the far arm of Sam's chair. He sipped at his wine, then set it down and cleared his throat.

"A lot of this is theory, Mitch, but I'll give it to you in layman's terms as much as possible. Simply put, Deirdre is changing; the poison in her blood has done more than block her memories. It's done something unprecedented, something I'd not have believed possible, if I hadn't seen it with my own two eyes. I went to reexamine the samples I'd collected from her just two days ago and saw that even in the test tubes, the cells were changing. Evolving. Transforming into something completely different from what they'd been before. And into something different from any blood cells I'd ever seen, human, animal, or even vampire."

"What?"

Sam shook his head. "I don't know exactly. I have my theories on it, of course, but I can't know for sure. In fact the only way I can know anything certain is to continue with my tests."

"Okay," I said, "Deirdre is changing. What exactly does this change mean?"

"It means," he paused and sipped his wine. Vivienne rubbed his shoulders gently. "If the poison can't be arrested or reversed, but is allowed to continue in its purpose, it means, simply, that Deirdre won't be a vampire for much longer. The change is occurring rapidly in the dormant blood samples. I've no way to gauge how quickly it could occur in her, but I can only assume the process will be accelerated."

"And when she changes? What then? She'll be human?"

"No, as far as I can tell she won't be human either."

I reached over, grabbed my glass, and drained half of it in one gulp. It didn't help. Laying my head against the back of the couch, I closed my eyes for a second, trying to get a grip on what Sam said. Deirdre, not a vampire? Not human? Transforming into what? What the hell else was there?

When I opened my eyes again, Vivienne nodded at me. I'd never seen her this serious. Ever. And with a cold slap of realization I saw that she was frightened. Frightened for Deirdre. Frightened for herself. Frightened for all of us. This very formidable woman had lived through the French Revolution, lived through the destruction of Cadre headquarters, lived through the recent years of persecution and through God knows how many other disasters and tragedies, and had managed all of it with a smile on her face, secure in her self and her powers. And she was frightened now?

Shivering slightly, I finished my drink and slammed the glass down on the coffee table. Both Sam and Vivienne jumped and I gave them a weak smile. "Sorry. It slipped. So what do we do now?"

Sam looked guilty. There was more he wasn't telling me. What on earth could be worse than what he'd already said? "We go and find her, if she's not already back, Mitch. And then we'll see what I can find out. There may very likely be a way to hold back the change, maybe even to reverse it. I feel sure of it. But I can't do anything unless she's present."

"And if there's not a way?"

Sam looked away, but Vivienne got up from her

perch on the arm of the chair, crossed over to me, and placed tiny cold hands on my cheeks, searched my face with gray eyes slightly misted over with tears. "She will die, Mitch, *mon amour.* She will die."

CHAPTER THREE

The abbey was deserted when we got there. No sign of Deirdre, no sign of anyone else either. Even by Whitby's tough standards it was a cold, wet night. And everything was so quiet. Too quiet, as they'd say in the old war movies I liked to watch. Even the sound of the ocean was muted, as if the world stood still.

All three of us took turns calling her name and only the eerie echoes of our voices answered back.

I pulled my black T-shirt over my head and un-buckled my belt.

"Mitch?" Sam gave me an odd look. "I doubt that she's swimming in this cold."

Vivienne gave a half laugh and patted him on the cheek. "No, no, *mon cher,* you misunderstand. He is going to change his form, which is an excellent idea. And I will join him. We can cover more ground that way, as well as get better scents. So turn your back, please, Sam, and we will get on with it."

I glanced at Viv, surprised at her modesty. She smiled and shrugged. "I do not wish to be observed during the change. Sam knows this, but he insists on trying to sneak a peek anyway."

"Research," he grunted. "No other reason than that." But he folded his arms and turned his back.

I undressed completely and moved into my wolf form almost immediately. Not a painful experience for me, the transformation was almost a celebration of life, of the power I possessed. Deirdre struggled with it, always, fearful of dropping her human form for too long. She clung to her humanity, nurtured it. I couldn't blame her, I suppose, we are what we are. I'd not have wanted her any different. As for me, though, I had no compunction about changing. During my years on the force, I'd seen enough of the horrors that humanity could produce to regard the human form with more reverence than any other.

I padded over to where a now naked Vivienne stood, folding her clothes, and I nuzzled her hand. She looked at me and smiled. "Excellent," she said, "you've been practicing, no?" Vivienne had been the one to teach me the animal forms, since Deirdre refused. I nuzzled her again. "I get the point, Mitch. *Adieu*, Sam, darling, we will be back soon."

She curled in on herself, and her fragile human form became that of a deadly lioness. I knew she was deadly, she'd swatted me more than once with those claws during our training sessions and both the Wolf and I remembered the pain.

I howled and she roared and we tore off down the hill behind the abbey.

In our animal forms, the cold and the rain had no effect, so we ran, tirelessly, searching the night air for the scent of her. Halfway through the search, we both switched to our flying forms and, as eagle and black swan, we scanned the empty moors from above. Then we dropped to the ground and became four-footed beasts again, covering the ground back to the abbey slower this time. We arrived back at the ruins hours later, exhilarated but despondent from the useless run. Deirdre was nowhere to be found. I knew it; hell, all evening, I'd known the truth somewhere in the pit of my stomach. What Maggie had told me in the kitchen was true. Deirdre was gone. I refused to let my mind add the word, forever.

In silence we changed back to our human forms and dressed. Sam waited for us on a bench overlooking the ocean. "Any luck?" he asked, walking toward us, holding something in one of his hands.

"Nothing, damn it, not one scent, not one hair."

"Ah. I was afraid of that. Because, you see, I found something, taking a stroll through the cemetery."

"Strolling through the cemetery?" Viv kissed him full on the lips. "Sam, *mon cher,* you are growing morbid on me. Show us."

I froze in my tracks. Suddenly I didn't want to know what Sam had found. In my mind, I sketched a horrible picture: Deirdre, sick and poisoned without memory of the world around her, crawling off to a far corner to die, like some wounded animal.

"Mitch, it's not her, calm down." Sam knew me well enough to recognize my upset. "It's the other dog, dead. And this." He held out an empty syringe. "Amitryptilene, probably enough to knock anyone out for quite some time."

I sighed with relief, remembering that drug well. It had been responsible for the deaths of many of the Cadre vampires during the Larry Martin affair. Not by its use, but by its paralytic properties and the fact that it had been given in an open area shortly before dawn. The drug had also been administered to me by my stepdaughter, Lily. It wouldn't cause Deirdre any lasting harm. "So she's been taken by someone," I said. "But who? And why?" Then I clenched my fists. "Maggie will know. She's known all night long."

"The Breeder?" Vivienne asked, a nasty edge to her voice. "Just who did her eldest son turn into, I wonder."

I had my suspicions. Eduard DeRouchard had a lot of atoning to do. Too bad he was already dead, I'd have enjoyed ripping him to pieces. "Let's find out." I said.

"What about the dog?"

"Where is he?"

Sam led me over to the far row of graves in the cemetery. Curly lay there, a poor little dead lump of fur, his eyes open and glassy. I leaned over, picked him up. "Chris will be heartbroken," I said. Then I looked up at the sky, gauging the time until sunup. "We'll bury him tomorrow night; for now, we have just enough time to get back to The Black Rose and find out what our little Maggie knows about all of this."

"She won't tell you, Mitch. Why should she?"

It didn't make me feel better to know that Vivienne was right. I was angry and itching to take it out on someone. "Oh, she'll tell me, if only to save her useless life."

"No, no, Mitch. That's not an approach that works with her kind. You don't know what they're like. She'll ensnare you, lie to you, and make you want more than anything in the world to believe her."

I gave her a cold, hard look. "This is Deirdre we're trying talking about, Viv. I'll do everything and anything I need to do to find her. If it means roughing up Maggie Richards in the process," I smiled unpleasantly, "so be it."

When we arrived back at the pub, the issue became moot. The entire place was in darkness. We were hours past last call, so of course Maggie had closed the pub. But normally there was a light on in the kitchen. Or a thin flash of light coming from under the door of Maggie's room. It could be that she and Chris had gone to sleep. I had no compunction about waking her up in these last hours before dawn. Gently, I laid the body of the dog down under one of the trees and opened the back door.

Entering the room, I noticed that there was an empty feel about the place. No sounds of breathing, no scents of occupation. But there was a very strong scent of death.

Next to me, Vivienne inhaled in a sharp gasp. The kitchen reeked of blood, so much so that I knew that a lot of it had been spilled here. Recently.

I ran my fingers through my hair, squared my shoulders, swallowed the lump in my throat, and opened the door to Maggie's room, fearing the worst. When I flipped the light switch it took my eyes some time to adjust to the artificial glare. That momentary pause didn't provide enough time to prepare me for what was there. True, it was not what I'd feared, but what I saw did not bode well.

The dog, Larry, lay on the floor of the room in a pool of thickening blood. His throat had been slit and the knife that had done the job was laying on the bed next to a small piece of paper. As Sam bent over the animal, I picked up the note she'd left.

The words jumped from the page in a script that was bold and black and somehow disturbing. "Mitch," the note read, "I have gone. Chris is with me. Do not attempt to follow us. It will do you (and your son) no good at all. Accept that you have lost and let it go."

"I'd guess," Sam said, coming over to me, wiping the dog's blood from his hands onto his pants, "that he died about three hours ago. Maybe longer. What does the note say?"

"Nothing good," I snarled. "Maggie's left and she's taken Chris with her. Damn it. Now what do I do? Deirdre's gone. Chris is gone, taken by the one person who has the answers."

"She called him Chris in the note?" Sam asked. Nodding, I handed him the piece of paper.

He read it. "I see," he said, his voice grim. "It's not a particularly good sign that she refers to him by the name of Chris, instead of Phoenix. Nor is it good that she calls him your son. She's already tried to kill him once."

"I should have given her twice the dose of Valium last night," Vivienne said. "Or three times the dose. Or drained her dry of blood. The Breeder doesn't deserve to live."

"Deirdre spared her life," I said, with a catch in my throat. "Maggie has the answers I need to find my wife. And she has my son. I've no choice but to follow her, regardless of her threat. I've never given up on a case in my life. 'Let it go?' " I gave a mirthless laugh. "She has no idea."

Walking over to the dog, I picked him up. "We might as well bury both of them before dawn. Or rather, you two should be getting back to your place and I'll bury them."

Vivienne shook her head and glanced at Sam, who nodded. "We'll stay, Mitch, *mon cher.* We need a plan and that can't wait until the next sunset. You and Sam can take care of the dogs and I will clean up in here."

When the burial duties were over, Sam and I came back inside. Vivienne sat at the kitchen table, holding the note in her delicate hands. "Where would she go?" she asked as we entered. "Where did she and that *monstre* Eduard live? That, *mon chers,* is where I would go. Back to the source."

"A good guess, my love," Sam said to her.

I bolted the back door, glancing at the clock afterward. "Let's get upstairs and settled in before dawn. We can do a little checking on the Internet. I remember from previous research that the De-Rouchard Funeral Home business began in New Orleans. That would seem to be the place to start."

We trudged back up the stairs and secured the apartment for daytime, bolting the steel clad door and closing the steel shutters. I started a fire in the grate and looked around. It was a small apartment, but without Deirdre's presence it felt overwhelmingly large and empty. Pulling a clean change of clothes from the stacked and folded pile on the dresser, I headed for the bathroom. "You two make yourselves at home," I said. "I'm going to take a shower to wash the stink of the night away."

Letting the water run hot first, I stripped off my clothes and looked at myself in the mirror, almost wishing the legend of vampires having no reflection was true. If it were true, at least I'd not be able to see the ravaged face of what I'd become staring back at me. My hair showed gray at the roots; fat lot of good the disguises had done us. The bastards had still found us and hurt us. Hurt *her*. And now, when, against all rational hope, they'd returned my son to me, Chris ended up in the control of a madwoman, a Breeder trained from birth to view the death of her children as acceptable.

I saw the fire of rage come up in my eyes and I wanted to tear and slash all of them. Pull their beating hearts out of their bodies and laugh as they died.

"Slow down, Greer, old man," I told my reflection. "Now is the time for thought. Cold and clear, unclouded by anger. Revenge and justice will come later."

I showered methodically, not noticing my actions, playing over the entire night in my mind. Finishing, I turned off the water and stepped out of the shower. As I dried myself, I remembered something Sam said earlier. ". . . it's not all bad news." Forgetting the need for clothes, wrapped only in a towel, I opened the door of the bathroom. Vivienne and Sam sat on the sofa, facing the fire and talking quietly.

"Sam," I called to him. "You didn't finish the joke. What's the good news?"

He turned. "Excuse me?"

"When we spoke earlier, you said it wasn't all bad news. So I want to know, what's the good news?"

"Ah." He cleared his throat and looked uncomfortable. "I'll need to test Deirdre again, of course, to be absolutely sure. There might be something in her blood or in the poison that falsified the results. Still, it looked fairly definite."

"What looked definite?"

"Deirdre is pregnant."

I started to laugh, but the serious look on his and Viv's faces choked it back into my throat. "Pregnant? But how is that possible?"

"Beats me, Mitch," he said, "But the results can't be argued with. Deirdre is pregnant."

CHAPTER FOUR

Deirdre Griffin: New York City

"Where do I go from here?" I pulled out of Max's embrace and crossed the room to the couch, sitting down and pressing my fingers to my eyes. The headache hadn't improved with the wine I'd drunk earlier. I couldn't think and I couldn't remember anything specifically about my life prior to waking up in this room. There were vague details, however, that haunted me—I knew Max and knew of Steven DeRouchard and the Others' method of attaining immortality through the murder of their newborn children. Perhaps some horrors could never be forgotten. Presumably I had other memories, better ones than the few I now held. "Where are they?" I whispered into my hands. "And where do I go to be healed?"

"You'll stay here with me," Max said, "at least until you are better able to function. I hope," his voice lowered, "that even then you will consider staying with me. I have loved you for so long, Deirdre, and it seems that fate has given me a second chance to make things right between us. I will do everything possible to keep you well and safe."

I slid my fingers from my eyes and gazed up at him. "That is all well and good, Max. But how did this happen? I have no memories. None. I may as well have been born right this very minute for all I know of my previous life. How will you ever make it right?"

"I can give you explanations if you insist." He reached behind the bar and pulled out another bottle of wine, pouring some into a glass and handing it to me. "But I'm not sure how that will help. Perhaps it's for the best just to move on from this point in time."

"For the best." I nodded and sniffed at the wine, noticed that he hadn't poured himself a glass from the same bottle. Not the same vintage as the other, it smelled strange, bitter and oddly medicinal. Suspicious, I set it down on the floor next to my feet. "Yes, Max, I can easily see where you might think that this is for the best."

"You can?" He seemed somewhat shocked by my statement. "That's good. We'll just pick it up from here and go forward then."

Laughing, I shook my head. "You misunderstand me, Max. I didn't say I agreed. I said I saw how you might think it. What you really mean is that not explaining is best for you. Best for me is for you to tell me exactly what has happened to me. Now."

Max stared at me for a while in disbelief and anger. "Is that a threat, Deirdre? What I've done has been for your welfare only. If it had not been for me, you'd be wandering the moors of . . ." He stopped abruptly and gave me a forced smile. "You'd be wandering aimlessly, defenseless and alone, sickened and dying."

I made a mental note of that pause. Realizing I had not been here in this place indefinitely changed everything. I knew from what he just said that I'd been living somewhere else. Before. It was a start, at least. Better than a start actually, since his mention of the moors triggered a flash of memory: I saw the stones of a ruined church, heard a restless ocean, and felt the gentle weight of a familiar arm wrapped lovingly around my shoulders. Maybe it had been Max's arm. It could have been, but somehow I didn't think so. There had been someone else; if only I could pull back something other than that brief flash. A face or a name or a place. Anything. I glanced at him, wondering if I could trick more information out of him.

"I vaguely remember being with someone else. Was I really alone when you found me, Max?"

"When I found you, yes, you were alone. There was no one else, Deirdre, except perhaps in your feverish imaginings. At the time you didn't know who you were, you didn't know who I was. I imagine you don't even remember the flight here, do you?"

He sounded so sure of himself. Sighing, I picked up the glass of wine and took a tentative sip. The strange scent didn't detract from the taste, so I drank more, draining the glass before I spoke again. Although the liquid was tepid, it seemed to warm me and took away the gnawing hunger in my stomach. "I'll tell you what I remember, Max. Waking up here. That is the sum total of my memory. Not much to build on, is there?"

"But you know me. You said my name. That must count for something."

I shrugged, not wishing to give him the advantage. I did know him, that much was true. Somehow the knowledge did nothing to make me feel more secure, since I also knew that I didn't trust him one bit. "And for what does it count? I say your name and I know that it is your name. But do I know you?"

"There's no one on this earth who knows me better, Deirdre. We've been together for a very long time."

"If you say so, Max. But that still doesn't explain a thing. You say you saved me. But from what?"

"The Others."

"But you are one of them." It was not a question. I knew what he was, just as I knew what I was. Or I thought I did. Resting my head against the back of the couch, I rubbed my eyes again. In reality, I knew nothing for certain. If only my head would stop aching, if only he would stop sounding so confident, so calm and self-assured, then maybe I could think.

"When the attacks on you were happening, I was not in control. I could not help the fact that you were poisoned, could not stop the effect of the drugs they'd introduced into your system."

"And now? Can you do something to stop this, to reverse the process?"

Max looked away from me and turned back to the bar, picking up that second bottle. Walking over to me, he filled my glass again, then sat down next to me on the couch. "Drink," he said, "it'll do you good."

"What is it?" I asked, suspicious again. "Why does it smell so odd?"

"It's a tonic, of sorts. A blend of nutrients, vitamins, minerals, and medications, sweetened with just a little bit of wine to help it go down. It will nourish you, for one thing, you have been a long time without any kind of sustenance. It will also help control the nausea you've been experiencing. And it serves as an antidote to the poison, flushing it out of your system. You have been very sick, whether you remember it or not."

"Sick?" I puzzled that over in my mind. "I haven't been sick, have I?" Sipping more of the wine, I strained to remember. "I can't have been sick." I was a vampire, wasn't I? By rights, I was immune to sickness, immune to disease, immune to death itself. How could I have been sick? How on earth could that be possible?

"Yes, Deirdre," Max walked over and sat next to me on the couch. I inched away from him, but he ignored my response. Instead he took my free hand in his and brought it up to his cheek. "You have been sick, Deirdre. Even now, I'm sure, your head aches. And I can tell that you are running a fever and may still be slightly delirious. I don't mind telling you, it was touch and go for a while; I feared you might die." He kissed my hand then and dropped it back down. I moved the wineglass to that hand, making a show of brushing back my hair with the other.

He crooked an eyebrow at me, not at all fooled by my casual avoidance of his touch. "The fact that you don't remember is a blessing. You ranted and raved and swore at the doctors I brought in." He got up from the couch and laughed. "You have always been a creature of great spirit, little one, one of your many wonderful qualities."

"If I was that sick, why was I here? Why wasn't I in the hospital?"

He turned his back to me and busied himself at

the bar. I felt he was trying to gather his thoughts. With every word he spoke a part of me screamed *liar!*

"A hospital? For you? I think not. I took care of you myself. Who better?"

"But first you had to find me? To save me? If we have been together as long as you say, why wasn't I with you when I was poisoned?"

Max knocked over a wineglass and it shattered on the floor. I sat up straighter on the couch and gave a small gasp, staring at him intently, as he picked up the fragments. *That,* I thought, *that sound is familiar.* He stood up, noted my interest, and a flash of dismay crossed his face. A bit of memory flew into my mind and out again as quickly as it had come. I slumped back down on the couch and closed my eyes. When I opened them again, he was watching me, an uneasy smile on his face.

"Surely you remember how clumsy I am, my dear? I can't remember the number of times that has happened in this office with you laughing at me. As for your question, I did not say that I wasn't with you when you were poisoned. I said that I could not stop it. After you grew sick, you ran away. Of course I did all that I could to find you. You are my love and my life. And find you I did. Then I brought you back here and nursed you back to sanity and put you on the road to health."

I drained my glass again. He was right, the liquid did make me feel better, my headache was almost completely gone. I relaxed slightly, the screaming voices in my head began to quiet, and his words suddenly made sense to me. Why was I fighting him? He saved me, he cared for me. Silently, I nodded and held the now empty glass out to him.

He refilled it with a smile. "That's right, my love,

this is good for what ails you. Drink up and see how you feel after that."

I did as he asked. It was true, I did feel odd. Nauseated. Hot and cold at the same time. As I sipped that drink, he spoke to me, telling me of things that we had done in our times together over the years. I took in every word, seeing the events in my mind and, as his voice droned on and on, I grew more and more relaxed, drifting along on the rhythm of his words. I hadn't even noticed that he'd come and sat by me again, until I felt his breath tickle my ear.

"And do you remember," he asked at last, "how we were walking down by the harbor when you were attacked?" I nodded, drowsily. Yes, there had been water nearby. "A dilettante, one of the remnants from my father's time," his voice acquired a sneering quality, "acting under no one's orders but his own. He hadn't recognized me when he struck, but he did just as he died. I snapped his neck and dumped the bastard's body in the water. One more mysterious death in a city full of them would never be noticed and he was never missed."

I nodded again. The movement seemed to take forever. "We saw when he smiled that his teeth were filed down to sharp points," I said, my voice sounding small and far away.

"Yes," Max said, "that's right."

"He had a crossbow." I paused for a while, it took such an effort to produce the thoughts, to sound out the words. "And a gun. With wooden bullets coated in poison. He spoke. We'd never heard them speak before. And you . . ." Here the memory failed me. I just could not seem to be able to fit Max's actions into my mind.

"Exactly." Max said with a light voice, patting my

hand. "I rushed over to you and gathered you up. You were already in shock, little one, the poison acted that quickly. I brought you back here to take care of your wound, but you got away from me."

Some of his words rang true. As for those that sounded false, I had grown too tired to care.

"But now you are here," he continued, "and you are getting better. I see it, I can almost feel it. Words cannot express how happy I am to have you home, safe with me."

He kissed my cheek, then got up, and returned to fill my glass again. I sipped it as he told me of his future plans, of places we would go and things we would do after I'd recovered. Of how we would fill eternity together. In my semiconscious state, everything he said sounded wonderful and reasonable. I wondered for a moment how I could have ever doubted him. The man loved me, you could hear it in the way he spoke. So I must love him back. *No,* a tiny voice rumbled in the back of my mind, so quiet it was barely audible over Max's talking, *no, you don't love him. You mustn't ever make that mistake again.* I shook my head and finished the drink in my hand.

When his voice finally stopped, I was almost asleep. I heard the sound of a door being unlocked and he came and stood over me. "You have done well for your first day out of bed, Deirdre. But you need your rest." He scooped me up in his arms and carried me into a small room through a door behind his desk. There was a bed, that was all I saw. He set me down on the floor, his one arm wrapped around my waist, holding me up. With the other arm, he pulled back the blankets on the bed and laid me down on it.

"We will talk more later, Deirdre, for now you need to sleep."

I murmured agreement, pulled the blankets up to my chin, and slept.

CHAPTER FIVE

Several days had gone by since I found myself in this place. Our days and nights had fallen into a routine of sorts. I slept during the day in the chill, windowless room off of his office, alone most of the time, with only dark thoughts and empty memories to keep me warm. On the rare occasions when he joined me, he would merely lie next to me. We shared no warmth, no love, and no sexual contact. I might have welcomed intimacy; it would at least have filled some of the empty moments, some of the dark void within my heart and my soul. But although he constantly referred to himself as my husband, he didn't act as if he were. And I didn't see him as my husband, that whole scenario just felt wrong. I couldn't deny the fact that his face was the only one capable of lingering in my mind. Yet, I did not trust him. Something in my very core shivered with his touch, recoiled at his presence. What did that inner piece of me know that my mind could not fathom?

When sleep would not come, I would read the

books or view the videos stocked on the shelves.
Many of the books, however, were in languages I
couldn't understand. Had I once, I wondered? Or
did these books not belong to me? And the library
of vampire movies on videotape? Had I collected
all of these? Or had Max put them here to enable
a return of my memories? The latter seemed un-
likely, for while they did inspire wisps of memories,
his face did not appear. It was all very strange to
me, very new, and yet something in the back of my
mind responded to the stimuli and I strained to remember.

At sunset, I would hear the sound of his key in
the door. We would go out to his office and talk
about our past life together. I would obediently
drink what he gave me until I fell asleep again.
And once asleep, the dreams would begin, most of
them grotesque and filled with blood and rage,
Max's blood and my anger. I felt the roughness of
splintered wood in my hands, saw the rush of surprise in his eyes as I pinned him to the office door,
laughed as his blood ran out of the wound and
pooled on the floor. And in the corner, in the shadows, there was . . .

This night started no differently than any of the
others, but the rasping of the lock woke me and,
before I could see his face, that face of the shad-
owed man in the corner, the sound roughly pulled
me out of the dream. Without warning an overwhelming rage grew in me. *Damn it,* I thought, *I'm
not going to play his game anymore.*

Max entered the room and sat down on the bed,
touching my arm. "Deirdre?" Feigning sleep, I gave
no response and he shook me gently. "It's no good,
little one," he said, "I know your habits too well. I
know you too well. Open your eyes."

I glared at him, staring at the glass he held out to me. "I don't want it, Max. Take it away."

"You must drink it, my dear. You know it helps you."

I knocked the glass from his hand, taking great satisfaction in seeing it fly across the narrow room and smash up against the wall. The thick red liquid flowed slowly down to the floor, staining the floral wallpaper and the carpet below it. "No, it doesn't help me. It helps you. Helps you control me."

"Is that what you think?" He reached over and ran the back of his hand over my cheek. "That I want to control you?"

I shied away from him and got out of bed. "What else am I to think, Max? That you're my doting and loving husband? That you keep me a prisoner in these rooms because you're protecting me?"

"But, Deirdre, I am protecting you. As I keep telling you, you have been very sick and you're still not fully recuperated. I understand your frustration, you've never been sick before, you have no defenses against what's been happening to you." He rose from the bed and moved toward me, reaching his arms out and gently grasping my shoulders. "I'm glad to see you rage a bit, Deirdre, since it means you are recovering, but I am not your enemy."

"Don't touch me," I said between clenched teeth as I shifted out of his grip. "I am in perfect health or would be if you allowed me to feed instead of forcing me to drink whatever that godawful sludge is you keep bringing. If you really want to help me, my dear husband, you'll bring me some clothes, some real clothes, not these silly little silk gowns. And let me leave these rooms so that I can hunt."

"Hunt? Other than what you have may have

learned in the movies you watch, what could you possibly know of hunting?" His voice sounded soft, indulgent.

Suddenly I felt dizzy as if his question knocked me off balance. He was right, what did I know of hunting? What, for that matter, did I know of anything? I closed my eyes and took in a deep breath, trying to summon the remembrance of something, any small detail that could be dredged out of the mystery of my past. When I opened my eyes again to see his face, I realized only that this was wrong. That *he* was wrong. He shouldn't be here and neither should I.

My dreams since I found myself here were full of death. *Yes*, I thought, *and it is his death of which I dream.* Some shred of my sleeping mind persisted in holding the belief that I had killed this man, killed him to save the life of someone. And now he was alive and where was that someone? The whole situation was progressively becoming so frustrating I wanted to scream. I wished to go back to my initial belief that it was all a dream. How blissful it would have been to wake up and have a laugh with that someone.

Then Max smiled at me, smugly, patiently. He reached over and touched my arm; the warmth of his skin on my arm was comforting.

I sighed. "I do not know much, but I know I need something, Max, something I cannot get from you, in this place. You say you are my husband. You say you love me. Then prove it, damn it. Let me out of here, let me breathe fresh night air. Give me my life back."

His smile faded and for one brief second he seemed angry. Then he laughed. "Finally," he said, "you are becoming yourself again. After all this time, I'd worried and wondered if you were going to stay spineless and submissive for the rest of your life. Worried that the poison and the sickness might have damaged your mind. But now, this is all the proof I needed that the real you has survived. You have always been a fighter, little one," his eyes lit up with a memory I couldn't share, "so it does my heart good to see your spirit revive, even if it's at my expense. Yes, it's true, a little fresh air won't do either of us any harm, but you must allow me to accompany you."

"Do I really need an escort?"

He nodded. "For your first trip out, yes. Humor me. You may find the world changed since last time you walked through it."

"The world has changed?"

"Not the world so much as your perception of it."

I gave a small laugh. "Since I can't remember much of anything beyond a few days ago, I doubt I'll notice a thing."

Max managed to produce clothes for me—a pair of black leather jeans and a red silk shirt. They fit perfectly, as did the pair of high-heeled black pumps and the pieces of underwear. A glance in the mirror shocked me, I recognized these garments. Here now was another piece of evidence that he was telling me the truth. And I didn't want to believe him.

I brushed back my short bleached-blond hair, noticed that the roots were growing back in a dark auburn shade. "Who are you?" I asked of the woman in the mirror. She didn't know, but gave me a bleak smile. "And why the hell did you do this to your hair?"

Something clicked in my mind then—a flashing glimpse of another woman, blond and vivacious, laughing at me and asking the same question.

"Deirdre?" There was a knock on the door of the employee bathroom where I'd been changing and the vision vanished as quickly as it came, leaving me in doubt once again. "Deirdre?" Max called again, "are you okay? Do you need some help? Or is there something wrong with the clothes?"

Damn it, just go away. I grimaced over the complete lack of privacy as much as over the loss of what might have been a memory. "I'm fine, Max, thank you so much. And the clothes are just perfect." *As you knew they would be,* I thought. *How can you be so sure about everything?* "I will be ready in a minute or two."

The cabinet above the sink held a few cosmetics, used by the waitresses here, I assumed. Brushing a little rouge on my cheeks and some mascara on my lashes, I took one last critical look at my reflection. *It'll have to do,* I thought, *unless I can talk Max into taking me on a trip to a late night hairdresser.* "Who cares?" I whispered. "I'm going to get out of here. Finally."

As I turned to leave the room though, my stomach lurched and I spun back to the sink and tried to vomit. It didn't do me any good, my stomach was totally empty and all I managed to bring up was a bitter splash of acid. Running cold water in the sink, I gripped the porcelain with one hand and wet the other to wipe my brow and mouth. I hadn't been sick since I came here to this place with Max, but I knew with certainty that I had been before. If only my head would stop aching so, I might be able to remember something other than fevered glimpses.

He knocked on the door again. "Deirdre?"

I sighed. Hungry and nauseated, I wasn't in any shape to deal with him tonight. But if I didn't come out soon, he would surely come in after me. I straightened up, squared my shoulders, and walked out the door, hiding my weakness as best as I could.

He wrapped an arm around my shoulders and his concerned smile seemed more like a smirk to me in the dimness of the hallway. I wanted to slap him, to lash out against his self-assured possession of me. Nothing would be gained by that, though, and so I swallowed back my anger and my pride and gave him my sweetest smile.

"I feel so much better," I lied, leaning in to him, "and I am looking forward to getting out."

"As I am, little one." We began to walk down the hallway; he paused at the entrance to the club. "But before we go I have some business to take care of. Would you mind terribly if I parked you at the bar for a while?"

He pushed the door open and I heard talk and laughter and music. During my stay in the secret room connecting to Max's office, these sounds had been muted, but I realized now that I'd been hearing them in the background, filtering into my mind. I smiled and took in a deep breath, feeling as if I had finally come home, feeling that if there was a chance I could regain myself, it would be here.

The club was relatively dark and it took a while for my eyes to adjust. When they did, however, I felt a joyful stab of recognition. I knew this place, knew it well enough that I didn't need to see to find my way around. The tables were small and heart-shaped, each of them topped with a Victorian-style lamp, complete with fringed and beaded shade. The wallpaper was comprised of red velvet swirls. It had taken me days to choose it. The whole decorating scheme, I remembered with triumph, was my creation, Max commissioned me to do the job when I'd first come to this city.

I gave a laugh of delight.

"What is it, Deirdre?" Max bent over me, his eyes concerned.

"Nothing, Max. I am just so happy to be out. So happy to be well."

"Are you? Then I am pleased too. I only wish you to be happy."

I ignored his comment, so enraptured I was with my glimpse of the club. My eyes drank in the entire scene: the decor, the dance floor, the layout of the bar, the positioning of the musicians, even the song that played was familiar and I hummed along with it. I *had* been here before. That much of what Max told me was true. I had danced here, flirted here. I'd drunk so many glasses of wine at those tables, at that bar.

And more than that, I realized with a flood of excitement. I'd fed here. I could almost taste the bitter, salty flow that kept life in my veins, could almost feel the exhilaration that came with the blood, with the drinking.

Max's voice pulled me back down to earth. "So you are sure you don't mind if I leave you alone for a few minutes while I tend to business? No one will bother you, I'm sure. And if you grow tired, you can always go back to the rooms."

Go back? Was he insane? Why would I want to go back? Here I was alive. I gave him the sweetest smile I could muster along with a quick kiss on his cheek. "Actually, I'm wide awake right now, Max. So you take care of what you need to take care of. I don't mind at all."

CHAPTER SIX

Max led me to an empty seat in the corner of
the bar, where I could watch the patrons on the
dance floor as well as those gathered into smaller
groups. The club was fairly crowded; I wondered if
this was a typical night and decided it probably
was. Even so, with our appearance, the bartender,
a young man with a goatee and a shaved head,
snapped to attention and immediately came over
to greet us.

"Derek will take good care of you until I can get
away," Max rubbed my shoulders lightly and nodded to the young man. "We'll need a glass of my
private stock here, Derek. And keep her glass filled
until I come back."

"Right away, Mr. Hunter."

I didn't bother to watch Max walk away, nor did
I watch Derek fumble behind the bar. The sight
and scent of a room so full of humans was en-
thralling, enticing. I licked my lips and inhaled
deeply.

"Mrs. Hunter?"

I heard the name and the voice, but couldn't take my eyes away from the dancers.

The bartender cleared his throat. "Mrs. Hunter?"

He had to say the name one more time before I finally realized he was speaking to me.

"I'm sorry, Derek. I wasn't paying attention. Did you want something?"

He shook his head, "No." He moved the glass he'd set in front of me a little closer. From the smell I could tell it was the same red liquid Max brought me every evening upon awakening and had me drink while we talked. "Just wanted you to have your wine."

I crinkled my nose a bit and pushed the glass back to him. "Actually, I am not thirsty. But thank you anyway."

"But," he looked across the room to where Max was speaking to a group of waiters, lowering his voice in nervousness. "Please, Mrs. Hunter, if you don't drink it, Mr. Hunter will think I'm not doing my job."

"And exactly what is your job, Derek? Are you a bartender or a babysitter?"

"Excuse me?"

I narrowed my eyes and glared at him for a second, trying to figure out where he fit into the puzzle. Was he like the dancers and the other patrons here: human and fair prey? Was he like me? Or was he a creature like Max? And had I known him before?

Derek leaned over the bar and whispered. "You'll feel better if you drink it, you know. You haven't been well at all and Mr. Hunter has been worried sick."

"Has he indeed? And what would you know of it?"

He smiled at me and winked. "Come on, Deirdre,

surely you remember me. I know you've been sick and are having some trouble remembering the past. But I thought we were friends, thought you knew that I was on your side."

"Side? I was not aware that there were sides."

"You know what I mean."

"Not really, Derek. Explain yourself please. Or go away and leave me alone. I do not need, nor do I want, someone watching my every move. Max already does more than enough of that to suit me."

He laughed at this comment. "You really are feeling better, aren't you?"

"Am I?"

"Yeah, you are." He nodded and pushed the glass of wine back to me. "I can tell. You're feisty again. You were always ready with a snappy comeback, always ready for a friendly argument."

"And have you and I had many arguments?"

He threw his head back and laughed. "When we were first setting up the club? You don't remember? I hated the tables and hated the lamps. Wasn't particularly thrilled with the wallpaper either. I was always surprised that you didn't ask Max for my head on a silver platter. He'd have obliged you, I'm sure. He really does care for you. His devotion is touching."

"Yes. Very. You were here when the club was opened? Just how long ago was that?."

"About seventeen years ago," he said, "or thereabouts."

"Pardon me for saying so, Derek, but you hardly seem old enough to have been here for seventeen years already."

He laughed again. "But I am older than I seem, Mrs. Hunter. You should remember that, if nothing else. I am one of yours."

"One of mine?"

"You made me what I am today. And I have never looked back. I'm eternally grateful, of course."

I nodded as if I just then remembered. "Ah. Then since you are one of mine, as you put it, you will take away this horrible drink and bring me a glass of your best Merlot. Won't you?"

He gulped and glanced around. I did the same. Max was nowhere to be seen, so I reached out and touched Derek's hand, staring into his eyes. "Max need never know. It will be our little secret."

Derek nodded. "Fine," he said, his voice a whisper, "if that's what you want." He removed the glass in front of me, poured it into the sink and refilled it quickly from an open bottle sitting at the back of the bar. I took it from him and sniffed. It was wine, nothing more than that. After sipping it, I gave him a smile. "Thank you, Derek. That wasn't so difficult, was it?"

"No." He went back to the other bottle and with another glance for Max, poured out the equivalent of a glass. *Such a sneaky young man,* I thought. *I'll know not to trust you in the future.* Then with a final nod to me, he moved away to the other end of the bar.

I stared after him for a minute. Was he really a vampire? And had I converted him? Neither his face nor his voice sparked one bit of recognition. Surely if he were mine, as he put it, I would feel some sort of bond with him. He sounded sincere, though; then again, he must merely be a better actor than I gave him credit for. Time would tell.

"Excuse me. I couldn't help but notice that you were getting good service over here. What's your secret?"

I looked up into the face of a conventionally handsome young man. He was tall, probably about six foot or more, well built, dressed casually in khakis and a button-down oxford cloth shirt, blond hair, blue eyes. A young barfly's dream come true. His smile seemed straightforward, but there was a look in his eyes that told me he was as far from that as a man could be. No matter. I didn't chose prey for their morals, quite the contrary.

Giving him a warm smile, I swung my body a little closer to him. "As it turns out, I know the owner."

"Ah. That's a good thing. So? Do you think you could get the bartender's attention for me?" He deposited a glass on the bar, empty but for the clank of ice, "I could use another. It was a rough week."

"It's Friday." I said it out loud, bemused about not knowing the day of the week until he spoke. He gave me an odd look and I backpedaled a bit. "I mean that it's Friday, and it's always harder to get served on a Friday."

"Yeah. Isn't it?"

"But I'll call Derek over if you like. What are you drinking?"

"Scotch on the rocks."

The mention of that drink seemed appropriate to me, for no particular reason. I motioned to Derek. "I see. You really are having a bad week, aren't you?"

"I was. But I'm not now." He shifted a little closer to me, twisting his empty glass around until Derek claimed it from him and refilled it. Dropping a five-dollar bill on the bar, the man accepted the drink, and took a long slow sip. "Why do you ask?"

I thought for a moment. Why did I ask? "No real reason. Although I think I must know someone who drinks that particular drink, at the end of a bad day. Or week. Then again, maybe I am just making conversation." Shrugging, I extended my hand to him giving him my most seductive smile. "Deirdre," I said. "It is nice to meet you."

"Tom." I could see that I puzzled him, intrigued him. That was what I was best at. He took my hand and kissed it. "Would you like to dance?"

"I thought you'd never ask." I looked at him and smiled, sliding off the barstool. Derek stared after us as we went out to the dance floor, I could feel his eyes following us all the way. If he knew me as well as he claimed, he'd know that this was normal behavior for me. And that Max wouldn't object. After all, Max never had before. And I smiled with that thought, knowing it was true. He had never minded. In fact he'd often arranged meetings like this, but that had changed when I'd met . . .

I scowled briefly until Tom took me in his arms as the band began playing a slow song and we danced. Laying my head against his chest, listening to his heart beat, I hid my triumphant smile. Finally, something familiar. I was remembering. It turned out to be as simple as being in an accustomed situation, meeting people similar to those I'd interacted with in the past. I knew now that there had been many men in my life, not lovers, but donors. And that Max had often arranged for me to meet them. Here in this club.

I would take them to a back room somewhere, not Max's office, but another place. And there I would bite them on the neck and draw their blood into my mouth, swallowing each mouthful and savoring their different tastes, feeling the rush of heat hit my stomach and spread through my veins. With each step of the dance, I inhaled the smell of the man pressed up against me, remembering the sweet touch of blood on my lips, on my tongue, the tingling of my gums with the growth of my fangs. I remembered!

Soon, I would take this man by the hand and lead him to a quiet room. I would slowly unbutton his shirt and welcome the warmth of his hands on my body. My eyes would meet his and hold him there; slowly and sensuously, my mouth would whisper the words of seduction, then come down on his neck and I would drink my fill, I would . . .

"Excuse me," I pushed Tom away and raced toward the ladies' room, barely making it into one of the stalls. Falling to my knees I vomited again and again, bringing up acid and bile and the Merlot I'd connived from Derek.

When I finished, I sat back on my heels. Women outside the door laughed and talked in stage whispers. "Can't hold her wine, that one."

"Poor dear," another said. "I remember the night I did three shots of tequila on an empty stomach. I didn't leave the bathroom for days." They laughed again and then pushed out of the door. As it swung shut behind them, I knew I was alone and felt hot tears stream down my face. *What had those bastards done to me?*

The door swung open again and there came a soft knock. "Deirdre? Are you okay?"

I sighed and got up, opened the stall and went to the sink, washing my hands and face. Snapping off the water, I turned to him. "No, Max, I am not. As well you know."

He shrugged and took my arm, leading me from the restroom back down the hall to his office again. "I would have warned you, my dear," he said as we walked, "if I had known that you were that desperate to feed. Or if only you'd drunk what Derek gave you, the urge would not have been so overwhelming. As always, though, you know best. Now maybe you'll stop fighting me and listen to what I have to say."

I settled onto the leather couch, accepted the drink he offered, drained it, and held the glass back out to him.

"That's better. You're acting like a good, sensible girl. When I say you've been sick, Deirdre, perhaps now you will believe me. You have been very sick. And now you are getting better. But it will take time. You must not rush it."

"But all I wanted to do was feed." I heard a whine enter my voice. So be it. If he wished to treat me like I child I would act like one. "I remembered, Max, really remembered how to do it. I remembered how it felt, what the blood tasted like. It was wonderful."

"And the operative word in that sentence, little one, is was." He sighed and sat down next to me, taking my hand and twining my fingers together with his. "I, too, remember. But I have changed. And so will you, it's happening even now and there is no way to stop it."

"What sort of change is happening, Max?"

Crooking an eyebrow at me, he smiled. "*You* know, Deirdre. Your body knows. Just as I'd planned, I have given you the gift you have always asked for, since the first day we met."

Given me the gift I'd always wanted? Warning sirens went off in my head. At first he said he'd saved me from the vicious attack of the Others. And now, he made it sound like the attack was his idea all along. I'd waste no more trust or belief on him from this moment on. "What gift? What the hell are you talking about, Max? I thought you saved me, now you're telling me that it was all part of some plan of yours. What have you done?"

"I've made it possible for you to be human again."

CHAPTER SEVEN

Mitch Greer: Whitby

"Pregnant? Even though it's not even remotely funny, please tell me that you're joking."

He shook his head. "I'm not joking."

"But even if it was possible, with all the changes you say are occurring, for her to get pregnant, surely I'm physically incapable of providing the seed. And she's not been with anyone else. Not that way."

Sam sighed. "I wasn't implying that, Mitch. Have you been drinking from the bags of blood I sent you?"

I thought for a moment. "Yeah. We both have. What does that have to do with anything?"

He looked away from me again and stared at the fire. "Those bags of blood were provided by the people for whom I was doing the blood research. Stupid of me, I know, to never actually look that gift horse in the mouth. The blood was tainted, of course. A nice little trap, if you will. Even without the addition of Maggie's blood, it's capable of causing change within those who ingest it. So, although you've not fully succumbed to the poison as Deirdre has, you are still affected, at least enough to cause your sperm count to be accelerated. So if she is pregnant, I can assure you with almost one hundred percent accuracy that it is your child."

I laughed. "That's actually the least of my worries, Sam." We'd certainly taken advantage of every opportunity available to make love. Just the thought of her made me ache with longing to be with her again. "Of course the child is mine."

"And no wonder, *mon cher.*" Vivienne gave a small chuckle, staring pointedly at my towel-covered privates.

Following her eyes, I stared down at myself, suddenly embarrassed, and clutched the towel tighter about my waist. "Look," I said, "just let me get dressed and we'll talk about it some more."

I went back into the bathroom and began to dress, unsure of what to think about what Sam had just told me. If it were true, Deirdre would be pleased. Regardless of everything that led up to it or led away from it, the birth of a baby would be a blessing for her. And for me? I slid the T-shirt over my head and looked at myself in the mirror. "Face it, Greer," I said with a grin, "you're pleased, too. You'd like nothing better than for this to be true."

When I came out of the bathroom, Vivienne was sitting at the computer, typing at the keyboard, a look of extreme concentration on her face. She hit the return key and watched the resulting screen load. With a triumphant shout of *"Voilà!"* she turned to us and said, "I've found her."

"Who?" I asked, rushing over to her and reading over her shoulder.

"The Breeder. She boarded a late flight to New York tonight with a connection from there to New Orleans the next morning. And apparently Chris is with her, since she bought two tickets and left this evening. We can't catch her now"—she looked at the clock—"since the sun has risen, but we can follow her."

I looked at Viv with disbelief. "How did you find all that out so quickly?"

She gave a little giggle and flicked her hand at me. "While Sam was occupied in customs, I was making the acquaintance of a very helpful man at the reservations counter. He was most kind, very willingly gave me his password and employee ID. If I understand the instructions correctly, I can even book us a flight to follow. Would you like me to try?"

I kissed the top of her head. "Vivienne, you're a marvel. Yeah, book us."

She typed some more and then reached over and turned on the printer. "E-tickets and boarding passes on the way for the night after next. If I remember right, it takes about five hours to drive from here to London. So we'll find a hotel close to the airport. I can do that online as well." She turned back to the computer and began to type, a look of delight on her face.

"You seem quite proficient on that machine," I said looking over her shoulder.

She laughed. "The Internet is a wonderful place, Mitch. Did you know you can shop any time of the day or night? No annoying sunrise to get in your way. And anything one could possibly ever want to know or to buy is all there, for the taking."

Sam looked up at me and gave me a sheepish grin. "What can I say, Mitch? You should see some

of the stuff she buys on auctions. I gave her a laptop computer and created a monster."

Vivienne pulled off one of the pieces of paper
on the printer and read it, then kicked her feet off
from the floor, spinning the chair around several
times. "Nonsense, Sam, *mon petit,*" she said, grin-
ning up at him when she finally came to a stop, "I
was a monster long before I met you."

"You seem in a better mood now, Viv," I said
with a smile. "More like yourself." Somehow the
knowledge that she wasn't afraid relaxed me, returned my confidence that we would beat Steven
DeRouchard at his sick little game.

She smiled at me, reached over and gently
touched my hand. "I am still upset, Mitch, but that
does none of us any good. We need clear heads
and clear hearts to survive. And as my head is so
clear as to be almost transparent, we will do fine."

"I don't believe that for a moment, Viv," I said,
"you have always been far from obvious. But you
make me feel better just by being you. Thanks."

"Who else could I ever be? Besides, Mitch, *mon
chou,* if Deirdre really is pregnant, we should be
happy. I shall be an aunt and isn't that a wonderful
thing? Somehow Lily has never counted as a niece,
coming, as she did, fully grown. But a baby," she
sighed and tilted her head, "a baby is different."

"Let's not get ahead of the situation, Vivienne,"
Sam cautioned. "We really know nothing certain
about any of this; there are all sorts of tests that
must be done first."

"Oh, foo, Sam." She stuck her tongue out at him.
"If I choose to be happy, not even you and your de-
plorable bedside manner can stop me."

The phone rang and I jumped, held my breath
and picked it up.

"Yeah?"

"Hi, Mitch. Can I talk to my mother?"

"Hello, Lily. She's not here."

"What? How can she not be there? It's past dawn. This isn't funny, Mitch. I don't care if she's busy. Just put her on."

"Trust me, Lily, I'd love nothing better than to be able to do that. But she's not here. Someone, Steven DeRouchard we believe, has taken her. Away. We don't know where."

"Kidnapped? Mom?" Lily paused and cleared her throat. "Someone must know where she is; maybe you should ask that Maggie Richards bitch. Or let me ask her."

"Maggie is gone as well. And she's taken Chris with her."

She gave a mirthless laugh. "Figures. We seem to be having a fire sale on missing persons these days. Victor is gone too, without a trace. What are you going to do?"

She wasn't going to take this well. "I don't have much of a choice, Lily. I'm going to have to go after Chris. We're worried about his safety and I don't think he understands just how unbalanced his mother is. I'm not sure any of us do."

Another pause. "And Mom? What about her?" Her voice raised in anger and I held the phone away from my ear. "What the hell do you plan to do about her? Just let this bastard take her away?"

Vivienne pulled the phone away from me. "Listen to me, young lady," she said, "we'll have none of this. We will find both Chris and your mother." Lily's screaming stopped, the pitch of her voice returning to normal, and Vivienne listened intently. "Of course, *ma cher,* you may come along, I would expect nothing less of you." Viv nodded. "And

Claude as well. I will make all the arrangements. Just see that the two of you are here as quickly as possible following sundown. We'll drive to London and stay over to catch a flight the next night. Now here is Mitch again."

She handed the phone to me. "Lily? It'll be okay, I promise. Can you and Claude drive one of the cars? Sam, Viv, and I will take the other one."

"Yeah," she said with a choked laugh, "I can manage that. We'll just have to watch out for Vivienne's cows on the way. See you tomorrow at dusk."

I hung up the phone, shaking my head and giving a small snort. "Cows again. I can't believe it."

"There were," Vivienne's eyes laughed and she crossed her heart with a flourish, "so very, very many cows on the road. I swear."

I shook my head then stretched and pushed my fingers through my hair. "Tomorrow night's going to be hectic. Let's try to get some sleep. You two take the bed, I'll take the couch."

Sleep evaded me even after Viv and Sam quit whispering and slept. I could still scent Deirdre in the apartment. Could still smell her on my skin, regardless of the shower I'd taken. I replayed the events that'd happened since we arrived in Whitby and had to admit that everything Sam said made perfect sense. All the signs were there. Deirdre's vomiting, especially after the taking of blood, the weakness and the fever and the pain, the inability to change her form, the way she couldn't tolerate the extremely hot shower she'd always loved.

Yet, it made no sense. How could it be possible? I punched the couch pillow. Life had become exasperating in the past few years. And just because something wasn't possible, didn't make it untrue. My own existence and the fact that my son lived again proved that.

I swore under my breath and stared at the dying fire. Then I got up from the couch and sat down at the computer, calling up driving instructions from Whitby to London and printing out two copies. Then I did a search on the name Steven De-Rouchard and found the transcript of the retraction given by Terri Hamilton on *RealLife Vampires* and a few references to the DeRouchard family funeral homes. There were no pictures of the man to be found; I'd once seen a photograph of him when he was a child, standing next to his brother and his father.

As I remembered, he'd been blond in that photo. That fact proved useless in identifying the man; even normal children's hair often darkened with age. As a man, an Other, he'd grow the body to match the soul. But whose soul? Who hated Deirdre this much to want to do this to her? My first thought had been Larry Martin, but since he'd died the same time Chris had, he was out of the running. I gave a grim chuckle while pulling up the information on the DeRouchard funeral homes. Too damn many dead people walking around these days and Larry'd already lived two lives. More than enough for a lunatic like him.

The DeRouchard funeral parlors seemed to be located in only two cities: New Orleans and New York City. No doubt the Others had similar setups all over the world. What better place than a mortuary for their murderous rites? The transfer of Chris occurred in New York City, but Maggie had chosen to go on to New Orleans from New York. Not that it made much difference. Finding a single person in either city was like finding a needle in a haystack. At least in New York I'd have the benefits of contacts in all the police departments. Certainly contrary enough, she probably avoided the city just for that reason.

I didn't like New Orleans; I'd been held prisoner there by Deirdre's daughter. And I'd faced the unthinkable monster of DeRouchard there. Victor, though, had eliminated him. Victor. I shook my head. And where had he gone? I'd never been convinced that there was anything wrong with him, mentally. All of the little poses of illness and insanity were the perfect cover for someone who'd always pulled the strings. I remembered Lily complaining that his mind had gone and how one night she'd come home and heard him talking to—

"Son of a bitch!"

Vivienne sat straight up in bed. "Mitch? What is it?"

"Max. Goddamn son of a bitch, I should have known all along. Who else could it be? Max Hunter is the soul occupying the body of Steven DeRouchard."

"Max?"

"It has to be. There's no other answer. The timing seems right. I wonder . . ."

"What is it? Is there a problem?" Sam's voice sounded sleepy.

"Go back to sleep, *mon beau,* you need your rest." She rose from the bed, affording me a quick glance of her silky white skin before she wrapped a blanket around herself and walked over to me. "Here," she said, giving me a little push, "you go open another bottle of wine for us and let Vivienne do her magic on the computer. I was out of the country for the blessed event of Max's death. What date, do you know?"

I thought for a moment. "Deirdre would know." I winced when I realized that probably wasn't true, by now she'd no doubt have lost all of her memories. "I don't recall the exact date. I was pretty badly beaten up and spent a lot of time in the hospital. Mid-December, I'd guess, seven years ago." I heard her typing as I went to the kitchen and opened another bottle of wine.

"Voilà," she said quietly as I came back into the room. "It is quite easy when one knows where to look. Steven DeRouchard was born, amazingly enough, in the same time period. Now Sam would say," she smiled, displaying her dimples, "that we haven't enough direct evidence to support this theory and that further testing is in order, but I have this feeling that you are right. I wish you weren't." She took the glass of wine I offered her and drank it in one long swallow. "Max has never been a creature to be fooled with. I don't imagine his rebirth as an Other will have given him a better disposition or made him any easier to handle."

"But why?"

"Eduard," she said the name with a growl in her voice, "would have thought him useful, no doubt."

"No, I mean why would Max go to all this trouble to take Deirdre? She killed him once; she'll do it again."

Vivienne laughed. "Killing him apparently does no good. Too bad." She paused for a moment and then gave a little gasp. "What if she is pregnant, Mitch? What will he do to the little one when it's born? The Others are not exactly known for their pleasant treatment of newborn children."

That horrible thought had never occurred to

me until she mentioned it. "No, Vivienne." My fists clenched and my voice rose. "No, that will not happen. I will not allow it."

I moved away from her and punched my hand into the steel shutters covering the window. The pain cleared my head, but did nothing for the lead weight in my stomach. "Damn it, I'd give my right arm now for the ability to go out in the sun. My wife and my child, possibly my two children, are in danger. And I'm stuck here, like some caged animal."

"Hush, hush," she came up behind me and rubbed my shoulders, then took me by the hand and led me to the couch. "Here," she said, taking my head into her hands and looking into my eyes with her gray ageless stare, "I will make it all better. You can do nothing now, Mitch. And what will be, will be. No amount of raging will change it. So sleep."

As I'd always suspected Victor was faking his senility, I'd also suspected Vivienne carried more power than she ever displayed. Now, I knew that was true. Somehow, she entered my mind and my eyes opened wide for one second in surprise, before they drooped and closed, barely leaving any time for my final thought. *Can she teach me how to do that?*

CHAPTER EIGHT

I woke later that afternoon, more than well rested. It looked as if Vivienne and Sam had been awake for a while. Sam had stacked their bags by the front door and was now washing the dirty glasses in the kitchen. Vivienne sat at the computer again. She glanced over her shoulder at me and flashed me a twisted smile.

"Sleep well, *mon chou*?"

I laughed and rubbed my chin. "You know I did, Viv. If you could bottle that power, you'd be a rich lady."

Her high-pitched melodic laugh filled the apartment. "I am already rich. The lady part, alas, has always been questionable."

"You won't be rich for long if you don't quit spending it," Sam called from the kitchen. "Seriously, how many black leather corsets does one vampire need?"

"That, my darling doctor, is a silly question. You might as well ask how many angels can dance on the head of a pin."

Ignoring their banter, I pulled a large duffel bag from the closet and began to load it with clothes, mine and Deirdre's. We didn't have much these days, having lost most of our earthly possessions when the Others took over Cadre holdings. The lack never bothered me and if it bothered Deirdre, she never let on. Collecting our items in the bathroom, toothbrushes, shaving kit, cosmetics, and hair dye, I grew angry again about what had happened. All the two of us had ever wanted was a life together, a place to call our own, and a little peace of mind. My stomach growled. "And a good meal," I said savagely, tossing the rest of our toiletries into the bag. "Are you sure we can't use that blood you provided, Sam?"

"Positive," he said, moving out of the kitchen after drying the glasses he'd washed. "We'll find an untainted supply soon, I'm sure. For now, though, it's better to be safe. I've emptied them all out and thrown the bags away."

"Good. Seal up the garbage bag and we'll get rid of that in the can out back. And then we'll be on our way."

"London," Vivienne said with a nod, "is a wonderful city; filled with all sorts of people. No one need go hungry for too long and we'll have hours before dawn to hunt after we arrive."

The phone rang. I didn't jump this time, but picked it up immediately. "Yeah?"

"Sundown, Mitch," Lily said. "Claude and I will be there soon. Do you want us to follow you?"

"Sure, but I also have driving directions for you in case we get separated. And Viv has your e-tickets and boarding passes. We should be all set."

"Great. See you in a minute or two."

Hanging up the phone, I looked around the

apartment. There wasn't much left of us and the life we shared here: crumpled blankets and sheets, a few bottles of wine, and a glass or two. Still, I took in one great gasp of air, pulling in what scent of her remained. It would have to do until I found her. And find her, I would.

Vivienne tilted her head to one side, laying a soft hand on my arm. "Are you ready?"

"More than ready," I said.

Downstairs, I dumped the garbage in the can, locked the back door, and turned out the lights in the kitchen. In Maggie's room, I left a note for Pete, so he would know where we'd all gone and promised to call when I got the chance to fill him in as much as I could. The calendar on the wall had his return date circled: two days from now. *Bad timing*, I thought, *if Deirdre shows up, no one will be here*. Useless to worry about that, somehow I knew she was far away by now.

Lily and Claude arrived, knocked on the front door of the pub, and walked in. "I'm sorry I acted like such a shit on the phone, Mitch," she said, giving me a hurried hug. "I'm so worried about, oh, about all of it. Maggie's taken Chris off somewhere, Victor's nowhere to be found and Deirdre's gone without a trace. It's so typical of her. Just when I was finally starting to like her, she up and disappears on me." Lily clamped her hand over her mouth, looking embarrassed. "I'm sorry again, I didn't mean that quite the way it sounded. But you know what I mean, right?"

I nodded. "Yeah, I do. Don't worry about it, kiddo." I kissed the top of her head.

"And I know why you have to follow after Chris

and I know what a bitch of a decision that is for you. I've been thinking about it all, and let's be realistic, Mom can probably take care of herself after all this time, right? In spite of how she seemed so frail the night before last—like one bad word would break her. She'll be fine, she's a fighter, isn't she?" Lily's eyes shone with unshed tears.

"Do not worry, child, it will take more than this to break my sister." Vivienne kissed Lily on both cheeks and then turned to reach up and pat Claude on the cheek. "Good evening, *mon petit chou.*"

Claude murmured a greeting and pulled a white handkerchief out of his pocket to wipe his brow, a hold-out habit from his human days.

"Now," Viv said, "if we are going to get anywhere, I suggest we leave now."

Claude groaned. "I hate the thoughts of crawling back into that tin can of a car, but let's get it over with."

"I'll drive," Lily said, "and you can just stretch out in the backseat."

I watched in amazement as Claude curled up into a car two sizes too small for him. Funny, how I tended to forget how large he really was; he was so quiet in manner and had developed an almost invisible stance in the world. In a strange way, he reminded me of Moe, the mastiff stray who'd adopted Deirdre. For all the good it ever did her. Or him. Damn.

I handed Lily her directions and her tickets, gave her shoulders a brief squeeze, then Sam and I loaded our bags into the trunk of his rental car. Like Claude, Viv took the backseat. "I may want to nap," she said, "it is always good to conserve one's energy until it's needed. I get a better view back here, as well, so I can watch for the cows." She giggled. "Such silly cows. And you can navigate for Sam. Even after all my centuries on this earth, I've still never learned how to read a map."

The night was clear and cold and felt strangely empty to me. I looked back once at the breath-taking view of the ruined abbey on the hill, then turned in the seat and left Whitby behind me. Even if we managed to get our lives back, we wouldn't live them here. I'd never return to this place.

The first hour or so we drove in silence. Sam concentrated on the road, pausing only to glance at the directions. Vivienne seemed absorbed in the landscape and I chewed on my own thoughts, try-ing to make some sense of it all.

Just as we merged onto M1, Sam turned to me and smiled. "That was the worst of it, from here on it's pretty much freeway driving. As long as I re-member which side of the road to stay on, we'll do okay."

I turned around in my seat and checked on the rest of the crew. Vivienne was sleeping and Lily and Claude were a few cars behind us. "I guess Viv's given up on spotting the cows."

Sam craned his head up to see her in the rearview mirror. "She's an angel, isn't she?" he said, smil-ing.

I shrugged. "She's pretty enough, but . . ."

"Yeah, I know. She's not Deirdre. Totally differ-ent personality type, for one thing. Our little swan is a sociopath, I'm afraid. But for all of that, I wor-ship the ground she walks on. Still, it takes some getting used to."

"You two seem to get along pretty well."

"Yeah, we do. Now. Once I realized that she was what she was, really knew, then we adjusted." He leaned toward me and lowered his voice to a whisper, "I don't quite know what I'd do without her. But I think I'm going to lose her. And maybe soon."

"Why would you say that, Sam?"

He shook his head and his hands tightened on the wheel. "We'll talk later, this next bit of road is sort of tricky."

The road didn't look tricky to me, but I kept my mouth shut. If the man wanted to confide in me, he would in his own time and his own way. The relationship between them was none of my business and I had more than enough other things to occupy my mind.

"I'm going to make a stop at the next service area." Sam's voice returned to its normal level. "You folks might be able to fly all night, but I need to stretch my legs and get a cup of something hot. Coffee would be nice, but I'll take tea if that's all there is."

There was coffee, it turned out, strong enough to keep Sam wide awake and alert for the rest of the journey. Lily and Claude followed us into the rest area, also looking for sustenance, but of a different sort. Lily found hers in the form of a gaunt boy dressed all in black leather with enough visible piercings to make me wince. Claude waited by our car, and when we came out of the little kiosk that held the food and drink machines, he held the door open for Vivienne to get into the car.

"*Merci,*" she said to him, curling up into the backseat. "See you in London. And tell Lily to watch out for the cows." She giggled to herself and Claude nodded seriously, then leaned in toward Sam who was seated once again behind the wheel. "I'll wait here for Lily, but you three might as well go ahead. We know where we're going."

"If you're sure," Sam said, putting the car into gear, "we'll see you there."

Viv turned and waved to him as we drove away. "He is a good man, no? Devoted and loyal."

"Yeah," I said, leaning my arm over the seat and looking back at her. "He makes a very good watch-dog."

She sighed then and started to say something, glanced at the back of Sam's head, and gave her head a small shake. "Poor Claude," she said finally. "Perhaps I should have left him in the blues club where I found him. I fear he is not happy with the life I chose for him."

"He does okay, Viv. And I'm sure you gave him a choice."

"Do any of them have a choice, Mitch? Is there a way to withstand the allure?"

"Sam's managed." I blurted it out, saw his hands tighten on the wheel, and wished I'd kept my mouth shut.

"Yes, but my Sam is an exception." She reached up and tickled the back of his neck. "Aren't you, *mon amour*?"

He laughed a humorless laugh. "Always the ex-ception, Vivienne, sweetheart. After all, someone has to keep you vampires amused."

"Just so," Viv said, then sighed again, resting her head against the side window.

I shot Sam a glance; his mouth was set and rigid. Shaking my head, I turned my attention to the never-ending English landscape. No need for me to get involved in whatever was wrong between the two of them.

And for the record, I didn't see one single cow on the trip.

Our hotel was right outside the airport. Vivienne had booked rooms for all of us on the same floor. "Safety in numbers," she whispered to me as the desk clerk distributed the keys, keeping Lily and Claude's since they hadn't arrived yet. Then she turned her attention to the clerk. "*Pardon, mon ami,* can you possibly recommend a good place in London where a girl can get a good drink and some pleasurable company?"

He mentioned a few pubs near Paddington Station. "And the Heathrow Express will get you there in no time, Miss. Or if you'd prefer, we have a fully staffed bar and restaurant here at the hotel."

"Ah," she said, with a smile that showed off her dimples, "fully staffed. It sounds *très* charming. What do you think, Sam?"

"I think I'm going to go up to the room and get some rest, Vivienne." He sounded tired and harsh. With good cause, I thought, he'd driven for over five hours in a somewhat tense environment. "I'm exhausted. But you do whatever you want."

She sighed and gave a little pout.

Sam smiled then and kissed her. "I can't resist you when you do that. Really, go and have some fun. Just come back to me when you're ready."

Viv tucked her hand into his arm. "Perhaps I do not wish fun after all." She turned to me, "Mitch, do you want to ride up on the elevator with us?"

I shook my head, "No, I think I'll wait here for Lily and Claude, I saw them pull up just a second ago. And then maybe I'll stop in the bar for a quick drink. Anyway, I doubt either of you need or want a chaperone."

They chatted quietly on the way to the elevator. I heard Sam laugh again, "Oh, I see," he said, his voice low and tender, "you don't have fun with me?"

The elevator door closed then, cutting off Viv's response. Lily and Claude walked into the lobby and came to the desk where I was waiting. Claude looked around expectantly. "Did Vivienne and Sam go out?"

"No," I said, "Sam was tired so they just went to their room."

"Oh," Claude said, failing to hide his disappointment. "I was looking forward to seeing a little of London. Are you up for some sightseeing, Mitch?"

"Not me," I said, "The only sight I want to see for the rest of the night is a dark bar and a bottle of scotch."

He turned to Lily who'd picked up their keys at the desk. "How about you?"

"Nope, not me either." She handed him the little envelope that held his key card. "Aren't we a sorry bunch of party poopers tonight?" She laughed and my heart ached, she looked so much like Deirdre it hurt. "All I want now is a nice hot bath and a soft bed."

Claude threw up his arms in mock dismay. "And you dare to call yourselves night people? Okay, I'll go by myself then, if I have to."

"Take the express, Claude," I said, "and have fun." I kissed the top of Lily's head. "Night, kiddo, have a good one."

CHAPTER NINE

The bar was dark, and the scotch came in the form of a twenty-year-old single malt. I charged it to my room, hoping Vivienne had enough credit to cover it. After that it was a simple matter, all I had to do was keep the ice from melting.

Three glasses in, the hunger hit. *Should have gone to London with Claude,* I thought, eyeing the emptiness of the bar, *it would have been quicker and easier.* As I got up to leave, though, a woman walked in. She was about the same height as Deirdre and the same weight, but the similarity ended there. Her straight dark hair shone in the light from the doorway, giving her the appearance of purple streaks throughout the black. She walked slowly, almost a saunter, and she had a lovely smile.

"Drinking alone," she said, as she slid onto the barstool next to me, "is no good. Didn't your momma teach you better than that?"

Her drawl oozed with pure southern charm and I smiled in spite of myself, extending my hand. "The name's Mitch," I said. "New York."

Her eyes laughed at me as she returned the handshake. "Diane," she said. "North Carolina. Leave it to me to find the only Yankee in the bar."

I looked around us at the empty seats. "Yankee or not, I'm practically the only other person in here."

"True." She picked up the bottle and examined it. "Nice," she said, "but a little too much for me after a flight."

"May I get you something?" I asked, motioning to the bartender.

"White zinfandel, thank you." She sipped the wine he brought. "Not bad," she said, "better than the swill they were serving on the plane."

"Here on vacation?"

"No, business. I write for travel magazines, free-lance. But it gets old real fast, you know? The planes, the cabs, the empty hotel rooms. How about you? You here for business or pleasure?"

"It's sort of hard to say. I'm heading ultimately for New Orleans by way of New York. And from there? I have no idea."

"And what do you do for a living?"

"I'm a retired policeman. Most recently I was a bartender."

"Two very useful occupations."

"Damn straight they are."

We clinked our glasses together. Diane had a effortless laugh and her skin smelled fresh and clean. When she inched a little closer to me, I didn't move away. Instead I motioned the bartender to bring her another glass of wine and watched her unwind before me.

After three glasses she was telling me her life's history, her words only slightly slurred. "You know, Mitch," she giggled, holding her glass up to what little light gleamed in the bar, "I only drink pink drinks."

"Pink drinks?"

"Yes, pink drinks. That same momma who told me it wasn't good to drink alone taught me that a lady is always a lady provided she only drinks pink drinks."

I laughed. "It's important to have a smart mother."

She nodded and hiccuped. "Excuse me," she said, "she also taught me to not overstay my welcome. I've enjoyed your company, Mitch, but I think I need to call it a night. I'm still on eastern time."

I nodded. "I understand."

As Diane got up from the barstool, the straps of her purse tangled around her ankles and she pitched forward, landing practically in my lap. "Oh, God, I'm sorry, I'm so clumsy."

"Not at all," I said. My hunger raged from the close contact and although I felt guilty taking from her, I knew that I would. I stood up and gently took her arm. "My momma taught me to never allow ladies who've been drinking pink drinks to walk home unescorted. May I walk you to your room?"

"I thought you'd never ask," she said, gripping my arm. The heat of her skin was more intoxicating than the scotch had ever been. I felt uneasy, though, unsure of how far to take this seduction. I liked her and didn't want to frighten or hurt her.

She solved the problem for me on the elevator by passing out, leaning up against my side. I felt the slackness of her body as all of the tension dropped out of her and I caught her before she could fall. From there, I carried her to her room and opened the door. She didn't move as I unfastened the buckles on her shoes and she didn't make a sound when

I laid her in the bed, pulling the covers up over her.

When my mouth came down on her neck, she reached a hand up and stroked the back of my head, making a low moaning sound. Her blood tasted as pure and clean as she smelled and I drank her in. When I felt as if I'd taken enough to sustain me, I forced myself to withdraw my fangs.

"Don't go," she murmured as I pulled away.

"I have to, Diane. You're a lady and I'm a gentleman and what would momma say?"

She laughed softly. "Momma would say 'thank you.' "

"No, thank *you*," I said. "Now you go to sleep and forget I was ever here."

She gave a contented sigh and dropped back into sleep.

It was good that I'd been able to feed before we hit Heathrow. Otherwise, I'd have been totally overwhelmed by the mass of humanity there. People were everywhere, pushing and jostling, different ages, different races and nationalities, single businessmen and women alongside large families with crying babies. The noise level was almost deafening, a cacophony of languages so disorienting it made my head ache.

Vivienne clung to Sam as if he were a life raft and Lily, I noticed, did the same with Claude. The line to check luggage seemed endless but was a necessity, if only so that Sam could have his medicinal bag when we arrived in New York. With heightened airline security there was no sense in trying to take his kit as a carry-on. Even at that, his papers were scrutinized closely and as his companions, the rest

of us were singled out for more thorough searching. At one point, I feared that Vivienne's shame-
less flirting with the guard would create a problem,
until I noticed that the man was having a hard time
keeping a straight face. With all the delays, we managed to get to our gate with only a little time to
spare before the flight. I held my breath when the
steward at check-in had to reissue our boarding
passes, complaining all the time of the inefficiency
of the person who'd issued them. Viv drew herself
up to her full height and leaned over the counter,
looking the attendant dead in the eye and convincing her finally that all was the way it should be.

Still, in spite of all the hassles we had boarding
the plane, once we took off I relaxed and the flight
started out rather enjoyably. Vivienne had booked
herself, Sam, and me into first class; Lily and Claude
were sitting in the first row of seats in coach. She'd
thought of everything from food preferences for
Sam to reserving two seats for Claude.

"You know, Viv, you should probably think of
opening a travel agency."

She laughed. "That would be something, wouldn't
it, Mitch? *'Bon soir, mesdames et messieurs,* I'm Vivienne,
come fly with me.' No, I think I'd rather keep
going as I have been, carefree and independent.
And gainfully unemployed. I'm so very good at it,
don't you think?"

Sam didn't join in our banter. He'd turned back
into the sullen man he'd seemed on the drive to
London. Something was still eating at him, that
much was easy to see. I wondered why Viv hadn't
picked up on it, but she seemed oblivious, chatter-
ing excitedly to one of the flight stewards, laying a
soft hand on his arm and asking to see the wine
list. And when she walked down the aisle with him

to inspect the bottle she'd chosen and didn't return in a respectable amount of time, I braced myself for Sam's anger.

Instead, he smiled fondly in the direction she'd gone. "If I know my girl, she'll be gone for a while. 'Never miss an opportunity to savor the wine' should be her motto. Although," and he gave a hoarse chuckle, "I doubt it's wine she's partaking of."

"And this doesn't bother you?"

He shook his head. "I don't know why it would; we both know it's nothing more than a desire to feed. But that's not what I want to talk about. I'm glad she'll be gone for a while. I need to tell you something and I'm coward enough to want to do it in a semipublic place, to avoid risking your temper. I've not been able to tell anybody, not even Viv. But it's tearing me up inside. I have to tell someone and that someone should be you. You, of everyone, have the right to know what I've done."

"Well then, talk away. Confession is good for the soul, or so you used to tell me when I was your patient."

He grimaced. "We're more than doctor and patient now, Mitch. We share a bond. And we're friends, or at least I hope so. Maybe you'll feel differently after I've had my say, but I won't."

"Yeah, we're friends and we'll stay friends. Come on, I know you well enough to know you're softening me up for something. What is it, Sam?"

"I hardly know where to start. So let's go back a few years, after the Others started their feud. Viv and I found a nice little place in Paris and played house for a while, it was like a vacation. But as the weeks stretched into months and years, I grew bored and I missed my work. There was no way I could do psychiatric work in France without all sorts of hassles and licenses. Then one day, I received a letter, addressed to me and forwarded from the old hospital."

"You told someone where you were?" I'd been in charge of the Cadre at the time and the rule was that we would not contact anyone we'd known before with our current whereabouts. True, Sam wasn't one of the Cadre, but I'd have expected him to obey the order better than that.

He rolled his eyes. "Yeah, I know. But it was just one of the nurses. She never gave the address to a soul, I'm sure of it. No one ever came knocking on our door, at least, so I assume she was trustworthy. I couldn't just disappear off the face of the earth. A life of nothing but drinking and dancing is fine for a while, but I've always needed more. Needed to feel useful."

I nodded. "And as you've said, you were relatively safe. Most of the attacks seemed to be on me and Deirdre. And now," the bitterness dripped from my voice, "we know why she was the primary target."

He continued without comment on my remark. "Anyway, when I opened the letter I found that it was an offer of work from a private clinic that wished me to do some blood research for them. They were looking for the key to triggering and intensifying the body's natural immune systems to fight fatal diseases. Cancer, AIDS, that sort of stuff. It seemed like interesting research and certainly worthwhile, to say nothing of the impeccable reputation of the clinic. So I agreed to their offer and they set me up in a little lab and provided all that I needed. Including the blood to test and experiment with."

"I knew all this, Sam. I certainly can't blame you for wanting to work, there's no need to feel guilty about it. The idle life is not for everyone; I'd not mind getting back into police work myself." I tried to lighten the conversation to put him at ease. "But the day shifts would be murder."

He gave a half-smile. "I don't feel guilty about wanting to work. But I should have been more cautious, asked more questions. I, more than any other doctor in the world, should have seen where this research was leading. Should have seen the purpose for the drug I was developing for them."

He looked out the window for a minute, sighed, and turned back to me, a bleak expression on his face. "I didn't know, Mitch, but damn it, I should have. I realize that now."

"What didn't you know, Sam?" I thought I could see where he was going with this, but I wanted to hear him say it. Hell, he needed to say it; this had been his problem since the beginning of our trip. Before that even. When he'd appeared at The Black Rose that night, I knew that he wasn't telling me the whole truth.

"I didn't know that the drug I developed would be used against vampires. Used against Deirdre. I never meant to harm her, never meant for any of this to happen. But it has. And it's my fault. If you want a scapegoat for the whole affair, you needn't look any further than me."

"I'm not looking for a scapegoat, Sam. And if I were, I've got Max Hunter who'll fit the bill perfectly. The blame belongs on his doorstep, not yours."

"Even so," he said, looking near tears. "I poisoned Deirdre, just as surely as if I'd fired that crossbow."

CHAPTER TEN

Deirdre Griffin: New York City

"Human? What the hell are you talking about?"

Max smiled again. "It's quite simple, Deirdre, you're becoming human."

"Human?" I said again almost as if I didn't know the meaning of the word. Then I threw my head back and laughed. "Max, that has got to be the most ridiculous thing you've ever told me to date. It's just not possible."

"As you say, Deirdre." He dropped his head, but not before I caught the angry gleam in his eyes. "You accuse me of not telling you what you need to know, of not telling you what is happening. And when I do tell you, you won't believe me. How am I supposed to win at this?"

"Tell me the truth. That's all I ask."

"And I have. You are, to the best of my knowledge, becoming human. Whether you want it now or not. If you could remember the symptoms of your sickness, you'd know I was right. Tell me if any of the following seem familiar: dizziness, wounds healing more slowly than normal, instability of body temperature with chills and fevers, extreme hunger, and vomiting after the taking of blood?"

I thought for a moment. "It's possible, I suppose, that I have had some of those symptoms in the past. But that doesn't prove anything except that I've been sick. And you admit that I was poisoned. Where's the proof it's more than that?"

"You will be the proof, Deirdre. Until we know about you for sure, this is all just conjecture."

"And exactly how will we test this theory? Sit around and wait for my hair to go gray? Wait to see if I grow old and die?"

"I think we'll know sooner than that, my dear." He refilled my glass. "A nightcap?"

I took the glass from him without answering. He continued his explanation of the process I was supposedly going through. "Here is how the poison works, Deirdre. It gets into your blood stream and converts that which made you a vampire into something else."

I shook my head. "That's not possible," I insisted for a second time. "Vampires are immune to everything."

"Apparently not."

"I am sorry, but I don't believe you, Max. I can't believe you."

"And what do you believe?"

Looking down at the glass I held, I noticed my hand shaking and willed it to be still. "I believe that this vile drink you've been pushing on me ever since I woke"—I tossed the glass across the room— "is the very thing that keeps me sick. I believe that if I hadn't drunk it, my memories would be returning. And my body would return to normal."

"You may choose to believe what you believe, Deirdre. It doesn't change a thing."

"Even so. I won't drink it."

Max looked angry, then shrugged and gave a short laugh. "Suit yourself."

"Damn straight, I will. I'm going to my room now, I want to be alone."

I spent most of the next day watching some of the collection of movies displayed on the book-shelves. They were all vampire movies, and, with the exception of one comedy, none of them seemed even vaguely familiar. And there was really only one particular scene in that movie that caught my at-tention. When the count (why did it always have to be a count?) gave his lady love the necklace, I re-membered the line before he said it. "It's a crea-ture of the night," I said with him, including the little flip of my hand. "It flies." Smiling, I saw the face of that blond woman again. We were laughing together over this very film. Tonight, I decided, I will ask Max who she is. He always said he was ded-icated to the recovery of my memory, but never re-ally seemed to want me to remember anything except what he told me.

And I would get him to take me out. I needed to see the night sky, needed to walk the streets. I'd al-ways been slightly claustrophobic and the days and nights spent caged up in this tiny room hadn't helped one bit.

The sound of the key in the lock interrupted my planning. Max stood there, a glass of that infernal liquid in his hand. I'd made up my mind the previ-ous night to not ingest Max's tonic, but stretched out my hand out to take it from him anyway. He seemed surprised but delighted when I seemed to take a sip without his encouragement. "That's better, Deirdre, you're not going to fight me anymore on this, are you?"

I smiled up at him over the glass. "No, Max, I'll be good. But," and I pulled at the skirt of my silk nightgown, "I'd like to get dressed tonight. And go out." He began to say something, a protest no doubt, but I interrupted him. "Not just to the club, but out. On the streets. I need to see the night. And I won't take no for an answer; you may consider it positive reinforcement for my actions." I punctuated the words by putting the glass to my lips again.

"Of course, my dear. But please allow me to accompany you."

Barely letting the liquid touch my tongue, I tilted the glass and took another "sip." Nodding, I then set the glass down on the nightstand. "Fine," I said, "but go away for a bit and let me get dressed."

Max raised an eyebrow. "You aren't fooling me, Deirdre. Drink it, now, or you won't get out of this room. Look around you, there's no place in here to dump it anyway."

I didn't say a word. There was no need to; he was right. Max came over and sat next to me on the narrow bed. "Why do you fight me, little one? I'm only doing this for you, for your health and your full recovery. The changes you are undergoing are difficult, but you'll come through them just fine, provided you do what I tell you to. You'll see."

"And then?"

"And then you can begin living the life you were meant to live—the one I took away from you over a century ago. Isn't that what you always wanted?"

I put my head into my hands for a minute then looked up at him and sighed. Maybe everything he said was true. "Hell, Max, how would I know?" Picking up the glass again, I choked down the bitter stuff, thinking all the while that I would find a way to vomit it up before we left the club.

He stood up, gave my shoulders a quick rub, and took the empty glass from my hand. "Get dressed," he said, "I'll wait in my office for you."

I slipped into the clothes I had worn last night, since they were all I had, and opened the door. "I need to go shopping, Max, I can't continue to wear the same outfit night after night."

He smiled. "See, you are feeling better already. Shopping it is."

As we passed the ladies' room, I touched his arm. "I'd like to put on a little makeup, if you don't mind. And, while we're at it, we need to add that to the list."

"Deirdre, you're beautiful to me, just the way you are."

"Thank you, Max. What a sweet thought. But this isn't for you, it's for me."

I walked into the restroom right behind a few early bird club goers. At least they would forestall Max's following me. Entering one of the stalls, I quickly knelt on the floor. Try as I might, though, I couldn't get rid of the offending liquid. I only had a small amount of time, I knew, before Max would come looking for me. There was only way sure way I knew to make myself vomit, I rolled up my sleeve and bit down hard on my own wrist, causing a quick splash of blood to enter my mouth. I swallowed quickly and no sooner did it hit my system than it came right back, bringing with it the drink Max had forced on me. Standing up, I felt dizzy, but that passed and I went to the sink and splashed water on my face. My wrist was still bleeding slightly, but

I held it under the cold water for a minute. Then I quickly applied the makeup, just a little rouge and some mascara for my eyelashes.

Max looked impatient when I came out. "I was just about to come in after you," he said. "What took you so long?"

I laughed, relieved that the offending liquid was out of my stomach. "That's a question one should never ask a lady, Max. It takes as long as it takes. But I feel better now, let's go."

I discovered that I knew more about clothing and the construction of clothing than I'd have thought. The act of turning a piece inside out to inspect the stitching seemed to be second nature. And there was something so terribly familiar about the rows of garments and the smell of new cloth. I found myself rejecting items as having shoddy workmanship simply by a glance at the label, almost as if I'd known the designer, as if I'd known what they were capable of. Fortunately, this shop was a high-end boutique and the selection was good, so I didn't reject many things.

Max proved more patient than I would have expected possible. And more generous. I knew he was wealthy, but I expected protests on some of the more expensive items I purchased. Instead, he smiled indulgently, complimented me continuously, and carried the bags—the very picture of a devoted husband. And somehow all of that just made me angrier; he couldn't be my husband. It made no sense that I'd feel the way I did if he were. Finally, when it looked like he could carry no more, I stopped. "Done?" he questioned, checking his watch.

"Yes, I suppose so. But I don't want to go back

yet. Could we stop somewhere for a drink or coffee or something?"

He nodded. "Not a problem, little one." He took
out his cell phone from his coat pocket and began
to dial. "Let me give Derek a call and he can come
over and take the packages back for us. Then we
can do whatever else you'd like, if you're not too
tired."

The truth was I was tired and feeling weak and
more than a bit queasy, but I'd have rather died
than admit that to him. The only way to get him
off guard and relaxed enough so that I could get
away was to pretend to be better. And so I laughed.
"Actually, Max, I could shop all night. It's been so
long since I've had pretty clothes."

"Has it?" He shrugged. "You're always pretty to
me. And besides, you were the one who ran off, taking practically everything you owned with you. Ah,
yes," he said speaking into the phone now, "Derek,
we're over at Slivers of Life, grab a taxi and come
get our packages, will you? Mrs. Hunter and I will
be going out for a while."

He folded up the phone and tucked it back into
his pocket. "Shouldn't take him too long to get
here, I'd think. Is there anything else you'd like
while we're waiting?"

While he'd been talking I'd been examining a
display of vinyl totes. "One of these, maybe." They
were cheap little bags, at an outrageous boutique
price, but they seemed to be well constructed, with
a strong seam at the base and a zipper with which
to close it. More important, they were the perfect
size for holding a glassful of liquid one might not
want to drink. I smiled. "Yes, these are nice, I'd like
one of these. The red vinyl one, I think."

Max shrugged again. "I'm not sure why you'd

want it, but if you do, it's yours." He took the bag from me with a smile and handed it and my other purchases to the salesclerk, who'd been hovering over us. "Anything else?"

"No, I think that'll do me. For now."

He laughed and turned to the clerk. "Ring all of this up."

"Cash or charge?"

He raised an eyebrow at the total on the register and reached into his pocket for his wallet. "Charge. Definitely. Even I'm not foolhardy enough to carry that much cash with me."

The salesclerk gave a simpering giggle as she accepted the card he handed her. "Thank you, Mr. Hunter."

As he signed the bill, he turned to me and smiled. "I hadn't expected that we'd buy quite this much."

I bit back an apology. If he was my husband, he was used to my extravagances. This shopping spree seemed too natural for it not to have occurred, with or without him, many times in my past.

The door opened, and Derek walked in, looked at the packages and whistled appreciatively. "A little shopping, eh?" he said, giving me a wink. "Nice to see you're feeling more like yourself, Mrs. Hunter. Is this all of it then?"

"Yes, thank you, Derek. We'll be back at some point in the evening. You have my number if there's an emergency. Other than that"—Max put an arm around my shoulders and hugged me to him briefly, guiding me to the door—"I don't want to be disturbed. Deirdre and I have a lot of catching up to do."

We walked aimlessly for a while, my arm tucked into his elbow. The air had an autumnal chill and when the wind blew it was downright cold. I shivered and my teeth chattered.

"Cold?" Max asked. "We can go back, if you want."

"No, not at all." Cold or not, I was enjoying being out in the open air, surrounded by the bustle of the city. I'd missed this place, I realized then, even without remembering it. And, I glanced up at Max and smiled, I'd missed him. Maybe he was telling me the truth. Now that I didn't feel like I was being held his prisoner, I could acknowledge that I almost loved this man. Something in me responded to him, I certainly felt completely comfortable in his presence. "But if you want to get a cup of something hot, I won't argue."

We crossed the street and arrived at a small diner, nothing upscale, I noted, but clean and presentable. "Here?"

"This is fine, Max."

The hostess sat us in a corner booth. "Coffee?" she asked, setting two mugs in front of us.

Max looked over at me.

"Coffee would be great," I said as she handed each of us a menu.

"Your waitress should be over in just a minute. Enjoy."

Opening the menu, I glanced over their offerings. I couldn't eat any of it, but there was something comforting about the thought of a slice of warm apple pie. "Are you getting anything?"

Max shook his head. "I'm not particularly hungry, my love, but you get something if you want."

I laughed. "That would be interesting. What would I do with solid food?" Then I stopped. What if he was right? If I were becoming human again, I could eat. But at the thought, my stomach lurched.

"No, I think I'll pass this time. I could use the coffee, though."

Max turned around and motioned to the waitress behind the counter. "Miss?" he said with a trace of impatience in his voice. "We'd like that coffee. Now, please." He turned back before the woman moved. She glared over at us, looked away, and then quickly looked back, staring intently at me. Her eyes opened wide and, as odd as it might seem, she appeared frightened. It was as if she remembered me from somewhere and no place good, I imagined. I wondered briefly if she would feed me the same line as Max had been dealing out. Would she try to reinforce the story as Derek had? Or did she know a different truth?

Without taking her eyes from me, she jerked a pot from the burner behind her. I heard the sizzle of the coffee on the hot surface. Then she squared her shoulders and hurried in our direction.

As she approached, I took more careful note of her appearance. She wasn't particularly imposing. Slight in build she had short, dark hair, and a pert little nose. She carried herself badly, though, as if slumping over could hide the cheap uniform she wore. Something in her attitude made me think that she'd not been working as a waitress for all that long. As she came closer, I could read the name embroidered on her breast pocket.

"Good evening," I said with a smile, looking up to where she stood in front of our booth. Her eyes still hadn't left my face and she extended the pot to pour but stopped short of the mugs. "I think we'll just have coffee for now, Terri, thank you."

With the sound of her name, Max's head shot up from his study of the menu.

The movement caught her attention and when

his eyes met hers, she gave a gasp of surprise. Terri stood totally still, eyes opened wide and staring, first at him, then at me, and then back to him.

That she knew Max was apparent. She gave him a smile that immediately turned into a sneer. "Coffee?" she said, her voice rising above the noise around us. "Coffee?" Her voice quivered and the range of emotions reflected on her face was fascinating. Rage, righteous indignation, fear, all of these flickered in and out of her eyes and her mouth twisted up into a snarl. "Coffee? I'm so very happy to oblige, you son of a bitch!"

And she poured the entire pot of steaming coffee into Max's lap.

CHAPTER ELEVEN

Max's reaction was almost serpentine in its swiftness and cruelty. Before I even had time to register what had happened, he was out of his seat, gripping her by the shoulders and shaking her violently. His voice was low and quiet, but I hadn't a doubt that the rest of the diner heard him. "You clumsy fucking bitch," he whispered, and I flinched at the obscenity. "You did that on purpose."

To give the woman credit, she held her ground, despite being shaken around like a rag doll. Her teeth clattered, but her voice came out clean and clear. "Damn straight, I did, you lying bastard. And I'm glad I did. You ruined my life."

"And I'd be thrilled to ruin it more, Ms. Hamilton, don't think that I wouldn't. If you say one more word, I can make you wish you were never born."

I stood up, thinking there should be a way for me to intervene. But Max ignored me and continued his tirade. "I suppose you thought waiting tables was a comedown from broadcasting? I'll fix it so you won't even be able to get a job cleaning out toilets in this city." He dropped his hands from her shoulders. "Now get the hell out. I never want to see your face again."

He pushed her away and turned to me. "I'm going to go clean up, Deirdre, my love." The instantaneous change of his voice from threatening to loving was terrifying. Who was this man, able to display bone shattering anger one second and tender concern the next? I nodded, unable to say a word. He was crazy, there was no doubt in my mind at that moment. Whoever, whatever he'd been to me in the past, he could not now be anyone I'd ever trust or love.

He kissed my cheek and I jerked involuntarily. "And then," he smiled, not noticing my fear, "when I get back, we'll go home." Spinning around, he stalked down the corridor to the restrooms.

Terri stared after him for a second, then looked over at me. "I hate this stinking job anyway," she said, scribbling something on her order pad, tearing it off, and slamming it down on the table. "He doesn't own as much of this city as he thinks he does. Egotistical bastard. And you? Jesus Christ, Deirdre, what the hell are you doing here? With him of all people? Don't you know who he is? Don't you know what he's done to you? I thought you were in Whitby. And where the hell is Mitch?"

Mitch? Who was Mitch? She must have seen the question in my eyes and she started to say more, but the manager of the diner came over, apologized profusely to me, and led her away. They had a brief, heated discussion by the front door and then she stormed out.

I picked up the paper she'd left, thinking it was the bill for the coffee and wondering at her nerve. Instead written on the paper was a phone number.

And one word. *Revenge.* Glancing guiltily toward
the men's room, I folded the note quickly, sliding
it with difficulty into the pocket of my skin-tight
leather jeans. Then I sat back down at the booth
and stared out the window at the retreating figure
of Terri Hamilton. Who was she? And what did she
know about me?

And who was Mitch?

A hand on my shoulder interrupted my thoughts
and I jumped. "Let's go," Max said. "We can get coffee at the club. At least there," he gave a choking
laugh, "they'll give me a cup out of which to drink
it."

I slid out of the booth, giving him what I hoped
was a consoling smile to hide the turmoil I was
feeling, a strange combination of triumph and fear.
In Terri Hamilton, I'd finally found someone who
knew me who quite obviously wasn't in Max's employ, someone who might give me the truth. I
doubted that she'd been my friend in my former
life; seeing her sparked no recognition at all, but it
was obvious she hated Max. That, if nothing else,
gave us a common bond. Running my fingers over
the lump of paper in my pocket, I gathered up my
purse and flashed him a cold smile.

"Friend of yours, Max?"

For a split second a wave of anger flooded his face
and I feared he'd begin shaking me, too. Instead,
the emotion passed as quickly as it came and he
laughed. "Not hardly, little one. She's a nobody.
Don't give her a second thought." He held the door
of the diner open for me and we both walked out
onto the street. "Now, do you want to walk or should
we take a cab back?"

Perhaps it was hearing those words, perhaps it
was meeting Terri Hamilton, hearing her mention

Whitby and someone named Mitch. Maybe it was a combination of all those things. Whatever the reason, I felt myself transported back to a different time and a different place. And the someone with me was different, too.

"Can't really afford it. Besides, I didn't bring any cash with me."

I hadn't realized that I said the words out loud until Max looked at me and gave a short barking laugh. "What a silly thing to say, Deirdre. We can certainly afford cab fare and I have plenty of cash. What would you need cash for?"

When he spoke the vision of another place and time, the sense of another man at my side, faded. I shrugged, "I don't know why I said that, Max. I think I must be tired. It's been quite a momentous evening for my first night free from captivity. Let's go back."

He hailed a cab and as we climbed in, I thought of the laughing face of the blond woman that kept flashing into my mind. "Who's the blond woman?" I asked.

"Blond? I'm not sure I know what you mean." Then he reached over and ruffled my short bleached hair. "You're blond now, of course. I've been thinking that we should do something about that. I'll make some calls tomorrow—see if I can get an evening appointment at some salon or other."

"That would be nice, Max. Thank you." Slouching back in the seat, I pressed my fingers against my eyes. *Damn him,* I thought, *every time I get close to recalling a piece of my past he changes the subject.* I tried to pull up the bit of memory again. And there, there she was. "Besides, that's not what I meant. I don't mean me. Hell, I don't even know why I'd do this to my hair. But I keep getting this recurring flash of a blond woman, usually laughing."

Max stared out the window. "That would've been Vivienne. She was one of mine, from a long time ago."

Vivienne? Although I could see her face in my mind, the name meant nothing to me. Then I caught Max's use of past tense. "Was?" I paused. "What do you mean by was? Is she dead?" Somehow that thought saddened me more than I'd have imagined.

He cleared his throat. "If not dead, she's gone so far underground, it makes no difference. Very few of the original Cadre vampires are left, Deirdre. Eduard DeRouchard did his job quite well. And what he couldn't finish, Terri Hamilton cleaned up with her work on television. She's a dangerous woman. Deadly." Max gave a humorless chuckle. "Even armed with only a pot of coffee."

"Terri? I am certainly no good judge of character, Max, but she seemed fine, perfectly normal. At least, that is, until she saw you. What did she mean? You ruined her life?"

"Does it matter? I did what I had to do at the time to save the life of the one person I care for above everyone else." He reached over and took my hand, bringing it to his lips. "I wouldn't waste my time worrying over the likes of her, little one. Nor about Vivienne. Neither of them are worth the trouble."

We sat in silence for a while as the cab stopped at a light. When we started back up again, he gave a little cough. "What did she say to you while I was gone? Did she imply that she knew things about you? She doesn't, you know. She only knows what DeRouchard fed her, most of which was completely false." There was a casualness in his voice that seemed forced and I knew he was lying.

I wanted to laugh. We were both so good at this

game, the giving and taking of lies. Once again I rubbed my fingers over the outline of the note in my pocket and smiled into the darkness of the cab. "No, there wasn't really time for conversation. She just said that she hated the job anyway and then the manager dragged her away. I am fairly sure he fired her."

"Ah. Well, that's good. I find it hard to believe, but she's even a worse waitress than she was a news reporter."

I murmured something noncommittal and the cab pulled up in front of the Ballroom of Romance.

"And here we are." Max's voice was cheerful again, as if arriving here put the dishonesty behind him and let him tread comfortable ground again. "Home, at last."

Home? I glanced at his profile as he paid the driver. This place wasn't any kind of home. Not for me. Not here and not with him. The easy feeling I'd had in his presence earlier in the evening faded into wariness. And a certainty—even if I knew nothing else, even if my memory never returned, I now knew one fact. A fact I must take care not to forget. Max was an imposter. He was not my husband. He was the enemy.

Max led the way through the crowd outside the door. Something in the combination of the crowd and the cold autumn air and the familiar entrance to the club clicked off a memory.

A tall, blond-haired man stood outside, admitting groups of people after checking ID cards. He looked up, saw us, and waved us in ahead of the others. "Just follow me," he said and as he said the words it was as if a transparent screen came down in front of me and memories from the past superceded the here and now.

Another blond-haired doorman had met me here before and escorted me to a table. I'd trailed after him, appreciating the breadth of his shoulders and the heady aroma of his cologne. There were times I'd regretted not getting to know him better, but as it turned out, it was good that I hadn't become romantically entangled with the man. Larry Martin had been a psychopath. Beautiful on the outside and totally evil within.

My mouth curved up in a triumphant smile. I remembered something, independent of Max's input or his tonic. The memories were returning, all I had to do was keep refusing to ingest the drink and soon I would be cured.

With the memory of that other time, came the certainty that Larry Martin was dead. Another scene from the past played out before my eyes. The cellar had been dark and the shot deafening. A sharp pain pierced my shoulder. Larry gave a gasp and fell to the ground, bearing me down with him, his blood flowing over me. There was a voice, a remembered voice, "Oh, God, Deirdre," he called from the top of the stairs. And then, "Jesus, look at you."

"It's okay, Mitch," I'd said. "I wasn't hit, all this is Larry's."

Mitch! I held my breath for a minute, waiting for the flash to subside, but unlike many of the other glimpses I'd had this memory remained, like a single star burning in the black of the night. And the emotions I'd experienced at the time were as clear and as fresh as if they'd happened just this night.

"Deirdre?"

Apparently I had stopped still on the street, surrounded by the crowd trying to gain admittance to the Ballroom. Max pushed back down the steps and held out a hand to me. I blinked my eyes, stunned at the return to the present.

"Are you all right?"

I nodded. "Fine. I was just distracted for a moment, is all."

He took my arm when we entered the club. "I think we'll take our drinks back in the office. The trip out seems to have tired you more than I would have expected. I certainly don't want you falling sick again, just when you're starting to come back."

"Yes, that would be a shame, wouldn't it?" I decided then and there to keep the extent of the memories I was recovering a secret from him. And to test my theory of the tonic he was feeding me. Somehow I knew that it was responsible for keeping the memories at bay. I could live for a while, I was sure, with no sustenance, turning human or not.

I pulled his arm closer to mine as we headed back to the office, hoping he couldn't feel the way touching him made my flesh crawl. "Thank you for taking me out tonight, Max. It was just what I needed."

He looked down at me. "I'm glad, Deirdre. I only want to make you happy."

I settled in on the black leather sofa, content to replay the few memories I had over and over again, having a silent chuckle every now and then at the remembrance of Terri Hamilton pouring that entire pot of hot coffee into Max's lap. *Touché,* I thought. *Good for you, Terri.*

Max fussed with some papers at his desk and listened to his phone messages. "Damn," he said, coming over to the sofa and pouring me a glass of the special tonic.

"Something wrong, Max?" I took the wineglass

from his hand, but he didn't urge me to drink for a change. Instead, he seemed distracted.

"Nothing really," he said, the tension in his voice belying his words. "I missed an important phone call while we were out." Lost in his thoughts and almost ignoring my presence, he walked back to his desk and sat down behind it. "One I'd been waiting for," he continued, talking more to himself than to me. "But I'm quite sure they will call back. They'd damn well better or they'll be very sorry they crossed me . . ."

His voice trailed away and I stole a glance at him. Max's face was set in anger, its finely sculpted lines distorted into a mask of evil. *Here,* I thought with a shiver, *here is the truth of the man.*

CHAPTER TWELVE

He continued to ignore me, giving me time to think, to plan. Now that I knew the truth of the matter, knew him for what he was, what on earth could I do about it? I glanced over at Max again, pretending to sip a glass of that horrid stuff, watching him tend to some paperwork at his desk. What did he hope to gain from all of this? Obviously not my goodwill. He had to be crazy if he thought that I'd stay with him after I learned the truth.

And yet, here I sat, wearing the clothes he bought, living in the shelter he provided, taking my sole sustenance in the drink he provided. Which one of us was the crazy one? Prior to this evening, I didn't know any better, but now that I did, what was I going to do about it?

The phone rang and I jumped. Max crooked an eyebrow and gave me a twisted smile. "Nervous, little one? Expecting a call? Guilty thoughts?"

Biting my lip, I shook my head.

"Hunter here." Turning his attention back to the call, he listened for a bit. "Good. Good. Are you

sure?" Then he glanced back to me for a minute
and a slow blush crawled up my neck. "Yes, of
course." His answer was cautious, but I knew somehow they were talking about me. "Where else?"

I struggled to hear the voice of the caller, but
the noise from the club outside drowned it out.
Max laughed into the receiver. "Yes, I'll be sure to.
Thank you for calling so promptly." His voice
dripped with sarcasm. "I'd expected to hear from
you sooner." A pause ensued and he drummed his
fingers on the desk top. "No. No. You don't seem
to understand. I don't care if there are problems.
You know what to do, don't you? Perhaps I wasn't
clear enough." He was scowling now. "Look, I don't
give a damn how you feel about it," he said. "You
know what you need to do. Just do it. And let me
know when it's done." He hung up the phone.

"That was Derek," Max stood up from his desk
and walked toward me. "He says he put all the
packages into your room. And he sends his regards."

He was lying, obviously. There was no way that
conversation could be so easily explained. But I
played along with him. "Ah. That's nice of him."

"Deirdre," he sat next to me on the couch, "are
you upset about something? You haven't seemed
well since we got out of the cab. You can't let that
little scene in the diner with Terri Hamilton bother
you. She's not balanced. She should be locked up
somewhere instead of out on the streets, harassing
innocent people."

I shrugged. "I'm tired, Max, that's all. And"—I
set down the full wineglass I'd been feigning to
drink from next to me—"I don't want anymore of
this. I just want to sleep."

"But it's hardly even midnight. What happened to my little night-owl?"

"She's not here, Max. I think I left her behind with my memories." Sighing, I stood up and stretched. "Remember that I have been sick. And I need my rest. Good night."

I felt his eyes follow me across the room. "I'll come in after a while to say good night properly."

My back stiffened as I opened the door, but I didn't say a word as I entered my little room, I didn't even turn around, but pushed the door shut behind me. The shopping bags full of the clothes we had bought earlier in the evening were lined up neatly against one of the walls. I had been so thrilled with the trip, and now I felt like sending them all back, or opening the door back up and tossing them all into his face. Somehow, I knew that their purchase now made me beholden to Max, made me feel pressured into accepting his properly expressed good night. I shivered and gave a humorless laugh. "Now that's a euphemism if ever I've heard one."

If the offer had come one of my other nights here, I might have welcomed him with open arms. I'd been so lonely, aching for comfort and touch. But now?

I shook my head and began to unpack the articles of clothing, either hanging them up or folding and laying them into the dresser. Inside both the armoire and the drawers there was a stale floral scent; I closed my eyes and took a deep breath to identify it.

Lavender, that was the scent. Without opening my eyes, I breathed in the aroma again. And the vision of the blonde burst into my brain. If I could believe Max, she now had a name. Vivienne. My mind provided the rest. Vivienne Courbet. I remembered her. It was as if I could feel her hug me, feel the feather-light brush of her lips on my cheeks. I could almost hear her melodic high-pitched laughter, like the pealing of bells. Not wanting to lose the vision, I kept my eyes tightly shut and smiled.

Then the smile faded. Max had said she was dead. Dead? "Not possible," I whispered. "He has lied to me about so many things. So she might not be dead. Not Vivienne."

I brushed away a tear and when I opened my eyes, Vivienne was still with me. I wanted to tell someone the good news, that it was all coming back to me. If one or two stars could break through the darkness, others would surely follow. But I dared not tell Max. Nor Derek. They, and now Terri Hamilton, were the only people I knew.

As I finished putting away the clothes, I noticed that the bottom drawer wouldn't close all the way. I pulled it out and set it on the bed, then knelt down on the floor. There, in the open space below the drawer, lay a pair of jeans, a flannel shirt, and a bra and panties. I pulled them out and as I did so, a small plastic tape cassette fell onto the floor, clattering slightly. Scooping it up immediately, I looked around the room for a tape player, but there wasn't one. "Damn."

With Max's impending visit, I couldn't have listened to it anyway, so I tucked it under the mattress. The jeans and shirt I held up to my face and breathed in their scent. They held the aroma of a wood fire and cigarette smoke. And something else, too faint to place as certainly as the others. Whatever it was, though, that scent was one of the most beautiful things I'd ever smelled. And I knew that it was the scent of Mitch. Looking over my shoulder at the door, I folded the clothes back up, wrapping them in one of the bags from my purchases, to keep their scents with them. Then I lay them flat so that they'd fit under the drawer I slid back into place. Tomorrow, I thought, I can try again tomorrow.

Knowing that Max might come in at any moment changed my nighttime routine. Ordinarily, I'd change into my nightgown and read or watch a movie before falling off to sleep. But I thought I knew what he meant by saying good night properly and I needed the protection of clothes, flimsy though they were. Remembering the piece of paper Terri had given me in the diner, I pulled it out of my pocket and tucked it under the mattress with the tape.

I lay down on the bed, fully clothed, turning on the television for background noise and began to make a mental list of what needed to be done. First, I'd have to find a tape player and listen to that cassette. It didn't have to be anything earth shattering to be of value—a song, a voice, something might trigger another memory like the lavender scent did. I'd have to get access to a phone so that I could speak to Terri Hamilton in private. And I'd have to find a way to provide nourishment for myself, so that I could get through without drinking what Max offered.

None of this was going to be easy, considering Max never left my side when I was outside of this room. I needed a way to make him trust me, so that he would ease up on his vigilance. And there was a way, one I hated to even contemplate. The thoughts of Max touching me in any sort of sexual way made my stomach roll. Perhaps there was a time in my past life when I welcomed his advances, but now it just felt wrong. Still, if I allowed him to have sex with me, he might actually believe that I was coming around to his point of view, might think that I could be trusted to be left alone for a short period of time. And a short period of time was all I'd need to get away. This was a big city and my instincts were still good enough so that I could lose myself in the crowds.

The door opened and Max walked in. Here and now, there was no place to hide. "You aren't ready for bed? I thought you were tired."

He clicked off the television. "You watch too much of this stuff, when you're supposed to be resting. I can hear the sound in my office."

"I am bored, Max. I've no idea what my life was prior to here, but I'm quite sure I kept myself busy."

"That you did, little one. Too busy, perhaps."

Rising from the bed, all thoughts of cooperation flying from my mind in a sudden rush of anger, I gave a loud screech of frustration. "I cannot stand being cooped up in this room, Max. I cannot stand being under your constant surveillance. This is not life. This is limbo. Worse than that, this is hell. It is not home for me, it will never be home for me. I would have refused to share your coffin space when this room was nothing but a crypt. Fancy wallpaper and soft carpeting notwithstanding, this place is still a goddamned crypt. I want out."

He raised an eyebrow. "A crypt? And when was this place ever a crypt."

"Don't be stupid, Max. I remember when this room held two coffins, one for each of us." Then I

stopped. Smiled. "Damn, I really do remember that."
Gone was the determination to keep any recovery
of memories secret, swallowed up in the delight of
regaining my past. "And I remember Victor." I
laughed, "I called him your Renfield. And I did kill
you. It wasn't just a dream, I know I did. You goaded
me into it. You wanted to die, I think, and couldn't
do it yourself. And you'd be dead still if it weren't
for Eduard DeRouchard."

Max shook his head. "Deirdre, I'm concerned
with this development. I really am. You seem to be
returning to your old delusions. When you were
sick, you would talk about all of these strange things
you thought you'd done. The fact is, my love, none
of that was real. You dreamed it, yes, you dreamed
all of it."

"No. That's not possible. These are real memories." I was not about to let him talk me out of the
truth.

"And what else do you remember?" His voice
sounded curt, angry, but I ignored the tone. I didn't
care if I angered him. These revelations were too
important.

"I remember Larry Martin. Killed in the basement
of the Ballroom. Shot." I stopped again as the scene
filled my mind. "Mitch," I said, unable to control
the softness in my voice. "Mitch killed him. To save
my life."

"Mitch? Who is Mitch?"

I stared at him, either he was a better actor than
I'd ever have imagined, or he was totally insane.
"Mitchell Greer. My husband."

Max thought for a moment, as if he were dragging the name up from the dregs of his mind. "You
mean Detective Greer? He was here a few years

ago, investigating some murders in the area. I hadn't realized you'd met him. He must've made a strong impression on you to feature in your delusions."

"They are not delusions, Max, they are the truth." My voice was not as sure as it had been just a minute earlier. What if Max weren't the crazy one after all?

"He's still working in the city, as far as I know, Deirdre. Would it make you feel better if I arranged for him to come and talk to you?"

My heart rose. Mitch? Here? Oh, just to see him again would be heaven. He was the someone I'd been missing. But what sort of game was Max playing now? Why would he risk the confrontation? I shook my head slightly and raised my hand, palm facing him. "Wait a minute. What did you just say? Bring Mitch here? Why on earth would *you* do that?"

"So that you can finally put all of this to rest. I want you back, little one, all of you. Just the way it used to be."

"It was never that way, Max."

"It was, Deirdre. And I can prove it." He put his hand into his pocket. "But we'll do that tomorrow. For now, I want you to sleep."

I didn't see the hypodermic in his hand until it was too late. But as the needle slid into my arm, I had another memory. He had done this to me before, on a hillside in another country, overlooking a restless ocean.

I wanted to reach out and rake his face with my nails, wanted to hurt him, to kill him, to make him let me go.

But the drug he'd pumped into my system worked too quickly for me to do anything but give a dismayed cry.

"Why?" My eyes grew heavy and I dropped onto the bed. He touched my arm and I hadn't even the strength to push him away. "Why?" I asked again, my voice not loud enough to be heard.

"It's for the best, Deirdre. You'll see."

CHAPTER THIRTEEN

Mitch Greer: New York City

I can't say Sam's revelation that he'd been the one
who developed the poison that afflicted Deirdre
came as much of a surprise. Using him made good
sense, from the point of view of the Others, as well
as providing a certain irony to the proceedings
that both Eduard and Max could appreciate. As for
his fear that I would be angry about his involve-
ment, he was dead on about that. I was furious that
he'd not been long-sighted enough to see the consequences, but I decided that I couldn't afford to
allow myself the luxury of anger. Too much de-
pended on him. When we recovered Chris and
Deirdre, they both might need medical treatment.
And it wasn't as if we could just check them into a
regular hospital—too many questions would be
asked.

Vivienne returned to her seat shortly after Sam
had made his confession. She smiled at him and
winked at me, making the motion of wiping her

mouth after a particularly tasty meal. The steward appeared at the entrance from the galley and began to take orders for drinks. He may have been a little paler than when we'd boarded the plane, but seemed none the worse for wear. I chuckled to myself. Viv probably supplied him with a lifetime's worth of erotic dreams in those few minutes she was gone.

She curled her legs underneath her in the seat and snuggled underneath a blanket, resting her head on Sam's shoulder. He kissed the top of her head and I turned in my seat to stare out the window, remembering other flights from England. Damn, I missed her. Only gone two days and already her absence made a huge gap in my life. And now with Chris gone I felt totally alone in the world. I gave a grim chuckle, thinking I should have throttled Maggie when I had the chance and saved all of us a lot of heartache.

The steward made his way to my seat and I ordered a double scotch on the rocks. I nursed the drink through most of the flight, drifting in and out of my thoughts. My traveling companions noted the choice of drink and left me alone.

The flight itself was easy sailing across the ocean, but there was a weather delay in touching down in New York and we ended up circling the airport for almost two hours. Our baggage seemed to take an unusual amount of time to be unloaded and, following that, the line to go through customs was lengthy, winding around in a serpentine pattern. Once we reached the officials, they decided to search all of our luggage. By the time we'd gotten everything back into order and hired cabs to take us all over to the airport hotel in which Vivienne had booked our rooms, there was only about an hour left before dawn. As much as I wanted to search for Deirdre during our stay over before the flight to New Orleans the next night, I reluctantly acknowledged that it was much too risky to take a cab into the city and hope to accomplish anything worthwhile at all before sun up. And where on earth would I start looking? I really had no idea if she was even in this city. In reality, she could be anywhere. If I had taken her, I'd have hidden her well in the least likeliest place.

No, there would be no search for her tonight. Finding Chris and Maggie had to be my first priority anyway. As much as I hated being separated from Deirdre, and as concerned as I was about Max's intentions (if indeed the soul inside Steven DeRouchard's body was Max's) I had the greatest confidence in her ability to take care of herself. Even without a memory, she had her instincts to fall back on. And, I smiled to myself as I closed the curtains and crawled into bed, her instincts for how to handle Max had always been dead on.

"All in all, you've bought yourself a pile of trouble, Max, old man," I said.

I didn't actually sleep much that day, being too keyed up about the tasks ahead of me, too worried about Chris and Deirdre. Had it not been for the soft talking coming from Sam and Viv's room next to mine, I'd have knocked on their door and asked her to put me to sleep, as she had that last night in Whitby.

I'd never become accustomed to the reversal of sleep patterns and being a vampire could be boring at times. When I was with Deirdre, the waste of the daylight hours didn't bother me one bit. We always found something to do, something to talk about. But without her, the hours just dragged on. I'd been a vampire for over four years now, and for the most part it wasn't a bad life, far preferable to the alternative of dying that night back in my old apartment.

Still, the restrictions of the lifestyle disturbed me more than I'd ever have let on to Deirdre. The avoidance of sunlight, the furtive feedings, the feeling that one must keep watching over one's shoulder, feeling all powerful at one point and completely vulnerable the next: all of that took a heavy toll on me. I understood now, much better than when I was human, the difficulties of the life and how easy it would be to fall into despair or degeneracy. As a result, I had tremendous respect for the accomplishments of Vivienne or Deirdre or Victor or even Max. That they'd lived as long as they had without going totally insane from lack of sunlight or lack of human touch, from the loneliness or the ultimate separation from all that one loved, amazed me.

I'd never have considered vampirism as a viable choice, though, had Deirdre not been one. The rush of sheer power was invigorating and exhilarating, true; the shape-changing, the euphoria of feeding, the intensification of emotions and senses made it a thrilling existence, but I still wasn't sure it could compare with sitting on a beach somewhere watching the sun rise.

Or, I thought as I got back out of bed and started to read the room service menu, *a steaming plateful of fettuccine alfredo with extra garlic.*

Looking into the mirror, I gave myself a twisted

smile. "Greer, you've got to be the only person alive who'd seriously consider trading immortality for a serving of pasta."

Since sleep seemed impossible, I flipped through the television channels a few times with nothing catching my attention. Then I sat down at the desk and began to make a list of all the people I knew that Deirdre knew in New York City. It wasn't a very long list, especially since I left off almost all of the Cadre. The list consisted of only two names: Betsy, the woman who bought Griffin Designs, and Max, who might not be alive. And if alive, he might not be here. The simple fact that it seemed right that Steven DeRouchard was also Max Hunter didn't make it true. Then again, I'd always been good about playing hunches and I'd have put good money down on this one without a worry in the world.

Picking up the phone book, I found the number for Griffin Designs and dialed.

"Good morning, Griffin Designs. How may I direct your call?"

"I'd like to speak with the owner, please. Betsy . . ." I hesitated for a moment, realizing that I completely forgot her last name. Fortunately the woman supplied it for me.

"McCain. And who may I say is calling?"

"Mitchell Greer. I'm Deirdre Griffin's husband."

"Hold please."

I barely had time to identify the Muzak song when Betsy's voice shrilled in my ear.

"Mitch! My God, it's been years. Are you in town? Is Deirdre with you? I'd love to see her. Did you know that her daughter stopped here a few years ago?" She paused for a second to give a hoarse laugh. "Imagine her having a daughter. And at first

I thought the girl was Deirdre. Amazing resemblance, isn't it?"

I shook my head. Nice to know some people never changed. Betsy was a brassy, fast-talking, cutthroat business woman. I never liked her much, to be honest, but she was the only hope I had right now.

"I'm in town, yes, Betsy. Staying over at the airport right now and I'll be taking a plane to New Orleans this evening."

"Lovely place, New Orleans, very romantic. A vacation for the two of you? A second honeymoon maybe?"

"Well, not really, Betsy. Here's the problem. Deirdre isn't with me. And I'm not sure where she is. I was hoping that you might have seen her recently."

"Haven't seen hide nor hair of her. You two have separated?"

"Not willingly, Betsy. It's kind of a complicated situation and hard to explain on the phone."

"Oh."

That one word carried a lot of suspicion and wariness. It was as if I could hear the thoughts running through her mind. *They'd had a quarrel or Deirdre had run off with another man or Mitch was a lousy control-freak bastard who was a bad husband.* Or worse, I shuddered a bit, remembering her hand on my knee at our wedding dinner, maybe she was thinking that I was now on the market.

"Complicated? I guess it is. But if you can't explain on the phone, we could maybe meet for lunch? Amazingly enough my schedule for today is completely clear and I'd adore to see you again."

"I'd love to, Betsy, but I'm afraid I can't. I'll take a rain check, though." *When hell freezes over.*

"Hold on for a second, Mitch, I've got another call."

I listened to the hold music again, still not able to identify the song, a different one this time.

"Mitch? Look, I'm sorry. I'd love to chat for a while but I've got an emergency here. If I happen to see Deirdre, I'll let her know you're looking for her. How long will you be in New Orleans? And where can she reach you?"

I checked the itinerary Vivienne had drawn up for us. "I've no idea how long we'll be in New Orleans. But I'm staying at the Hotel of Souls." I gave her the number, she repeated it back to me.

"Got it," she said. "You have a safe trip. And don't be such a stranger in the future, okay?"

"Okay. And thanks, Betsy. Talk to you soon."

The whole conversation killed no more than a few minutes, even counting the time I spent on hold. I lay back down on the bed and tried to clear my mind of all worries and thoughts. Eventually, I slept, but only fitfully, waking every hour to check on the slow progression of the clock.

Relieved when the time finally reached four o'clock, I got out of bed and took a shower, which helped to fight the grogginess. *When this is all over,* I told myself while shaving, *I'll sleep like one of the dead.* Technically, though, there was something to be said for classifying me in that category right now. But I didn't feel dead, just tired and angry.

The phone rang. "Yeah?"

The call sounded far away, scratchy. "Mitch?" I didn't recognize the voice.

"Yeah, this is Mitch. Who is this? Deirdre? Is it you, sweetheart?"

There was no answer, but the caller drew in a

ragged breath. "I've changed my mind, Mitch. You need to find me. You need to help me. Chris is gone. And God help me, I can't do what I need to do unless you come to me . . ."

"Maggie? Where are you?"

She made a noise. She sounded like a wounded animal and I couldn't tell if she was laughing or crying. "You should know where I am," she said finally, her words halting and quiet. "You're the detective, aren't you?"

"I know you went to New Orleans," I said. "Are you still there?"

"Yes," she breathed the answer.

"And Chris? Is he with you? Is he okay?"

"I don't know," she said, "I don't know." She paused, then started again. "I don't know, I don't know, I don't know . . ."

I interrupted her, keeping my voice as calm as possible. She was panicked enough for the both of us. "How can you not know, Maggie?"

"Ooohhhhh." She dragged out the word. "Please. Don't ask me anymore questions, Mitch. I can't answer them. My head hurts. Just come."

The line went dead and I stared at the receiver for a moment before hanging it up. When I did, it rang again instantly.

"Maggie?"

"Maggie? Why would I be Maggie? And why would you even need to ask me that? This is Viv, of course."

"Sorry."

"Mitch, *mon amour,* you sound strange, you must have been dreaming. Are you awake now? Are you decent? And if not, shall I get rid of Sam and we'll fly away together?"

"Good morning, Vivienne. Sleep well?"

"Always. It's one of the benefits of having a clean conscience."

I managed a laugh. "Or none at all."

"Oui," she giggled, "that is also a possibility. We have coffee over here and croissants for Sam, dirty rat that he is." I heard his mock protest through the phone. "We've a bit of time until the flight. Would you care to join us?"

"Give me a few minutes to dress and I'll be right over. Can you give Claude and Lily a call as well? We need to make plans. And I need to tell you all about the call I just got."

I threw on a clean pair of jeans and a black T-shirt, ran my fingers through my tangled hair. The black dye I'd used to cover my now natural gray was fading away, but the roots still showed. When everything returned to normal, I'd do something about that.

Normal. I took one last look in the mirror and sighed. What was normal? Certainly not the life I led. And if what Sam said was true, it never would be. What sort of life would Deirdre and I have, if any? And Chris? Where was he? What had Maggie done to him? I couldn't bear the thoughts of her killing him or hurting him in any way. He had to be alive. But what did that mean in his case? How would Chris adjust to being back among the living? Would he become one of the Others and breed children only to murder them at birth to preserve his life?

I hoped I'd taught him better. But what sort of fatherly example did I set? Being a vampire hardly exemplified family values.

I tried to silence the questions as I stowed away

the few items I'd removed from the duffel bag. *If there were answers,* I thought, picking up the bag and going out the door to Viv's room, *I couldn't find them on my own.*

CHAPTER FOURTEEN

When Sam opened the door to me, I could see they were all in high spirits, lounging around the room, drinking coffee. Lily was sitting on the floor by the television, her legs crossed in front of her. Claude had settled in on one of the beds. Vivienne lay curled up on the other and Sam was pacing the room. I nodded to them all and took the large armchair in the corner next to Viv's bed.

"But Vivienne," Lily said, "you forget. I've seen all the teen slasher movies. What else did I have to do with my time? So I know that separating to find Chris and Mom is like committing suicide. They'll pick us off individually."

"Lily, my darling girl, there is no they in this situation. Or if there is, then they are us." Vivienne laughed. "We are the monsters, *ma petit chou,* you must never forget that."

Lily gave a mock sigh. "And here all the time I thought I'd been cast in the role of the teenage heroine. You know, the one who lives through the movie? Someone's gotta star in the sequel after all."

"Sequel?" Claude feigned shock. "I was hoping for a nice tidy ending in which everyone gets everything they want and we all live happily ever after."

"With," I said, joining the discussion, "the emphasis on the ever after."

"Can we drop the movie analogies now?" Sam looked uncomfortable, possibly because he was the only one in the room without at least the promise of immortality. "We've got"—he glanced at the bedside clock—"about two hours before we catch the flight to New Orleans. In addition to making our plans, I feel like I need to update all of you." He gave me a grim look and continued, "On certain recent medical discoveries and how all of this came about."

"Lecture time from Dr. Sam," Vivienne said with poorly disguised laughter in her voice, "sit up straight, boys and girls."

He gave her a scathing look and the smile positively melted from her face. *"Pardon,"* she whispered. "You are right, Sam. We all need to know all that we can."

He proceeded to tell Lily and Claude what he'd told Vivienne and me back in Whitby of the changes that were taking place in Deirdre. How it seemed she was evolving away from the vampiric and into something that was human and yet different as well. When he got to the part where he surmised her mother might very likely be pregnant, Lily scoffed.

"Yeah, right. The rest of it you might get me to believe; I saw her that last night and we all know how bad she looked. And Mitch can vouch for the fact that her memory was deteriorating. But pregnant? How is it possible that a woman over a century old is capable of producing viable ova? Or that Mitch, even after just a few years of being a vampire, would be capable of fertilizing these?"

Sam shook his head. "I can't explain it, Lily. But why don't you tell me how it's possible that any of you can sit here and talk to me, with your bodies perfectly preserved at the exact moment of transformation? For Mitch and Claude it's not that much of a marvel, I suppose, and not out of the realm of normality. But for you, Lily, it's impossible. And Vivienne?" He shot her a warm smile. "She's a bloody miracle, born in 1719 and not a scratch on her."

She buffed her nails on her shirt. "Thank you, Sam, *mon cher,* I'm so very glad you noticed."

"All of you," Sam's voice raised just a bit, "take your lives for granted. But we're dealing in impossibilities with you all. And the Others? Completely out of the realm of reality. And yet, here you are. And there they are. Chris is alive again due to the Others. You can't doubt the evidence. So why is Deirdre being pregnant such an obstacle?"

Lily looked properly chastened. "I guess, Sam, when you put it that way, it all makes perfect sense. And," a smile softened her face, "a baby. Yeah, a baby. That fucking rocks. A baby would be wonderful. A sister for me, a niece for Auntie Viv, a daughter for Mitch."

"Or a son."

"Oh, foo," Vivienne said, rolling over and giving my knee a little push. "You already have a son. We'd like a little girl, wouldn't we, Lily?"

Sam cleared his throat. "Before we start reciting the litany in praise of babies, I'd like to say a few more things. It's entirely possible that Deirdre will begin recovering her memory on her own, depend-

ing on the circumstances surrounding her. If she is
in a familiar place or with a familiar person, as we
are surmising she is, wherever and whomsoever that
may be, small things will start to trigger flashes.
Something as simple as a scent or a touch or just a
random phrase can pull back entire events. Unless,
and this is a big unless, the person who has her is
supplying small doses of the poison to keep the
memories muffled. It's entirely possible that if we
find her . . ."

I must have made a sound of some sort, because
Sam looked over at me and amended his statement.

". . . when we find her, she won't know any of us.
If I had abducted her, I'd keep her as subdued as
possible and hidden away. Whoever has her has
certainly got to know we will be searching."

"And," Vivienne said, her voice soft, "we must not
forget that it looks like she is with one of them.
One of the Others. It is not a place I'd want to be
in if I were with child."

"Shit." Lily twisted her mouth into a snarl. "That
hadn't even occurred to me. So help me, if he hurts
my mother or my sister, I will kill him with my bare
hands."

"I am afraid, it's not that simple, Lily. Mitch and
I have good reason to believe that the soul inhabit-
ing Steven DeRouchard's body is none other than
our old friend, Max Hunter."

"If so," Claude nodded at Vivienne, "he's proved
remarkably difficult to kill in the past."

"And since Deirdre's already killed him once,"
my voice sounded agitated and I took a breath to
calm myself, "he's likely to be more wary around her
this time. It would be my guess that Maggie took
off with Chris at his orders. He knew that I'd have

to follow her to protect Chris. That way, he could keep me off his trail and out of the picture for a while."

"Or permanently," Sam said. "Let's not forget that Maggie is extremely unbalanced right now. She may always have been, I don't know. I would believe her capable of anything; a woman who is willing to kill her own son with a corkscrew is not to be taken lightly."

"I had a call from her," I said, "right before Vivienne called.

"From Maggie? What did she say? How did she sound?"

"Honestly? She sounded totally insane. I asked her where Chris was but all she could say was that she didn't know. She asked me to come after her and confirmed that she was in New Orleans."

Sam frowned. "I don't like it. Not one bit. Why would she call you and ask for you to find her? It makes no sense."

I shrugged. "She said something about not being able to do what she needed to do unless I came for her."

"I don't know, Mitch," Sam said, "maybe it would be better if you didn't go to New Orleans. It sounds like Maggie's setting you up for something. And I doubt it's anything good."

"Of course she's setting me up," I agreed. "Since I first met her that's all she's ever done. And I know she's only a decoy at this point in time, to keep me off the trail of Deirdre. But it doesn't matter, I have to go after her. Chris may be in danger. I can't let anything happen to him. Not now."

"I know," Sam said. "Chris has to be our first priority. But I still don't like it. So we'll go to New

Orleans, but I'd feel better if you kept a low profile while we're there. Let the rest of us find her."

I snorted. "Not on your life, Sam."

He smiled sadly. "Somehow I knew you'd see it that way."

Viv looked at the clock and sat up, swinging her legs over the side of the bed. "So we're all settled then, no? I still need to pack up a few things before we leave, Sam. Is there anything else we need to know?"

He rubbed his fingers over his eyes and made a small groaning sound. "Yes. There is." I gave him a nod of encouragement, knowing what he was reluctant to say.

"None of you have asked how all of this happened. How did the Others just happen to find a poison that could wreak such havoc on the vampires of the world?"

"Does it make a difference, *mon chou*?" She walked to the closet, began folding clothes and packing them. "Obviously they found some stooge, a doctor or research person, to study the situation. Money would have been no object, they had all of the Others' funds at their command as well as the holdings of the entire Cadre. They probably provided him with money and materials and equipment, set him up a nice little lab somewhere with coolers brimming with little bagged blood samples and . . ." She broke off her statement and stared at him from across the room, the truth growing in her eyes. "Oh, no. It can't be that, can it? Sam? Please tell me that I am wrong."

"No, Vivienne, I can't tell you that. It's true, all of it. My terrible secret. And the fact that I had no idea my research would be used against you all"—

he gestured around the room—"doesn't make it any less terrible. Or any less of a betrayal. But," his voice broke, "you must all know that I meant no harm to Deirdre, no harm to any of you."

The room was totally silent. I rose from the chair; his statement was less of a shock for me since I'd heard it before. He'd never given me reason to doubt his sincerity and his trustworthiness for a moment the whole time we'd known each other and I didn't doubt him now. I valued him too much to not let the others know exactly how I felt. So I walked over to Sam and pulled him into a rough embrace. "Forget about it," I said gruffly. "What's done is done. You shouldn't beat yourself up. We'll need you in good shape to fix everything once this is all resolved."

I could almost feel their collective relief. After all, if I wasn't upset with him over this betrayal, none of them should be. Vivienne still seemed disturbed, but she'd adjust to the idea. That's what she was best at, adapting. And really, some of the blame, if there needed to be blame, was hers. She'd been right there and even assisted Sam with his research. I walked over to her, gave her a quick kiss on the cheek and she brightened up.

After that, everyone began to prepare for the upcoming flight. The timing was a bit tricky on this leg of the trip, since most of the flights to New Orleans took off in the daylight. The one Vivienne had booked had a departure time about forty-five minutes after sunset, but that didn't allow us much time to get through the airport.

Still, we all boarded in time and in a little over three hours we'd touched down in New Orleans. From there it was another wait for luggage and then a dispute at the taxi stop.

"Why do we all have to stay at the hotel?" Lily sounded tired and more than a little petulant. "My house isn't all that far away and it's free. Besides, I'd like to see if Victor's come back. We've all been so worried about Chris and Mom that we've forgotten all about him."

"I haven't forgotten him," I said, "and I'd like to talk to Victor anyway. I suspect he knows where Max is."

"How could he know that, Mitch?"

"Don't you remember, Lily, about telling us how he'd been talking to Max one night? We all thought he'd lost it, or was pretending to have lost it, but what if he really did speak with Max?"

"Hmmm." She thought for a moment. "I'd never even considered that he really had talked to Max. It was one of his bad days and he just rambled on and on. I didn't hear another voice in the conversation."

"But Other children have no voice and he may not have been totally transformed then."

"Excellent point, Mitch." Vivienne smiled at me. "This isn't a problem, anyway. We'll go to Lily's place first and there's still plenty of time to check in at the Hotel of Souls."

"Finding Victor might very well solve everything and it would certainly make me feel better. I miss the old bastard." Lily waved a cab over for us, looked at Claude and shrugged, then waved for another. "Why don't you and Sam and Vivienne take the first cab, Mitch? Claude and I will follow." She opened the passenger side of our cab and gave the driver her address.

We rode in silence, each of us deep in our own thoughts. I would rather have gone straight to the hotel. Lily's house held bad memories for me. But we needed to stay together.

Vivienne sat still for most of the ride, her head back on the seat, her eyes closed. Sam kept opening his mouth as if to say something, then seemed to think better of it.

We were maybe two blocks from our destination, when Vivienne opened her eyes and took Sam's hand in hers, bringing it up to her face.

"What?" he said, a half-smile on his face.

"Nothing, *mon chou*, I merely wanted to let you know I was still here. For you. With you. And that there is no place I would rather be."

She kissed him then, full on the lips. I turned away and watched out the window.

CHAPTER FIFTEEN

Lily's house was dark when we arrived. We waited around outside for a few minutes until she and Claude showed up. When she got out of the cab, she had a disgruntled look on her face and reached into her bag for the keys. "I don't think Victor's here, somehow. He doesn't really need light, but he will normally turn them all on anyway." She chuckled. "One of his more endearing qualities."

Still, when she opened the door, she called for him. "Victor? Hey, you old coot, are you here?"

We didn't need the silence that followed to tell us the house was unoccupied. Empty houses have a certain feel to them.

We all dropped our bags in the living room. "Excuse the mess," Lily said, "I'm not much of a housekeeper and I left in a hurry. Let's go into the kitchen. I'll make us a cup of tea or something. And I'll make a phone call and see if I can round up Angelo."

I remembered Angelo well. Too well. He'd cut off the hand of the man he'd procured for me to

feed on while I was prisoner here. Quite by accident, really, but totally avoidable. The complete lack
of concern he showed in the situation cinched my
opinion of Angelo. He was a snake, not to be trusted.
An obscene excuse for a human being who'd cut
off your hand gleefully if it served his purpose. Lily
read the expression on my face.

"I know, Mitch, I know. He's impossible to deal
with. And you of all people have good reason to
distrust him. For that matter, though, you also have
good reason to distrust me. And you don't, do you?"

"Not anymore. I know you better now."

"And I know Angelo, probably better than anyone, especially since Moon died. He's self-serving
and manipulative, but he's also the eyes and ears
of this city, more than anyone else I've ever known.
If something interesting or out of the ordinary
happens, Angelo is the first to know. And if anyone
can help us find Maggie and Chris and maybe even
Deirdre, it'll be 'Lo. I'm afraid you'll have to trust
him, just a little."

"I'll trust you, Lily. Is that good enough?"

"It'll have to do, I guess." She opened the cup-
board under the sink, then banged the door shut.
"Damn, there's nothing in here to drink. I'll have
a hard time convincing him to help without something liquid and alcoholic to hurry along his cooperation."

"I'll go out and get some, Lily," Claude volun-
teered. "Brandy, right?"

"Yeah. Either that or some Mad Dog. Whatever
you can find. Thanks."

The rest of us sat down at the kitchen table and
Lily smiled over at us. "Home sweet home," she said.
"I know it's not much, but I'm happy to be here at
least. I just wish Victor had been home." She put a

tea kettle on the stove and turned the burner on. "I worry about him. Stupid of me, I know. Compared to him, we're all children. Which, I guess, is as it should be, since we *are* his children. He's the eldest, you know. And maybe the very first. I've never been able to get the story out of him, the hows and whys and wherefores, but I'm pretty sure he's the original deal. It's gotta be an amazing story."

Rummaging around in one of the cupboards, Lily produced a couple of cans of loose tea and some mugs. She measured the tea into a tea pot that had been sitting in the dish strainer and set the mugs in front of us. "And he has such a depth of sadness in him, surpassed only by his capacity for caring. It would be a great loss to all of us, and maybe to the rest of the world, if he were gone for good."

She wiped away a tear. "Sorry. I get silly about that old man. And I know he's somewhere still. There are times when I feel him inside my mind. He's still pulling our strings. And loving every minute of it."

Vivienne reached over and patted Lily's hand. "You are right, Lily. I've felt for years that Victor was in control. And I'm sure he's fine. No one has lived as long as he has without perfecting the preservation instinct. So no more tears, *ma chér.* Make your phone call and then you can show us your charming house."

"Not all that charming, Vivienne." Lily picked up the receiver from the wall phone and began dialing. "It's certainly not large enough for a full-fledged tour, is it, Mitch?"

"True. But you should see what she has tucked away in one of the bedrooms."

"Now that sounds promising," Vivienne turned

to Sam who hadn't said a word since we arrived. "Does it not, Sam?"

"Yeah, I suppose so."

"Sam," I tried to meet his eyes over the table. "It's okay. No one here is upset about your role in this whole thing."

"Except me," he said quietly. "I've built my life around a solid desire to do some good, to help people in trouble. I'm not used to being a destructor. There must be something I could do to make it up to her and to all of you. Open a vein, maybe?"

"Staying alive and ready to help out would be the best option. Honest."

"Rudy?" Lily's phone call must have connected finally. "Hi, it's Lily." She paused and laughed. "Yeah, yeah, I know. Just like a bad penny. Say, have you seen Angelo around lately?" The kettle gave a shrill whistle and we all jumped. She cradled the phone between her shoulder and her ear, still talking while moving the kettle off of the stove and pouring the water into the teapot she'd prepared earlier. The room filled with an herbal aroma and Vivienne sniffed appreciatively. "Okay, well, when he comes in, tell him I'm home. And that I need to see him." Lily laughed again. "Yeah, for sure, I know exactly how he is. But make sure he knows that if he doesn't find me, I *will* find him."

She hung up the phone, shaking her head. "Fine. Now while we're waiting for the tea to steep, let's take that little tour."

There wasn't all that much to see. Lily's bedroom, still decorated from her teenage years. A small bathroom. "And this"—Lily said, opening the last door—"used to be Moon's room."

"And for a while," I said, giving Lily a smile, "it was my room."

Vivienne seemed very interested in the holding tank. "I understand this is exactly like the ones Victor had built in Cadre headquarters?"

Lily nodded. "Down to every last detail. Except for one thing. Victor built a few secret safeguards that only he knew about in the others. This one has none of those. Unless the door is opened, the person or vampire or whatever staying within is completely incarcerated." She gave a twisted smile, "Even Harry Houdini couldn't have gotten out of this one."

"Take my word for it, Viv," I said, "it's fully functional."

"But," Sam asked, examining the dials and controls that regulated air intake and the speakers, "why is it still here?"

Lily gave an uneasy laugh. "Victor wanted me to keep it, intact and functional. Just in case. And periodically he'd sleep in there. Don't ask me why; the whole idea gives me the willies. He always said it was very peaceful."

I laughed. "Yeah, I guess it would be, at least as long as you know someone's going to let you out."

Lily gave the tank one last look and turned out the light. She walked out of the room and waited for all of us to leave, then closed the door and went back to the kitchen. Vivienne, Sam, and I settled in around the kitchen table again. Lily fussed with the teapot on the counter. "There were times," she said, "when I thought of leaving him in there, days and nights when it seemed he'd completely lost his mind." She shrugged, checked the tea, and poured out four mugs, "You know, I love him and I miss him, but there are times he scares the ever-loving shit out of me."

Vivienne picked up her mug, inhaling the aromatic steam. "What is this, Lily?"

"Moon's special serenity blend. Catnip, lemon balm, and just a touch of lavender. It's too bad she's dead. For many reasons, actually, most of them incredibly selfish on my part." She sat down at the table with us, her hands wrapped tightly around the warmth of her mug, a wistful expression on her face. "But right now because she'd just be tickled to see who was sitting at her kitchen table."

"Oh, she can see all right, Lily. Don' you worry none 'bout that." Recognizing the voice, I turned in my seat to stare over at Angelo, standing in the kitchen doorway, framed by the huge bulk of Claude behind him. He flinched slightly as my eyes met his and tried to retreat, but Claude gave him an ungentle nudge in the small of his back and Angelo shot forward, laughing uneasily.

"Good to see you again, Mr. Greer." I half-expected to see him wring his hands, instead he slumped down just a bit and nodded his head. "No hard feelings from last time we met, I hope."

"None at all, Angelo. You almost did me a favor, since the circumstances were the only reasons Lily would let me out. I can't afford to dwell on the past, anyway, so you have no worries on my account."

"Good, good." He looked at Vivienne and gave a broad smile. "Very pleased to see you again, missy. Always with a handsome man, always the same strong heart. Solved your problem from last time we met?"

"*Oui*, Angelo. That I did." She laid a hand on Sam's arm. "And this is Dr. John Samuels. Sam, this is Angelo. You've heard a lot about him."

"Mostly good stuff, this one hopes." Angelo reached out a hand to greet Sam who seemed rather surprised at the strength of his handshake. Angelo looked frailer than he was.

Claude moved into the kitchen and handed Lily a brown paper bag. Angelo's eyes hungrily followed the exchange. "As chance would have it," Claude explained, "he was lounging around the liquor store when I got there."

"Not chance," Angelo watched hungrily as Lily broke the seal on the bottle. She poured some into an empty jelly jar and he reached for the drink. "Thanks much, Lily. It never be chance. I feel you back in town, Lily girl. And feel your need in the night air. The spirits, they whispering to me, always whispering." He drained his drink in one swallow and set the glass down on the counter. "Now let me have a good look at you, Lily. You changed some since last we spoke, round 'bout the time that Greg man end up with the nickname of Lefty." Angelo gave a long, wheezing laugh, shot me a quick glance, and grew serious again. "But you, Lily, you no longer a little girl, are you? More like the dark queen of the night."

Lily's mouth twisted. "Yeah, right, Angelo. Whatever you say."

"No," Angelo pulled himself up straighter and laid both of his hands on Lily's cheeks. "There be a strength deep down inside you that weren't there before. I glad to see it, Lily child. And Moon, she be so proud of how you become what you should be."

She filled his glass again and handed it to him, turning away quickly, but not before I caught the gleam of unshed tears in her eyes. "It's not as if I had a choice in the matter, 'Lo. So let's drop it, okay?"

He nodded to her and then to the rest of us. "There always a choice. Always." Angelo drained his glass again, giving a loud belch when he'd finished. "Pardon," he said. "So, the fine Claude man here tell me you need some information from ol' bow-legged 'Lo. That true?"

"We're looking for a woman and her son. My son. She's tall, with dark curly hair, green eyes, very pretty. And the boy is about twelve or so, but might seem older."

"Your son?" Angelo gave me a questioning look. "I thought you married Lily's mam and had only one child from before. And they say he be dead many years now."

"They?"

"The spirits whisper, Mitch. I only listen."

I was beginning to lose what little patience I had for the man. I reached out and gripped the front of his shirt. "And what do the spirits whisper of the Others, Angelo?"

"Your son one of they?" He shook himself out of my hands. "That a powerful magic at work. And the woman one of they, too. Only female and a Breeder, eh?"

"Exactly. Have you seen her?"

He pursed his lips. "Maybe I see her. Maybe I don'. Either way, there be payment needed for getting into it with such as they."

"How much, Angelo?" Lily sounded almost as frustrated as I felt.

"We ol' friends, Lily. I don' cheat ol' friends. Five hun'red be good enough for me."

"I have it," Vivienne got up from the table and went to her bag in the hallway. When she came back, she handed Angelo five crisp hundred dollar bills. "Payment," she said, "but if what you say isn't worth the price, *mon chou,* be prepared to give it back in trade."

"Trade?" Angelo voice cracked slightly as he stuffed the bills into his pants pocket. His eyes darted around the room, as if searching for escape. Finally though he looked back at her, giving a slight shiver as he caught the full brunt of her gaze. "Trade? What trade?"

Vivienne didn't say a word. She merely smiled, exposing her fangs and licked her lips.

Angelo got the message. "That woman is down in the French Quarter right now. I see her go into her little house earlier, a pretty house with wisteria crawling all 'bout it. But she not pretty, nor do she have an eye for pretty. I see into her soul as she pass me on the street and she crazy, blood red crazy and hungry for death. She walkin' with murder and death wrote all over her. But the boy, he ain't with her. No sign nor scent of him."

"Can you take us to her?" I asked.

He laughed, a croaking, wheezing sound that seemed to explode from his throat. "I show you, sure. Why you so bound and determined to see her, I can't even figure. But I show you only from a distance. Me, why I already been close enough to her to last me the rest of my life."

"Thank you, Angelo," Lily said, handing him another glass of brandy. "That'll be fine. For now."

CHAPTER SIXTEEN

Deirdre Griffin: New York City

I finally awoke the evening of the next day. I felt woozy and shaky, but more importantly, I thought, rubbing the sore spot on my arm where the needle penetrated, I was angry—so angry I wanted to take Max apart with my bare hands. I couldn't even begin to imagine his rationale on drugging me. Once again everything he'd been doing to me made no sense.

The sound of his key in the lock made me wild. I sprang out of bed and hurtled toward him, hands extended, nails crooked. He caught my wrists and roughly pulled them down. "Awake, I see," he said, a twisted smile distorting his classically handsome face.

"No thanks to you, Max. Was it necessary to drug me without my knowledge? This sort of action goes above and beyond the bounds of spousal duty, don't you think?"

"You were in a rare mood last night, little one.

You'd worked yourself up into a fit complete with full-fledged delusions of a life that never existed. All that nonsense about Larry Martin and Mitch Greer and my keeping coffins in this room." He laughed and I bristled to feel his condescension. "In a mood like that, you'd be capable of anything, so I took what action I deemed necessary. You are my wife, after all."

"Your wife?" I gave a snarling laugh, sounding almost hysterical even to my own ears. "More like your prisoner, I would say. So what is on the agenda for tonight? Whippings? Interrogations?"

He looked hurt. "Why do you persist in making me out to be your enemy, Deirdre, when you must know, deep down in your heart, that I only want what's best for you."

"Then let me go, Max. That would be what's best for me."

"You say that, but you are still——"

I practically howled in frustration. "Sick? Yes, yes, yes. I am willing to admit I've been sick. I even vaguely remember the symptoms you've described. But I also remember other things, vivid things, important events which, no matter how hard you try, you cannot control or change. You may deny it all you like, but still, I know I have led a life that did not involve you. And that life was chosen by me in lieu of what you had to offer me. A life led with another man in another time and place."

His voice lowered a bit, seeming, if possible, to be filled with love and pity. "Oh, Deirdre," he said, "my sweet little one, I very much wish that things had turned out differently for us. That you hadn't been struck with this damned sickness holding you in delusions and false dreams. We were happy together once, surely you can remember that?"

And as he said the words, I realized that, in some small way, what he said was true. We *had* been happy together. At some point in my forgotten life, I had wished for nothing more than a chance for the two of us. In that moment I softened toward him, wanting more than anything to be held in his arms. It would be so easy to quit fighting, to swallow my pride, to abandon my delusions as he called them and reclaim the warmth and safety of his protection. Mouthing a soft word of consolation, I took a step toward him, stopping short when I caught the triumphant gleam in his eyes. *What the hell am I doing?* I thought, *this is Max. He's manipulating me. As he always has.* I swallowed and hardened my heart. "No, Max," I said, glad to hear that my voice sounded steady and calm. "There was someone else; he and I were happy. You and I, as a couple, as man and wife, never existed and will never exist. As much as you keep denying these facts, you know they are true. Otherwise you wouldn't hold me so close."

His mouth narrowed. "And you are still insisting the man in question is Mitchell Greer? Detective Mitchell Greer?"

"Yes."

"Good. Then we will put this delusion to the test. Do you recall what Greer looks like?"

I closed my eyes for a second and a face formed in my mind. Blue eyes, so very blue they were almost electric, his nose, strong and hawklike, and his hair, gray. I remembered the sound of his voice and the feel of his arms around me. I felt his body moving above mine and could taste his lips and his skin and his blood. My mouth curved into a smile, and I felt a contentment wash over me, the first wholesome emotion I'd experienced since waking up in this place. "Oh, yes. There's no doubt in my mind. The man I was married to is Mitch Greer. And I would know him anywhere."

"Good."

Good? His pleasant response threw me off balance. He should, by all rights, be in a rage. How could he think any of this was good?"

"With your permission then, I will try to arrange to have Detective Greer visit us tonight. If I remember correctly, and there's nothing wrong with my memory," he gave me a wink, "he's still working in the same precinct as he did when you met him."

That sounded wrong to me. Mitch hadn't been working as a policeman for years. Had he? We'd been away, for quite a while. I felt the truth of that in my very bones, but I kept my objections to myself. What if Max really could get Mitch here? The possibility took my breath away.

"And if you meet him," Max continued, not noticing my hesitation, "you will know him, right?"

I nodded, wondering what Max hoped to gain by this tactic. It would do him no good, since as soon as Mitch knew I was here, he'd take me away and we would resume our lives. I felt quite sure that being in Mitch's presence and with enough time all of my memories would eventually return.

"And so, when he is not the man you expect," Max continued, "will you allow that I might be right, that all of these flashes you take for memory may indeed be nothing but delusional dreams?"

"If. Not when. And it won't happen the way you say, Max. When will he be here?" My heart pounded wildly and I felt flushed with excitement. Mitch. Here. With me. Finally the nightmare was over for good.

Max glanced at his watch. "The sooner the better, my dear. I'd like to close this issue right now."

I wanted to laugh at him. Wanted to gloat about how I'd been right all along, to throw back into his face the fact that he was not the one I chose to spend eternity with. Yet there was something unsettling about the certainty he exuded, the willingness he showed in offering to arrange this meeting. Did he not know how it would turn out? How on earth was this to his advantage? I might not have remembered all that much, but I knew for a fact that Max never did anything from unselfish motives. It was difficult to reconcile this Max with the man I thought I knew. "You surprise me, Max," I admitted. "I'd think the last person in the world you'd want me to meet at this point in time would be Mitchell Greer."

He inclined his head, hiding his eyes from mine, but not before I caught that same triumphant gleam I'd seen before. "I've told you, over and over, Deirdre, that all I want is what's best for you. And this meeting will be good for you. Will be good for us."

"Finally," I smiled at him and kissed him on the cheek, "we are agreed on something."

"And afterward you will be able to resume the life you once led, the life we once led, free of the delusions and the fevered dreams."

Again his certainty disturbed me, but I said nothing.

"Then it's settled. Now, why don't you get dressed in one of those pretty outfits we bought last night. I'll try to get in touch with Greer and I'll wait for you outside."

I noticed then that I was wearing a nightgown and

not the clothes I'd had on earlier. I shuddered; the thoughts that he'd undressed me and re-dressed me while I was sleeping offended me, frightened me. What other liberties did he feel entitled to take upon my inert body? I glared over at him but he ignored my glance and walked out the door closing it softly behind him.

"Bastard," I whispered. "I still can't imagine what you hope to gain by this, but it will finally be made right. Mitch will make it all right again."

Smiling, I looked through the armoire and tried to determine what one should wear to be reunited with one's husband.

Something about the arrangement of colors—all black, red and white with one touch of green—and the scent of new garments triggered a flood of memories that had been tickling my mind since our shopping trip. I saw an office, filled with racks of clothes, my clothes, but not ones I would wear. Rather they were clothes that I had designed. Another missing piece clicked into place. I'd been a fashion designer in that other life. The recognition of that fact combined with my vision of the office invoked memories of late nights spent working on sketches and materials invoices and pattern constructions. There seemed to always be the smell of strong coffee in the air along with a faint whiff of roses. There were voices lifted outside of the office along with laughter and the face of a good friend. Her name rushed into my mind like a giant gulp of air—Gwen DeAngelis. And along with the name came a great wash of sadness and anger. I saw Gwen, staked to a bed, her bright blood coating the walls and floors, the victim of a crazed attack by Larry Martin. Mitch had been there, too. I remembered the comfort of his arm tightening around my shoulders just as clearly as if his arm were resting there now.

And what was it about Larry Martin? There was something about him that continued to haunt my thoughts. Mitch had killed him, I remembered that, but there remained a nagging doubt that his death hadn't been the end. Try as I might, though, the way forward remained blocked. The memories had a perverse way of staying just slightly out of focus. No matter, I knew that I was now reconstructing my prior life. Perhaps it was the fact that I'd quit taking the drink Max provided me. Perhaps it was just a natural progression as the sickness that had enveloped me abated.

Whatever the cause, I still believed that being with Mitch again would solve everything. "But," I laughed to myself, "you can't meet him wearing this nightgown." So I tried on three of the outfits before finally deciding on the last: a pair of skin-tight black velvet leggings and a loose-fitting hunter green sweater that hung to midthigh. Once again Vivienne's face came to my mind. She was laughing, she seemed to laugh a lot, and she was saying how green would compliment my complexion. I insisted the color was unlucky for me, not knowing why. I felt silly thinking it at the time and I felt silly now. Luck is what one makes out of life. I would wear the sweater, regardless of its color.

I slid into a pair of ankle-high black suede boots and began to apply some of the makeup I'd bought, using the armoire mirror. Then I stood back to check my image, running my fingers through my short bleached hair, wishing I'd had a chance to stop at a beauty salon. "But it doesn't really matter," I told my reflection. "Mitch loves me regardless of how I look. I know he does."

The eyes that stared back at me were filled with a combination of hope and doubt. "He does," I said with more conviction than I felt. "You know it's true." I dared not say out loud what I was thinking. What if Max was right? What if it were all only a dream? Why else would he allow me to meet Mitch? My throat closed up in momentary panic, I drew in a ragged breath. My mouth felt dry and cottony. "Damn Max," I said, balling my hands into fists until I felt my fingernails bite into the skin. "Damn him to hell. He's wrong. He must be wrong. Has to be wrong."

CHAPTER SEVENTEEN

Taking a deep breath, I exited my little room into Max's office. He was talking on the phone and when he looked up at me, he lowered his voice a bit while giving me an appraising glance. I noticed a hint of caution in his tone as well as a proprietorial approval of my appearance in his eyes. For some reason, his look annoyed me. He didn't own me, he'd never own me, and I hadn't dressed for him.

"Good," he said, glancing back at his desk and turning his chair so that his back was turned to me. "I'll expect to see you in an hour or so. I needn't remind you that this is extremely important to me. See that you get it right this time."

His words held an unspoken threat and I wondered briefly if he was talking to Mitch. The thought disturbed me; it sounded as if Mitch was in Max's employ. Could things have changed that much in just a short time? However, when the person spoke from the other end of the phone I recognized the

voice. "Practice makes perfect, Max," Derek said.
"I promise you won't be disappointed."

"I'd better not be," Max said and hung up the
phone.

"Instructions to the watchdog?"

"Watchdog?"

"Derek. For one of mine, he is quite attentive to
you."

He stood up. "You've not been available lately to
give him instructions. I had to take over the men-
tor role with him and his loyalty transferred in the
process. I assure you, though, that he is still yours.
Nothing can change the bond between the creator
and her creation. You should remember that,
Deirdre, if you remember nothing else. It is that
same bond which you and I share."

I shrugged. "I do not quite think of it in those
terms. And I'm still not sure that I created Derek.
One would think there'd be some spark of recognition."

"There will be." Max gave a brief laugh as if at a
private joke. "By the way, you look quite lovely. I've
always liked you in that color and I've never been
sure why you don't wear it more often. It brings
out the green in your eyes." He smiled as he walked
past me and over to the bar. There he poured out
a glass of red wine and held it out to me.

Immediately suspicious, I sniffed at it. It seemed
like an ordinary red wine, a Merlot, I thought, or
one of the blended reds. But what if he'd drugged
it? What if he'd spiked it with something to ensure
that I was out cold by the time Mitch arrived?

As if sensing my thoughts, Max laughed, poured
himself a glass from the same bottle and drained
it. "It's quite safe, Deirdre, I assure you. After our

last battle, I've quit trying to give you the medication you so desperately need. I daresay that by now, your natural immunities will carry on and you'll recuperate well enough without it, albeit a bit more slowly."

Max? Giving in to me? *It must be a trick,* I thought as I sipped my wine slowly. But I detected no trace of drug in the wine, nor did it have the bitter taste the tonic had. I took a bigger swallow. Just plain wine.

"Why won't you trust me, Deirdre?"

"Let me give you a hint," I said. "You bring me here and keep me a prisoner, you tell me lies, and why, wasn't it just last night that you slipped a needle into my arm? Hardly seems the sort of behavior that inspires trust, does it?"

He laid a hand on my shoulder and I shrugged him away. "It breaks my heart the way you won't open up to me."

"Heart? That is a good one, Max. When have you ever had a heart?"

He sighed. "What little you remember of me, Deirdre, is totally wrong. How can I convince you of that?"

"You can't. It's that simple, Max. I remember more than is necessary to know that you can't be trusted. Why else would you drug me, poison me, lie to me and keep me prisoner here when all I want is to be let free."

"This is about Mitch, isn't it? The man you've built up in your mind to be the perfect husband. The perfect mate. How many times do I need to tell you? He doesn't exist, Deirdre. I hesitate to bring him here—"

"Because you know I'm right."

"No, little one." He came over to me and wrapped

his arms around me, holding me tightly. I did not pull away, but neither did I respond to his attentions. His touch made my skin crawl. "I hesitate to bring him here, because I fear how you may react. The truth may be too big a shock for you. You may lose what little grasp of reality you now possess."

"There is nothing wrong with my sanity, Max. Despite what you want me to believe, I know what I know. I am fine. Healthy and strong. Or would be if you'd just let me go."

He held me out at arms' length. "You're more trouble than you're worth sometimes, Deirdre. I don't know why I bother. If I didn't love you so much, if I didn't care what happened to you, I would just let you go. Surely you can see that?"

I shrugged. "No, Max. All I can see is you. Standing in my way. Along with the vision of you, staked out solidly on your office door."

His hands on my shoulders tightened and I thought for a moment that he might hit me. Instead, he pulled me to him again and kissed me, hard and long on the lips.

I reacted this time, pushing him away with all my strength. "Don't you ever touch me again," I hissed, backing away from him until I reached the door of my room. "I killed you once," I said softly, "I can do it again. And will."

"Threats, Deirdre? Has it come to this?"

"Damn straight." The use of one of Mitch's favorite phrases fortified me. "Do not push me too hard, Max. You might be the one to break."

"Suit yourself," he said, walking over to his desk and sitting back down. "After the meeting with Detective Greer, you may see things differently. Or not. Right now I'm not sure I care. You've got nowhere to go but here anyway. No money, no friends, no prospects. You should be damned thankful I take care of you. I doubt that sleeping in a subway tunnel with the homeless and the rats would appeal to you."

"The company would be better, at least." He refused to comment, but I could tell from the tightening of his mouth that he was angry. And suddenly I was tired, too tired for this verbal sparring match. "I am going back to my room. Call me when he gets here."

He shook his head and busied himself with the stack of papers before him.

Just as I started to enter my room, there was a knock on the external door. Max gave me a quick glance and nod, and got up from his desk. I pushed the door closed behind me and leaned back against it; my heart pounded, my stomach rolled and my feet seemed rooted into the ground.

"Thank you for coming so quickly, Detective," Max said to the man at the door, his voice pleasant and calm, all traces of anger gone. "I promise we won't take up too much of your time."

"Wasn't a problem, Hunter," the man said. "I'm off duty and this was on my way home anyway. Now what can I do for you?"

My view was blocked by Max, until he stepped aside to let the man in. Still leaning against the closed door, I stared at the toes of my suede boots, afraid to meet the man's eyes. It sounded so much like the Mitch I remembered. Or thought I remembered. But surely he could see me standing here. Why didn't he say something?

Max moved over to me and took my arm, leading me across the room. "Come on now, Deirdre, this is Mitch. You wanted to see him, didn't you?

Don't be rude, the man's gone out of his way to accept my invitation."

All of a sudden, this whole situation seemed like a huge mistake. I dared not move or speak. Max nudged me forward a bit more. "This is Deirdre," he said, draping an arm around my neck. "Do you remember my wife, Detective Greer?"

I had no choice, I had to look up into his face. And my eyes met his. It was Mitch, my Mitch. Just looking at his face brought back so many memories. I could hear his laughter, feel his touch on my skin, his kiss on my lips. I remembered how we would run through the forests of Maine and over the moors of Whitby, he as the Wolf and I as the Cat. I could replay all the silly arguments we'd had and how we'd spend the next day making love as an apology and an affirmation. I remembered further back, before we were married. Chris had urged me to visit him in the hospital. I could see his haunted eyes as clearly as I saw them now.

He extended his hand to me. "Mrs. Hunter? Yes, we met briefly a few years ago. You've changed your hair, haven't you? If I remember correctly you were a redhead last time I saw you."

I couldn't say a word, couldn't take the hand he offered. It didn't matter that I longed for the touch of that hand, that everything about him was exactly as I remembered, that I knew this was indeed Mitch Greer standing in front of me. My heart fell. All I needed to know was in his eyes. They were the same blue, they had the same intensity I remembered loving, but they were, when they looked on me, empty—completely empty and devoid of any special emotion. I could have been anyone in his eyes. Or no one. My heart stopped and I backed away from him as if he were threatening me.

"Mrs. Hunter?" I noticed his quick panicked glance at Max, before turning his attention back to me. "Are you okay? You look pale. I know you've been sick, Max told me all about it. Maybe you should sit down."

I shook my head in response. "No," I said quietly, my voice betraying tears. Clapping my hand to my mouth, I continued to retreat from him, until my back was once again up against the door. I took one last look into those eyes, at once so familiar yet so very distant, dropped my head, turned swiftly, and after fumbling with the doorknob, went back into my room.

That fumbling enabled me to hear Mitch's subsequent comment to Max. "Is she okay? Should I go after her?"

"No," Max said, "she's just had a shock. It's for the best."

"Did I say something wrong?" His voice sounded distant, different somehow, but I assumed it was muffled somewhat by the closed door.

Max's laugh, on the other hand, sounded perfectly clear and caused a chill to run up my spine. "No, Detective, you were perfect."

CHAPTER EIGHTEEN

To my great surprise, Max was smart enough to leave me alone for the rest of the night. There were no knocks on the door, no attempts to enter my room and offer comfort, or, what would have been worse, to gloat over his seeming triumph. Had he entered, had he even spoken one word through the keyhole, I would have killed him. And I knew with certainty it wouldn't be the first time. Although the man I saw was not the Mitchell Greer of my memories, just his presence in Max's office, his face, even his voice triggered a flood of memories. I *had* killed Max, there was no doubt in my mind about that. I'd staked him through the heart and left him hanging on his office door like a scarecrow. For all the good it had done me. Eduard DeRouchard had made it possible for him to live again.

I deliberately turned my mind away from Mitch. It was unthinkable that he may never have existed the way I remembered him. Unthinkable that Max could be right all along. How could this have happened? How could I have been so wrong?

And yet, my heart ached with the loss. So much of my life had been tied up in his, along with my hopes for the future and my desperateness for release from this impossible impasse with Max. With the destruction of those hopes, I plunged as deep into despair as I believed I'd ever been. Rock bottom. The worst part of it was that the pain wedged itself tightly into every inch of my body and there was no release. The pain would never leave, I knew. And for the first time in my life, I could not cry.

Instead I sat on the edge of the bed for what must have been hours, arms wrapped tightly around myself, rocking slightly, hearing no sound but that of my ragged breathing. As that began to steady, as my pulse began to calm, my mind began to formulate a plan.

Although it was true that I remembered very little of my life before Mitch had walked into it, I knew somehow that I'd done fine on my own. Independent and alone, I'd lived for decades. And I would again. Even if it appeared Max had been telling me the truth all along, I did not have to accept the life he offered. And if Mitch had been nothing but a fevered dream, a delusion, then so be it. It was time, way past time, to wake up and take control.

First order of business was to get the hell out of the Ballroom of Romance and away from Max. I glanced at the clock and did some calculations. The sun would rise in about four hours; plenty of time for me to get away and find shelter. Max may have thought I was too fastidious to spend a night in the subway, but he severely miscalculated my desire to escape. Besides, I realized as I looked around the room deciding what I should bring with me, I did know someone in this city. Or at least someone knew me. From underneath my mattress, I pulled the slip of paper with the phone number Terri Hamilton had given me along with the cassette tape I'd found in my jeans pocket and slid them into the large tote bag. Those, plus a change of underwear, a comb, and my makeup were all that I cared to take. I didn't want to be hindered by luggage. This was an escape, not a vacation. The clothes Max had bought me could remain; I didn't want to wear them anyway.

The only other thing I needed to consider was the issue of getting past Max. It wasn't that I couldn't fight my way out of here. I may have been sick, but I suspected I was still more than a match for him. He was, after all, a human now. One with an indefinitely prolonged life, but he'd not yet demonstrated any of the powers that Eduard DeRouchard had. Like vampiric powers, Others' powers must have had to be acquired over time.

What I wanted was to be able to leave without Max even knowing I was gone. And what I needed was a disguise, a way to walk through the crowded club without being recognized by Derek or any of the other watchdogs I felt sure Max had in place.

Since I woke up in this place, I had been watching the vampire videos stored in my little room, hoping for a scene or a bit of dialogue that might trigger a memory. The vampires in these films had powers of many sorts, some of which rang true to me. True, I had memories of transforming into a wildcat, yet that vision had been part of my memories of Mitch and couldn't be true. Could it? In any event, transformation into an animal form would do nothing but call attention to me. But what if I could just manage to alter my features a bit? I could become someone else for a short period of time, that would serve my purpose, as long as Max wasn't in his office when I emerged.

"It can't hurt to try," I said to my reflection when I opened the armoire doors. "It has to be easier than turning into a wolf or a cat. So who shall we try to be?" *No one in particular,* I thought, *so as to be anonymous.* "Let's start with the hair. I hate what it looks like anyway." Closing my eyes, I concentrated on my hair, envisioning it as a mousy brown, about chin length. Feeling a tingling in my scalp, I began to resculpt my face, shortening my nose, thinning my lips, imagining wider set brown eyes and lower cheek bones. When the picture was complete in my mind, I opened my eyes and a stranger dressed in my clothes stared back at me.

The clothes, I decided, would have to go, too. I wanted nothing to clue Max into who this person really was. I opted for changing into the jeans and flannel shirt I'd found and when I was done changing, I appraised the results. I untucked the shirt and concentrated on bulking up the flesh around my waist. The jeans grew tighter and I looked slightly pudgy.

I had done it. No one, anywhere, would recognize this person as Deirdre Greer. The whole process, though, was more difficult than I'd expected. My face and scalp ached with the transformation. And my new features would blur if my concentration wavered. I held the vision of my new self and walked slowly over to the door to Max's office, pressing my ear up against the wood and listening for sounds of movement.

From without, there came the faint sound of shuffling papers and the outer door opening.

"Max," Derek said, "there's someone at the front door asking for you."

"Handle it for me," Max growled. "I don't want to leave this room."

"I can't." Derek's voice sounded apologetic and frightened. "You really need to talk to this person."

"Goddamn it, Derek. What do I pay you for anyway?" I heard the creaking of Max's desk chair as he rose. "Fine, I'll deal with this. You stay here and watch."

"Watch for what?"

"Her. I don't want her leaving this place."

Derek gave a nasty laugh that made the hair on my neck stand on end. "I don't know, Max. I'd think that after the performance she got from Mitchell Greer, she'll be holed up in there crying her eyes out."

"Is that what you think?" Max's scornful tone came through loud and clear. "Quite the cocky bastard, aren't you? But I'm afraid you don't know her very well. I'd wager a bet that she's planning something right now. So regardless of what you think, you will still stay here and keep watch. I'll be back as soon as I can."

The door opened again and closed with a slam. I heard Derek walking restlessly through the room, muttering to himself, then heard his footsteps move toward the bar.

I needed to make my move now. I stood a better chance of getting past Derek. Max knew me too well, knew me better, it turned out, than I did. Hearing the sound of clinking glasses, I slowly cracked the door open and watched Derek pour himself a glass of wine. Then he settled in on the black leather couch which fortunately faced away from the door. I slid out and closed it softly behind me.

He seemed tired as he sat there, sipping his wine, with his breathing accelerated, as if he had just run a marathon. While I watched he gave a huge yawn and tilted his head onto the back of the sofa. His breath came slower now, steadier, and his eyes closed.

It's now or never, I thought, knowing that Max would not stay away for long. Moving softly, I crossed the room and opened the outer door wide, turning back to face him. "Oh," I said, forcing a slight nasal twang into my voice, "I'm sorry; I'm looking for the little girl's room."

Derek turned and looked at me without giving me a second glance. "Three doors down on the left," he said and moved back around in his seat.

"Sorry," I mumbled again and went out into the hall. Max, I knew, was at the front door talking with his visitor. But I also knew that there was a side exit to the club, one that had not been connected to an alarm, at least not during my time spent here. I had to take the chance, and quickly, before Max returned and saw me here. Somehow I felt that my disguise would not fool him one bit.

I moved down the dark hallway, clutching my tote bag, opened the first exit door I found, and ended up on the side street outside.

Free! I relaxed slightly, feeling the tension ease out of my shoulders and back. I started walking, slowly so as to hold my new features, and when I arrived at the corner, I turned left. Behind me I could hear the murmur of the crowd waiting for entrance to the Ballroom. Not daring to look back, I kept walking and didn't stop until I'd put four blocks between me and Max. Maintaining the transformation sapped my strength and I felt myself begin to sweat in the frigid night air.

My original plan had been to ransack Max's desk for available cash. I needed money, if only for the phone call from Terri Hamilton. After that, I wasn't quite sure what would happen. Terri would either take me in and use me to further her plot for revenge against Max, or I'd find a convenient subway tunnel in which to spend the day. Both of these options were preferable to staying one extra minute in Max's presence.

I checked my reflection in the window in front of me, I'd managed to hold most of my features, except for the eyes that appeared too old for the face I'd concocted. Widening them a bit helped give me a more youthful appearance which might serve me better in begging some of the passersby for money. No sense in showing my true self while trying to get away without a trace. Even now I thought I could sense Max's pursuit.

The first couple I approached turned me down without even giving me a glance as did the second. But luck was with me on the third person to pass, a lone woman, middle aged and plump, but with a pleasant expression on her face. "Excuse me, ma'am," I said, keeping a faint twang to my voice. "I wonder if I could bother you for a little change to make a phone call."

She stopped and smiled at me, looking me up and down. "You certainly can. And"—she rummaged in her oversized purse, pulling out her wallet— "I'll give you a little more than that." She handed me a twenty dollar bill, a handful of change, and a small white card giving the address and phone number of the Angel of Mercy Mission. "This'll get you a phone call and a good hot meal, child. If you don't mind my saying so, you look cold and hungry."

The truth of the matter is that I was ravenous. But not for anything money would buy. My proximity to this woman brought out a hunger for her blood.

I shook my head. "No, ma'am," I said, my voice muffled slightly due to the growth of my fangs. "I'm fine." I pushed the bill and the change into my pocket. "Thank you very much."

"Not a problem. And if you need a place to stay, for the night or even for several nights, come to the address on the card and if I'm not there, mention that I referred you. I'm Marie, by the way." She held out her hand to shake mine.

I took it and she held it between her two hands. "You're chilled and shaking, dear. Are you sure you wouldn't want to come along with me now and I'll get you a place to sleep."

"No thanks, ma'am. I'm fine and I have a place to stay, I just need to call a friend."

"What's your name?"

I felt so relaxed with her that I almost gave her my real name. "Dei— er, Dee. Short for," I paused, what would Dee be short for? "Dorothy."

She smiled. "And do you have a last name, Dee?"

Between the terrible hunger that threatened to overwhelm me, my need to get some shelter before dawn, the strain of holding my transformation, and the terrible feeling that Max would find me soon, I couldn't think. "Um," I said, "er, Smith?"

Her eyes raked over me. "Are you sure?"

I nodded.

"It's okay, honey." She reached out and took my arm. "It's not a good thing for a young girl like you to be out on the streets by herself this late. Come with me."

"No," I pulled away from her. "I do not wish to be rude, Marie, but I am fine. Thank you."

I turned and began to walk swiftly away from her, realizing that my voice had reverted back to its normal pitch. And from the tingling in my face and scalp, I felt sure that my disguise was failing. Even exhausted as I was, I began to run, and didn't stop for four or five blocks until I came to a pay phone. My hands were still shaking as I dialed the number.

On the sixth ring she answered, sleepy and indignant. "Yeah? Do you have any idea what time it is? This had better be an emergency."

"Is this Terri?" I asked, "Terri Hamilton?"

"Yeah, that's me. Who is this and what the hell do you want from me? Don't you people ever sleep?"

"What?"

"It's a little late for a telemarketing call, isn't it?"

"But this isn't a telemarketing call, Terri. This is Deirdre Greer." There was a silence on the other end of the line. "Please," I said, not realizing at the time the great irony of my next statement, "I need your help."

"Oh." She paused again, then said, "Yes, of course you do. Where are you?"

I looked up at the signs and gave her the intersection. "Not too far away from me then," she said, and proceeded to give me directions to her place. "Think you can find me?"

"Yes. I'll be there soon."

She gave a small, vicious laugh and I wondered for a minute whether calling her was a good idea. But what choice did I have? "You'd better make it soon, sweetie, it's almost dawn."

CHAPTER NINETEEN

Mitch Greer: New Orleans

Vivienne's threats to Angelo paid off. He wasted no time in leading Sam and me directly to Maggie's house in the quarter. Just like he'd said, it was a pretty little house, for what that was worth. As we drew closer, though, we heard the sounds of hysterical sobbing, adding an eerie touch to an already tense atmosphere.

Angelo stopped just short of the front walk. From where we stood, we could see Maggie quite clearly, she sat on a glider on the front porch, rocking back and forth, crying and shaking. I nodded to Angelo, and he scurried off down the street. Chris was nowhere to be seen. "Let me talk to her," I whispered to Sam. "She knows me."

Sam nodded and moved back into the shadows of a nearby tree.

"Maggie?" I called her name softly as I walked toward the house. "It's me, Mitch. Are you okay?"

"Go away," she said, "you don't want to be here,

not with me. I'm more of a monster than any of you ever will be. I killed my children. Didn't you know that??"

"But you called me, Maggie. You said you wanted my help. And I know all about your children, Maggie, and it's okay. Both of your children are alive."

"No! They are dead. Eduard saw to that. He took care of everything. And I let him do it. That means their blood is on my hands just as if I'd held the knife myself. I know that and you know that." She gave a choked laugh. "We all know that."

"Where's Chris, Maggie?" I tried to keep my voice calm and conversational in tone. In the past, I'd handled criminals in this sort of shape, demented, damaged, and totally capable of doing absolutely anything. It had never frightened me before, all part of the job, but this time was different. I didn't want to lose my son a second time, and she was the only link to him now.

"Chris?" She repeated the name back to me as if she'd never heard it before.

"Phoenix?" I asked using the name she'd most often called her child. Maggie recognized that name; her eyes sought my face in the darkness and I stepped forward. "Mitch? You found me, that's good. I just want you to know right now that I'm sorry, Mitch. I couldn't help it, couldn't help any of it. I didn't want to, I don't want to. But I had no choice, I had to. He made me."

"Who made you, Maggie? And what did you do?"

"Steven. My son. I murdered him. Didn't you know?"

I looked over at Sam and motioned him to move farther away. We weren't going to get anywhere with her, not while she was so agitated. And Sam was a stranger to her. She didn't seem as if she'd noticed him yet, but if she saw him, she might be more intimidated. I wanted her relaxed and more likely to talk.

"Maggie," I said softly, approaching her more slowly, holding my hands out in clear view so that she would know I wasn't armed. "I've just come to talk to you. No one wants to hurt you."

She threw her head back and laughed. Somehow the sound was more unnerving than her crying had been. "Why not? You should *want* to hurt me. All of you should. And if you don't want to hurt me now, you certainly will eventually. It's all I'm good for. Eduard knew that. And so does Steven. Phoenix hasn't hurt me yet, but I know it will just be a matter of time."

"Where's Phoenix?" I asked the question of her again, a little less gently this time, not liking the turn her mind seemed to be taking.

"Gone, Phoenix is gone. Before he could hurt me like all the rest of them . . ."

I moved forward, but Sam stopped me. "Don't threaten her," he whispered. "We need to get her away from here. Some place unfamiliar, with nothing around to remind her of the past. This house probably feeds her insanity, all those unhappy, horrible memories haunting her. You have to try to lure her from the porch and lead her somewhere else. Somewhere we can watch her and keep her safe."

I nodded. "Maggie? Why don't you come with me? We were all friends back in Whitby, weren't we?"

She smiled and a flash of her old mesmerizing beauty shone through her madness. "I always did like you, Mitch. You had a way of treating me like I was a person who mattered."

"You do matter, Maggie. Why don't you come with me? It's a pretty night and it's just a short walk to Lily's house from here and we can talk."

I extended my arm and she came toward me. Behind me, I felt Sam tense up, but I could tell by the way she was holding herself, erect and proud, that Maggie had recovered some of her composure.

She took my arm and we walked, talking of the weather and the city and not much else. When I tried to steer the conversation into the direction of recent events, I could feel her tremble. I shot Sam a glance over my shoulder to where he walked a few yards behind us. He held his hand positioned awkwardly in his pocket, so I knew that he was keeping a tranquilizing syringe close, in case it was needed. Though it seemed that the farther Maggie moved away from her house, the saner she became.

By the time we'd arrived at Lily's house, she'd progressed to joking and flirting and seemed much like the carefree woman who'd arrived at The Black Rose. It was hard to believe that had only been a short while ago, so much had happened. My whole life had disintegrated in front of my eyes; I'd regained my son, then lost Deirdre and him. And the instrument of this torture, walked dangerously close to me, laughing up at me and being totally charming.

I shook my head.

"What is it, Mitch? Did I say something wrong?"

"Say something wrong? No. But do something wrong?" I pulled away from her so that I could look straight into her face. "Where's Chris, Maggie? Where's Deirdre?"

Her eyes darted back and forth nervously. "Chris? He ran away from me. I think I must've been acting pretty crazy. And I don't need to tell you I don't really know where Deirdre is, do I? I can tell you, though, that you'll not see her again. Steven has her."

"And just who is Steven? What soul did your bastard husband put into his body?"

She laughed mirthlessly and I felt a chill. "You know who it is, Mitch, I can read it in your eyes. He almost killed you once but she interfered. She shouldn't have done that. You should have been a dead man and she should have been his, that's all he's ever wanted. Fortunately, Maggie is here, ready to obey orders, and more than willing to rectify those mistakes."

Her abrupt switch from friendly to hostile took me completely by surprise, as did the knife she drew from her sleeve.

"You can't kill me with that, Maggie. You of all people should know better."

Still she lunged at me, her grin reminding me of the Other assailant that first poisoned Deirdre. I drew back and her smile broadened.

"Yes, you are a clever one, aren't you? The blade is poisoned, of course. I've just been waiting for you to show up, counting on your arrogance to ensure you'd come alone. I'll take care of the rest of your little group of friends after you're dead."

I grabbed her wrists to keep the knife away. She may have been strong, but I was stronger. And more determined. I only had to hold her still for a moment for Sam to arrive and administer the tranquillizer. Her eyes widened then drooped closed, the knife fell to the ground, and I managed to catch her before she fell on it. Asleep, in my arms, she looked like an angel.

"Thanks, Sam."

He grinned at me. "Quick Draw Samuels," he blew a puff of air on the tip of the needle, "Yeah, they all call me that." Then he grew serious. "No problem. I'm glad I was here."

I carried Maggie the rest of the way to Lily's house and Vivienne greeted us at the door. "I see the poor little lamb is asleep again. She is safer that way, no? Did she tell you anything before Sam stepped in?"

"Yeah, she did. Seems like Chris is alive, although we weren't all that sure of it at first. He ran away from her and is hiding out somewhere."

Viv smiled at me, showing off her dimples. "This is true, *mon cher.* But first things first. Have you thought where we would stow the sleeping beauty?"

"I thought Moon's room would make the perfect guest bedroom," I said, heading down the hallway with Maggie's limp body. Vivienne went ahead of me and opened the door to the tank. I entered, not without a shudder for the remembrance of my stay in the same place, lay Maggie down on the small cot, and, after making sure the oxygen supply was turned on, closed and locked the door.

"Now, what were you saying about Chris?"

Viv gave a little high-pitched giggle and took my hand. "Come with me to the kitchen, *mon chou,* and all will become clear.

More than clear, actually. There, sitting at the kitchen table with Lily and Claude, was Chris, my son, none the worse for wear.

He stood up when I walked in and came over to give me a quick hug. "Is Mum okay?"

I nodded and clapped him on the shoulders. "After she sleeps off whatever it was Sam gave her, she'll be fine. But how did you know where to find us?"

"I didn't. I'd gotten away from her finally. You

know, I didn't really want to leave her. I mean she was acting so crazy, and I was afraid she'd hurt herself. But she pulled a knife out of the kitchen drawer and threatened me. 'You're already dead, anyway, so doing it again won't matter. And I will kill you, if you don't get out of here now.'" His voice trailed off and his eyes grew sad. "I know none of you really understand it but I can't help myself. I love her, I have to love her. She's the only mother I remember. And she wasn't always this way."

Vivienne laid a hand on his shoulder. "One must never apologize for loving their mother. We do not judge you, Chris."

"Thanks," he said, sitting up a little straighter. "Anyway, I ran and ran and eventually found myself in a huge open cemetery After all the running, I was tired so I sat on the steps of some mausoleum for a while. Seemed fitting, somehow, since part of me rests in a place like that." He held his hands up in front of his face, examined them, then shrugged. "It's funny. I can't imagine having another body, lying in a grave somewhere, rotting. It's almost like I feel about Mum, this is the only thing I remember."

I nodded. "Yeah. I can't imagine it either."

"Anyway," Chris continued, "there I sat, on those cold, hard steps, trying to think, but trying not to think, you know? I heard this funny wheezing whistling sound and noticed an old man, at least he looked old, but he was walking upright and steady through the graves. He came up to where I sat. 'You lost, young man?' he asked.

" 'Not really, just resting.'

"The man laughed at that. 'Many folk restin' here, but you, young man, you must be special. Most of 'em restin' can't talk about it.' Then he moved closer to me, squinted his eyes and sniffed at me, as if he were a dog catching my scent. 'You got the smell of Other about you, boy. So you must be Chris.'

" 'Yeah, I am. How did you know?'

" 'I know lots of things, boy. And it ain't your place to wonder why. But I can take you to your father and his friends, if you like. Do it for free, even, since it 'pears this old man owe your papa a debt. I did him a disservice once and returnin' you will balance that. Ol' bow-legged 'Lo don't like staying in anyone's debt.' He gave a wheezing laugh, I could almost hear the air rattling around inside his lungs. 'Besides, I need to stay on the good side of that blond one. So I do it for her too. You be sure to tell her I say this.'

" 'Vivienne?'

" 'Just so, young man. Come along now.'

"We walked a few blocks and he led me up the steps. 'Take care o' your mam and your pap, young one, and all be well. The spirits, why, they like you. They leadin' you to a good way. And there ain't nothin' wrong with that.'

"He slapped me on the back and when I turned back to thank him, he had already disappeared down the street. And that's it."

I shook my head. "I'm glad he found you. But I still can't figure that man out. Whose side is he on, I wonder?"

Lily laughed and handed me a glass of scotch and ice. "That's an easy one, Mitch. 'Lo is on 'Lo's side, of course. For him there's no right or wrong, no good or evil. There's just 'Lo."

CHAPTER TWENTY

We all sat at the kitchen table with our various drinks. "Tell me what happened," I said to Chris. "Why did you go with her? You could have waited for me to return."

"There's not that much to tell, really," he said, "I came with her because I thought someone should take care of her. She seems strong at times, but that's just an act. She's always been the most emotionally fragile person I've ever know."

I made a scoffing noise and he stared over at me. "Yeah, I know what you think, Dad, but before you start on me, all I can say is that, yeah, I know that she tried to kill me twice, but that fact doesn't really make that much of a difference. Like I just said, she's my mother and I love her. It really isn't her fault that she's the way she is. I blame that on Eduard. And Steven. I thought that if I stayed with her it might make a difference. She said she was leaving you a note."

"Yeah, she left me a note. And another dead dog."

"Larry?" Chris's voice cracked just a bit and for a moment he resembled the lost child called Phoenix. "Ah, man." He rubbed his hand over his eyes. "I didn't know, honestly. I was waiting out in the cab in front of the pub and she told me to wait there. 'I need to leave Mitch a message,' she said, 'so that when he finds Deirdre he can meet up with us.' It was a fairly long while before she came back out. I remember thinking that the cab fare was going to be horrendous and I hoped she'd have enough money. And when she got back into the cab, she reached over and patted my cheek. Her hand was slightly damp. 'Sorry it took me so long,' she said, laughing. 'First I had to find a pen and some paper, and then when I was finished with that I decided I'd better make a stop at the loo before we left.' I had no reason to believe she'd hurt the dog. I'd have stopped her if I'd known."

Chris' eyes slid away from mine. Either he wasn't being completely honest with me, or he was ashamed that he hadn't known how far gone Maggie actually was.

"She was fine on the plane ride to here. She seemed her normal cheerful self, turning on the charm for everyone." He laughed a bit in remembrance. "She's got more than her fair share of charm."

"Yeah," I said, "I've noticed. She's got a gift, no doubt about it."

"Anyway, it wasn't until we arrived at the house that she started acting odd. She kept talking to me, but if I'd respond verbally, she'd start to cry. As long as I kept quiet, she was calm. I noticed that she avoided looking at me and if she caught my eye, she'd wince. It was nothing I couldn't handle. I'm kind of used to her little eccentricities. But then

she picked up the phone and called Steven. After
that all hell broke loose. She went to her room for
a while, and when she came out she was crazed,
tossing glassware against the walls and overturning
the furniture." Chris shook his head. "She's really
quite physically strong, you know. When she started
on the ranting about how she'd murdered her children, and pulled the knife on me, well, I just
couldn't deal with it anymore, so I left. I doubt she
even noticed when I'd gone."

"Actually, she knew you'd gone. And I think she
was relieved that you left. Maggie doesn't really
want to hurt you, Chris."

He rubbed his arm where she'd attacked him
with a corkscrew that night in Whitby. "Maybe. But
you know, it's getting more difficult to believe that
with each passing day." His voice then acquired a
wistful note, making him sound younger than he
was. "What are you going to do to her?"

I sighed, combed my fingers through my hair, and
held out my glass to Lily for refilling. "I have no
idea. Keep her from killing any of us, I guess."

"She tried to kill you?"

I nodded and Sam cleared his throat. "I have
her under observation and she's safe in the tank,
no danger to herself or to others. I'd like to see
her get professional help, though."

Chris nodded. "That'd be good, I guess."

"For now," I said, "there's not a whole lot we can
do. You were my first priority. Now that you're safe,
all I want to do is find Deirdre. Can you help me?
Have you remembered where Steven is? We think
that the soul placed in his body is Max Hunter,
and Maggie hinted at it as well. But we don't know
for sure."

He gave me a sad smile. "I'm sorry to hear that,

but it makes perfect sense. And it sure would explain why I hated him when we were growing up. I can even do better than remember for you. When Mum was done with her phone call, she went to her room. I could tell she was more agitated after that, and I was curious, so I hit redial. She'd called the Ballroom of Romance."

"Merde," Vivienne said, "so it is Max. Did he tear down all of my renovations? And my lovely dungeons?"

Chris laughed. "To tell you the truth, Vivienne, I didn't ask. I hung up when he answered; somehow it just didn't seem like a good time for a brotherly reunion. But if he's doing business as the Ballroom of Romance again, I'd expect so."

Vivienne pouted a bit then brightened up. "No problem, *mon gars*, I was getting bored with it all anyway. And now I suppose we will be needing tickets to New York. Lily, dear, did I see a computer in your room?"

"Yeah. Go work your Internet magic, Vivienne. But I think Claude and I will stay here. That way we'll be able to talk to Victor when he comes home. And you can leave Maggie here as well and we'll keep an eye on her."

"Actually," Sam said, "I'd like to take her with us and see if I can't get her admitted to my old hospital. We can't just keep her locked up indefinitely so we might as well do something positive for her as soon as possible."

"Fine," said Vivienne, "so that will be five seats on the next evening's plane to New York." She gave a small giggle. "Let's see if my airline friend has noticed yet that I've lifted his ID and password."

"Viv? You are paying for these tickets, right?"

"But of course, Mitch," she stuck her tongue out

at me and winked. "I may be a monster but I am not a thief. Having the airline employee information just makes it all much simpler. And there is nothing wrong with simple, nothing at all. Especially when everything else around one is so complicated."

She left the room and I checked the clock, then looked over at Claude and Lily. "I don't know about the two of you, but I'm starving. Haven't fed since that night at Heathrow and I've a feeling I'll need to be at my full strength to deal with Max tomorrow night."

Claude got up from the table. "We've got a few hours until dawn and I know a few places that never close. I'll come along."

"Lily?" I glanced over at her. She was hunched over her cup of tea, staring into the liquid. "How about you?"

She jumped. "What?"

"Did you want to go out?"

Lily shook her head. "No, I'll stay here if you don't mind. Besides, don't you need to check in at your hotel? We could squeeze everyone in here, if you all didn't mind, but somehow"—she cocked her head back to her room where Vivienne was making airline arrangements—"I doubt it will suit everyone."

"Damn. I forgot about that."

"It should not be a problem, Mitch," Vivienne said, entering the kitchen with printed copies of tickets and boarding passes. "There's time for you and Claude to go out for a bite and still make it to the hotel on time. As for me, I had a lovely meal on the plane the other night." Her eyes practically sparkled with amusement. "Sam and I will go ahead and make sure that the rooms are in order."

"Chris?"

He laughed nervously. "I know you don't want me to come along on your hunt, Dad. And to be honest, there are aspects about it that give me the creeps. Nothing personal. So, if Lily doesn't mind, I'll just stay here and keep watch over Mum tonight."

"I'd be happy to have the company, Chris. No offense, but the thoughts of Maggie, locked into that tank gives *me* the creeps. And," a faraway note crept into her voice, "Victor might come back. You never know."

Claude and I took to the streets. "There's a little club not too far from here," he said. "I used to play piano there, back before I met Vivienne."

I laughed. "That must've been a wild time."

"Actually, it wasn't at all what you'd think. She came in one night and picked me out of the band. I was flattered at the time. Let's be honest, how often does a woman like her even notice a man my size? Let alone pull him aside to whisper sweet French nothings in his ear? I fell in love with her instantly."

I nodded. "That would be easy to do. Viv is an incredible woman."

"You underestimate her, Mitch. She's also an incredible vampire. And trust me, you never want to make her angry. The night Cadre headquarters blew up, I encountered her in full rage. She may seem fluffy and soft, but she is anything but."

"I know."

"She led me out into the alley behind the club and told me what she wanted of me." He pulled out a white handkerchief and dabbed his forehead with it before stuffing it back into his pocket. "The odd thing was that I didn't doubt her for a moment. If she'd said she was the queen of England I'd have believed her, despite all evidence to the contrary." His laughter echoed down the streets. "I've never regretted it. Not once. Except maybe when the Others made all of us into walking targets. And then, my biggest problem was not having her around."

I looked over at Claude. "Does she know how you feel?"

His laughter had a hollow sound now. "How could she not, Mitch? She's my creator, my life. But she doesn't let on and I certainly feel enough of a fool most of the time without exposing my heart fully. I serve her the only way I can, the only way she will allow me to."

"It must be hell," I said, thinking out loud, "to think of her being with another man."

He gave me a keen glance. "You, of all people, should know."

"Yeah. I do." The bitterness and anger I felt spilled out in the words. "Look, let's get moving. I'm starving and we don't have all night."

We quickened our pace. "I know where the rough sections of town are," Claude said, "if you'd prefer a quick feed. Otherwise we could hit the clubs."

"No clubs, no lights, no music. The rough section suits me perfectly."

He led me down a series of dark streets and stopped at one of the alleys. "Around there," he said, "there's always one or two ruffians hanging about. You take this one and I'll be a couple of streets over."

It didn't take me long to find someone who was looking for trouble. And he found it. I'm ashamed to say that my hunt this night lacked even the slightest hint of the civilized man I once considered myself. Instead of establishing contact, I sprang on the first shadowy form I saw and fed on him savagely, tearing at his skin, being far rougher than I needed to be to subdue him and drinking far too much of his blood. My mind was carried away by the taste of his blood flowing into me, warming me, invigorating me, and for the first time ever, I lost control. His tortured gasping brought me back to my senses and I let go of him. He flopped to the ground like a wet rag.

"Damn," I said, angry at myself, angry at him, angry at the entire world. Bending over him, I felt for a pulse and to my relief found one. I peeled back his eyelids and his eyes focused on me.

"What happened?" he asked, his voice sounded faint and shaky with a note of fear but it was strong enough. He'd live.

"Nothing," I said, "you were like this when I got here."

"Shit," he said. "Son of a bitch sneaked up on me. I never saw him coming."

"Yeah," I said. "It happens. Want me to call an ambulance?"

"No way, man, but thanks for asking. I'll be fine."

He walked away from me slowly, clutching his hand to the wound on his neck. I turned away and went back to the street to wait for Claude.

After about five minutes, he came sauntering out of another alleyway, dabbing at his lips with his white handkerchief. "Want to go back?" he asked. "Or do you feel like hitting the clubs now?"

I shook my head. "I'll go back, but you can stay out longer. I'll see you back at the hotel."

"No," he said, stuffing the handkerchief back into his breast pocket. "I'll walk with you. I wanted to ask you something, anyway."

"What's that?"

"Did you have any trouble learning how to change your shape?"

I laughed. "The only trouble I had was with Deirdre. She absolutely refused to learn the skill and couldn't understand why I'd want to. Why do you ask?"

Claude looked down at the sidewalk. "I've never been able to do it. Change, I mean. So I was just wondering if it was something I needed to work at or if it was second nature to our kind."

"Actually, it's probably a combination of both. Didn't Vivienne teach you? She's the one who taught me."

He gave a nervous laugh. "I couldn't do it."

"Well, it's an acquired skill, it'll come with time."

"No, I don't think you understand. Vivienne tried to teach me, but I never got past the first lesson. I couldn't"—he looked around furtively—"take my clothes off in front of her."

"No?"

"No way," he said, gesturing to himself. "Can you blame me?"

"As I said"—I clapped him on the back—"Deirdre refused to change for years. But when she needed it, the change came to her. Give it time, Claude."

"Yeah, I guess so," he said. "Time I've got."

CHAPTER
TWENTY-ONE

Claude and I checked into our rooms at the Hotel of Souls shortly before dawn. An utterly fascinating establishment, the hotel catered to vampires, placing us on the upper floors and providing the rooms with luxuries such as steel shutters, heavily draped windows and a curious coffin-sized box at the foot of the bed. I'd also heard that the staff would often act as donors for their select clients. As I'd fed well just an hour ago, I had no need to test out this rumor.

The bed was comfortable enough. Like Deirdre, I shunned the confines of a coffin, knowing that others of our kind would be extremely uncomfortable without it. We were all different, it seemed, and much had to do with our creators, our mentors in the life. I tossed and turned for a while, but eventually fell into a fitful sleep, interrupted frequently with dreams—nightmares in which the principle figures were Max and Deirdre. My subconscious dredged out every fear, even some I hadn't known existed. From the scenario of Deirdre, lying bloody and lifeless with Max standing over her body gloating, to the totally absurd vision of Deirdre and Max, living as a happy couple in my absence. Maggie figured into the dreams as well. She was alternately trying to kill me or attempting to seduce me. That she could succeed in either was disturbing.

Finally, around three o'clock, I gave up on sleep, showered, dressed, packed my belongings in the duffel bag and flipped on the television. As always there was nothing much to watch, but I did manage to find an old war movie and drowsed in the chair. At five the telephone rang.

"Mitch? *C'est moi.* Sam has gone over to the house to get Maggie and Chris; they'll leave from there and meet us at the airport. I've scheduled a cab for us to arrive at sundown, which should give us plenty of time to catch the flight. It's a joy to deal with a hotel staff that understands our special needs. I would feel better if we weren't transporting a crazy woman, but Sam is sure he can keep her manageable with medication."

"He's the doctor," I said, "and crazy people have always been his specialty."

Vivienne laughed, then sobered up instantly. "Maybe so, but I fear he is playing the hero to make up for his role in the poison manufacture. He denies it, of course, but I am not so sure. I've asked Claude to come with us, I feel the need for extra protection."

"Good thinking, Viv. Claude always seems to get left behind anyway."

"He is a good man."

I thought of Claude's revelation of love last night. He would be pleased to have the opportunity to protect Vivienne. I hoped the plan wouldn't backfire; it's not particularly easy for a man to see the

woman he loves constantly in the arms of another
man. Look what it had done to Max.

"Yeah. I'll meet you in the lobby at dusk."

We met with no surprises and no hassles at the
airport—a pleasant surprise. I'd gotten damn tired
of jumping into an airplane every other day though,
and vowed to myself that once this was all over,
Deirdre and I would take a long vacation. Somewhere secluded and secret. The thought that perhaps we wouldn't be together after all crossed my
mind. Max had always exerted power over her; I
could only hope that for the sake of our love, she
would hold on. If, that is, she remembered me at
all. And that thought was unthinkable. I ordered a
scotch on the rocks from the flight attendant and
spent the rest of the trip staring out into the dark
skies, feeling old and weary.

Still, when we landed in New York, I felt revived.
This city was home for me, always would be. And
Deirdre was here. I had felt it when we'd touched
down here earlier in the week and I felt it now. We
would find her. As to what sort of physical or mental state she'd be in, well, I couldn't worry about
that now. I remembered that we'd talked about this
once in Whitby and I told her that we'd build new
memories if worse came to worse. And we would.

Getting off the plane seemed to take forever as
did getting through the terminal and hailing a cab.
I'd already arranged to have Vivienne and the rest
check into the hotel. There was no damn way I
would spend another night alone and away from
Deirdre if I could help it.

I paid the driver and got out of the cab in front
of the Ballroom of Romance. I always hated this

place, from the first time I set foot in the door. I'd been secretly pleased when Vivienne bought it from Deirdre and turned it into Dangerous Crossings. Standing outside the place now, though, it was as if I'd jumped back in time. And I didn't like it, not one damn bit.

I elbowed my way to the front of the crowd, glaring down any opposition. Half-expecting to see Larry Martin at the door, I approached the doorman. "I'm here to see Max Hunter."

"Mr. Hunter is not available right now, sir." He glanced up at me briefly, then turned his eyes downward to study the seating chart in front of him. "Perhaps if you'd stand in the back of the line and wait your turn, he'll be free when you get admittance."

"Not available? Like I don't know what that means. He damn well is available for me."

The man really looked at me this time and I could tell from his eyes that he recognized me. Shorter than I and younger in appearance with a shaved head and a goatee, he looked like a normal human being, especially dressed in his uniform/tuxedo with the small brass name tag that read "Derek." But there was something disquieting about him, something odd about his eyes and the way the features of his face seemed to blur. He reminded me, ridiculous though the thought was, of Larry Martin.

He continued to size me up, his hands curled into tightly knotted fists, but his voice remained calm and even. "Whom shall I say is calling?" he said, keeping up the pretext of politeness.

"You know damn well who I am, Derek. Just tell him I'm here. He must be expecting me. He'd be a fool if he wasn't. And Max is many things, but not a fool."

He didn't say another word, but motioned to

another employee to come over where we stood. "Take over for me, will you?" Derek said, "I need to talk to Max. Keep *him* here"—he pointed a thumb at me and scowled—"until I come back."

I didn't wait too long, maybe five minutes at the most, before I heard a familiar voice. "So good to see you, Detective Greer. What can I do for you?"

"Can it, Max. I'm not a detective anymore. And we both know why I'm here."

He smiled at me and I felt the gorge rise in my throat. He'd been a particularly nasty bastard as a vampire and now that he was an Other, I had no idea what he was capable of. But last time we'd met, I'd been merely human. Now, at least, the scales were somewhat more balanced.

"I'm disappointed in you, Greer. You're so predictable. No 'hey, long time no see, glad to see you looking so good' small talk? Civilized beings preface their interactions with polite conversation."

I smiled back at him, exposing my fangs. "Okay, I'm not civilized, big surprise. And our last encounter certainly gives a new meaning to the word 'polite.' Let's just cut to the chase. You have her. I want her. I can go through your dead body just as easily as look at you. I think I'd like that, actually. So what's it going to be?"

Max laughed. "So very 'Dirty Harry' of you, Mitch. I hadn't realized you were a movie buff. As far as my having her, as you say, I can only say that I don't know what you're talking about. Whom do I have?"

I reached out and tried to grab him by the collar but my hand seemed to bounce off of him. It was then that I noticed that the crowd outside the Ballroom had disappeared. I could see them, wending their way away from the club in groups of twos and threes, completely oblivious of this confrontation.

Max nodded. "Yes, you're right. I have that ability, Mitch. Bequeathed to me by my doting father, Eduard. Quite a handy attribute actually. Our business can be conducted, here, in plain sight of the whole city of New York and not one person will see or hear. The combination of vampiric powers still present in my soul and the Other powers given to me by this"—he pointed to the thick scar around his neck—"make me invincible. Just give it up. Even if I had her here, you must realize by now that she's changed. She wouldn't know you. Right now," he gave a smug smile, "I doubt she'd even speak to you."

Without thinking about what I was doing, my arm shot out and I punched him, a hard right to the jaw. He went down like a lead weight. I gave a harsh laugh. "Invincible? Not bloody likely."

Stepping over him, I moved quickly through the bar, past the drinkers, the dancers, and the band and into the back area of the club. I hesitated only one second at the door of Max's office, marveling at how it was all exactly as I remembered it. Then I pushed the door open.

I'd expected the office would be empty, but instead Derek was sitting on a black leather couch, a glass of wine in his hands. He jumped up when I entered and the glass crashed to the floor. "Hey," he said, his voice sounding sleepy, "how'd you get in here?"

"Max sent me," I said, "to pick up something that belongs to me in the back room."

He moved to stop me. "Don't even think about it," I growled at him. "Whoever the hell you are you're no match for me."

I crossed the room and flung open the door to Max's secret hideaway. Inside, though, there was no Deirdre. The bed was rumpled and there were clothes on the floor, but they were clothes I didn't recognize.

"Deirdre?" I called her name anyway, feeling foolish as I did it. I'd been so sure, so certain that she'd be here. The armoire door was open, filled with the clothes of a stranger.

I turned back to see Max and Derek standing in the open doorway. They exchanged a look that told me many things. One, Max was as shocked as I was to find the room empty. Or maybe even more so. And two, if I were Derek, I'd head for the hills as soon as I could. Someone had screwed up, big time. And Max didn't reward screw-ups.

Max, however, covered his surprise. "I told you, Mitch. She's not here." He rubbed his jaw and gave me a smile. "Nice punch, by the way; it's good to know you haven't lost all of your charm. But if you'd just believed me, we all could have saved ourselves a lot of trouble."

I pulled in a good long scent of the room. "Don't bullshit me, Hunter. We both know she was here. I can smell her, for God's sake."

He smiled and stretched his arms out. "As anyone can plainly see, she's not here, Mitch," he said with finality. "I'll give you five minutes to leave the premises before I call the police. We're on good terms with them now and I'm sure they'd be interested in finding out how far one of their own has fallen. Somehow I don't think you'd like to spend a day in jail."

Derek was laughing as I left the room. Before I was even out into the club, though, I heard a loud crack, perhaps the sound of the back of a hand hitting someone's face. Then there was the thump of a body falling on the floor and the laughter stopped.

Back out on the street, I looked around. "Not here," I said to myself. "How could she not be here?" If I had read correctly the look Max gave Derek, she had been there. She must have escaped.

I smiled. "Good girl, Deirdre. But where on earth would you have gone? And how will I ever find you now? It's a big city."

The rest of the night I spent walking the streets, searching. I asked at the hotel in which she'd lived when we first met. They'd never heard of her. Neither had anyone seen her near where I used to live, an old brownstone in a somewhat less desirable area of town. I even went to the building that housed Griffin Designs but the security guard would only say that Miss Griffin had sold the business years ago and that if I had any further questions, I'd need to see Miss McCain in the morning. Finally, I had to admit that I was out of ideas and out of time. The night was ending when I hailed a cab and went back to the hotel.

An ambulance pulled away as we approached, lights flashing and siren howling. A crowd of people stood around the hotel entrance. "What happened?" I asked, out of curiosity.

"Somebody was stabbed." A man in a business suit with a briefcase and a paper stashed under his arm answered. "They say he might be dead."

Glancing down at the pavement, I noticed a trail of blood leading out of the door and to the curb. "Thanks," I said to the man, "are the cops here yet?"

"Upstairs, I think. Seventh floor, I heard someone say." He shook his head. "And my travel agent said this was a safe area."

"It's New York," I said with half a smile. "You're not really safe anywhere."

CHAPTER TWENTY-TWO

Deirdre Griffin: New York City

I hesitated before ringing the buzzer marked with Terri Hamilton's name. Her hatred of Max and her desire for revenge were not exactly solid grounds for cultivating a relationship with a former enemy. Then again, I had no other choice. No one who knew me would think to look for me here.

"Deirdre?" Terri's voice sounded scratchy on the intercom.

"Yes."

She give a brief hard laugh. "Come on up." The door made a buzzing sound and I pulled it open, entering the hallway and rushing up three flights of stairs. Once in the actual apartment hallway I felt safe from sunlight, unless this invitation was a horrible ruse to expose me to the sun's rays. "So be it," I said softly to myself and knocked.

Terri answered immediately. She must have been sleeping when I called. She was wearing a short, pink nightshirt and her hair was disheveled.

"Come on in," she said, "I welcome you to my humble abode." The apartment was huge but empty except for a few folding chairs, a card table, a boom box, and a pile of blankets and pillows on the floor. "The emphasis is on humble, I'm afraid. When I lost the *RealLife Vampires* job, I had to sell all my furniture. In a few months what little savings I have will be eaten up by the mortgage here and I'll have to find some other place to live."

I didn't know what to say. "I'm sorry for your trouble, Terri. For what that's worth."

She raised an eyebrow at me. "You really don't remember me, do you? I'd think that you would be cheering at my downfall. After all, between Bob and me, with a lot of encouragement and support from Eduard DeRouchard, we managed to convince the world that you and all like you were blood-thirsty demons from hell."

I shrugged. "I can hardly be angry about something I can't recall. You've given me a place of refuge in need. I would think that would cancel all scores."

"Yeah. I guess it does. So, tell me, Deirdre, what the hell are you doing in New York with Max? Last I heard you were hiding out in Whitby with Mitch."

"Mitch? He never existed."

Terri looked at me as if she might explode with laughter. "That's the biggest bunch of bullshit I've ever heard, Deirdre. Of course he exists, I have pictures of him and you and all the others. What's Max Hunter been telling you?"

"That everything I managed to remember from my former life was all part of a fevered delusion on my part."

"And you believed him?"

The sun rose outside the drawn curtains of Terri's

windows. A small crack of sunlight filtered in, making me feel weak and slightly woozy. I glanced over at the chairs, they were out of the direct path of the window. "He presented me with conclusive evidence to prove the point. May I sit?"

She looked over her shoulder at the window. "Oh, yeah, sorry about that. Cheap drapes. And I'm being a bad hostess. Please, go ahead and sit down. I'm going to make a pot of coffee, can I get you anything?"

"Oh, coffee would be wonderful. Thank you."

She looked surprised. "You drink coffee?"

"Of course. What exactly do you know about me? About," I hesitated as always before saying the word, "vampires?"

"Not all that much, just what DeRouchard told us. At the start, I actually believed it was all the truth. But even before the end, I began to have doubts. But the money was good, and..." Her voice drifted off and she frowned. "That's no excuse, I know that now. Anyway, let me go make the coffee. Then we can talk. Do you need to stay the day?"

"Now that the sun is up, yes. I hope that is not an inconvenience for you."

Terri laughed on the way into her kitchen. "No problem, sweetie. I'll just cancel all my other pressing appointments today."

I heard the water running in the kitchen, heard Terri bustling about, opening drawers and cupboards, all the while humming a little tune. For a woman hell-bent on revenge she acted inordinately cheerful and normal. Or maybe it was all an act. It didn't matter. She said the words to me that I most needed to hear. Mitch did exist. He hadn't been part of a dream or delusion, he was real. He was real! And we should have been together. My being with

Max was exactly what I'd thought it was from the beginning—nothing but a lie.

"Ow!" Something clattered to the floor in the kitchen. "Oh, shit," Terri said.

"Are you all right?"

"Yeah, just clumsy and stupid." She came out of the kitchen, sucking on her finger. "Cut myself," she said, taking the finger from her mouth and examining it. "On the coffee can." She twisted her head to one side and grimaced. "It's pretty deep. Damn it."

I could see the blood dripping from her finger. Worse than that, I could smell it. Closing my eyes, I took in a deep breath and crooked my fingers around the edges of my chair.

"Deirdre? What's wrong? Surely you don't get faint at the sight of—" She stopped midsentence. "Oh. Yeah. Jesus, I can be a stupid bitch at times. Hold on, let me get a bandage."

She hurried down the hallway and rummaged around in her medicine cabinet. I started to laugh softly as her obscenities reached my ears. When she came out, her finger was wrapped tightly in toilet paper.

"Out of bandages," she said, shrugging. "I forgot them last time I was at the store. I think it's stopped bleeding, though. Sorry about that. I didn't mean to bother you."

"I am fine, Terri. Don't give it a second thought."

"Okay," she said, "coffee time."

Back into the kitchen she went. I felt tired just watching her bounce from room to room. "What do you take in your coffee?" she called from the kitchen.

"Just coffee, thank you."

"Ah, good thing, actually. I think the milk's gone sour."

Terri came out from the kitchen bearing two mismatched mugs. She handed one to me and sat down on the other folding chair. "Cheers," she said, clinking her cup up against mine.

As I sipped my coffee I noticed that my hands were trembling. The sight and scent of Terri's blood, even for that small amount of time, made me ache with hunger.

She noticed as well. "Deirdre? Are you okay?"

"Fine," I said, taking another sip, "I am just hungry. But don't worry, you are quite safe."

Her eyes acquired a curious glint. "How long has it been since you've, um, fed?"

"Unfortunately, I don't remember. Max had been giving me some particularly vile mixture to drink, a combination of wine, blood, and some sort of drug, I think. Whatever it was, it satisfied my hunger a bit and calmed the nausea, but tasted horrible, bitter and medicinal. After about the third or fourth day, I refused to drink it."

"I don't know Max all that well, but somehow I can't imagine he took too kindly to your refusal."

"No," I smiled at her over the rim of the mug, "but I can be forceful when needed."

"I'm sure you can. You said you had nausea? Is that normal if you haven't fed for a while?"

"Not at all. Until recently I don't believe I was ever sick. But right now I don't wish to discuss my health; to be honest, I've heard nothing but talk about that since I woke up at the Ballroom of Romance. I want to talk about Mitch." I sounded breathless, like a young girl talking of her first love. "Tell me all you know about him."

"Yeah, we kind of got sidetracked, didn't we? Hold on a second, I'd like to have a cigarette if you don't mind."

"I don't mind at all, Terri. In fact, I'll have one as well."

She choked a bit on her coffee. "You smoke?"

"I started so that I could fit in with the crowd. Not peer pressure, you understand, but the desire to blend in with everyone else. Now I find it relaxes me."

She nodded, got up and went back into the kitchen, returning with a pack, a lighter, and an ashtray. She lit one for herself, then offered me the pack and the lighter. "So let me get this straight. You drink coffee and wine and smoke cigarettes. Do you eat regular food, too?"

"No, anything liquid is fine, but solids don't get digested. And one loses the craving for them, they simply don't seem appetizing after a while."

"This is fascinating, Deirdre. Really. Eduard always maintained that your kind acted exactly the way you're portrayed in movies. Instead you're nonthreatening, charming, and, I hate to admit it, nice." She sat for a while, staring into her cup of coffee. "To be honest," she said, "I'd rather you weren't. I'd feel like less of a, oh, I don't know, murderer may be too strong a word."

"Or it may not. But what's done is done, I'm not here to judge you. Tell me about Mitch."

As she spoke of what she knew of the two of us, I felt some of the events fall into place in my mind. There was that first attack on us by one of the Others and I remembered how totally clueless we were about what this would mean to our life. All the subsequent attacks, all the way up to the very last one, the one that had introduced the poison into my system, became clear in my mind. As an added bonus, details surrounding the attacks revealed themselves, details to which she'd never have been privy. As times and dates fell back into line, I was able to reconstruct places we had been and call to mind people we had known. Terri told me of our wedding. As she went through the event I remembered it with her, right down to the green dress I wore that night. I could even smell the perfume I wore—lily of the valley.

At one point she got up, brought us more coffee and even produced some photos of that occasion and others.

I smiled at her when she finished. "You cannot know how much this has helped me, Terri. I only wish there were some way I could pay you back for the kindness you've done me."

She laughed. "For starters, you can pay off my mortgage on this place."

"Anything else?"

Her eyes dropped away from mine. "No, not really."

"Ah."

"Except . . ."

"What is it, Terri?"

She got up and began to pace the room. "This is going to sound very strange, Deirdre, especially coming from me. And well, I don't quite know how to say it."

"Just say it. I daresay you know more about me than I do. So you'll know how I'll react."

"Funny. But I'm being serious. Before I got involved in the whole *RealLife Vampires* thing, before I entered the employ of Eduard DeRouchard, I always had a thing for vampires. I thought they'd be exciting, thrilling to be around. You know."

I nodded. "Like in the movies."

She gave a nervous giggle. "Yeah. And, well, anyway, I know now that you don't kill the people you feed from and I'd sort of, well . . ." Terri blushed. "Shit, I feel like a real freak saying this."

"Just say it," I said again, gently. "I think I know where you're going on this and I'm old enough that very little shocks me."

"Okay. This is so embarrassing and lame, but I want you to feed on me, just a little, so I can know what it feels like. And since you're hungry, well, it's a way of sort of paying back all the misery I've caused you and your friends over the past few years."

"Terri, you're not thinking straight. What if I decided that all of your blood would be the proper payment? Do you want to die for this thrill?"

She glanced over at me. "You wouldn't kill me. Like you said, I know you better than you know yourself. You just don't have the killer instinct."

I gave a mock sigh. "Yes, you have guessed my deepest, darkest secret. I'm not a killer."

"So? Will you?"

I moved toward her. "Why not?"

She tensed up and giggled nervously. "I can't do this," she said, "if I see you coming. Why don't you come around behind me?"

I felt awkward also. "Yes, that might be better."

Turning her back to me, Terri set her shoulders and sighed. Silently I moved closer to her, so close that my breath on her neck made her shiver.

"Terri," I said softly, whispering the words, "we don't have to do this if you don't want to."

"I do. Honest."

"Fine." My feeding instincts had been turned up with the scent of her blood earlier. Standing this close to her, I caught a whiff of her skin, soapy clean and fresh smelling. I put my mouth on her neck, my gums tingled and my fangs grew in response to my need. My bite was as gentle as I could make it, but still she gave a short surprised intake of breath and tried to move away from me. I hesitated before drawing on her blood, this had to be a willing gift on her part or it was wrong.

"Don't stop," she said, her voice muffled.

Wrapping an arm around her waist, I held her close to me, pulling in small swallows of her blood at first, savoring the taste of her and the warmth that flowed down my throat with every drop. She relaxed and I pulled on her again, more aggressively this time. Visions of other feedings and other prey rushed through my mind as if each drop of her blood restored a vital piece of my vampiric nature. I wanted to stay there forever, slowly drinking, lost in the taste and the song of her blood rushing through her veins. Instead I forced my mouth away from her neck and withdrew, still supporting her with a gentle arm around her waist.

"Terri? Are you all right?"

She sighed. "Wow. I had no idea. That was amazing. It tickled at first and itched a bit but then after the initial bite I felt like I was floating away." Terri turned back to face me, smiling. "Sort of like Percocet, only better."

"Someone once said to me that being fed on was like being pulled through a velvet tunnel."

She laughed. "Well, that's about as Freudian as you can get. And while we're deep in the throes of clichés, how was it for you?"

Suddenly, the euphoria of feeding faded away, replaced with a gnawing sense of nausea.

"Deirdre? You don't look that good."

I pressed my lips together, closed my eyes, and held up a hand to stave off her comments, willing the sickness to leave. It didn't.

My eyes shot open and I doubled over from the pain in my stomach.

"You're scaring me, you know that, don't you? Is there something wrong with my blood?"

"No," I managed to gasp, "it's not you. Excuse me."

I ran down the hall, found her bathroom and dropped to my knees in front of the toilet, vomiting up every drop of blood I'd taken. When the pain subsided, my stomach was empty and I felt the same. I curled up into a ball there on the rug in Terri Hamilton's bathroom and whimpered, "What the hell is wrong with me?"

CHAPTER
TWENTY-THREE

When I finally felt that I could stand, I rose and splashed water on my face. Then I went back to the living room. Terri had gotten dressed. She wore jeans and a *RealLife Vampires* logo T-shirt. I smiled when I saw it and she shrugged.

"It's all that's left of my former glory," she said, pulling out the front of it. "I'm worried about you though. Were you sick? I mean, did you throw up?"

I nodded.

"Does that happen usually?"

"Not at all. And once again, you have no need to worry. The problem isn't yours, it's mine. Apparently I can no longer ingest human blood. What a fine vampire that makes me."

"But why?"

"Max told me my metabolism was changing and that it would even out after a while. I thought at the time he exaggerated the facts, so that I would take the drink he kept for me, the drink that kept me mildly sedated and docile. And here I thought everything he told me was a lie," I said dryly. "I think I can assume he told me the truth. About this, at least."

"Had to happen sometime, I guess," Terri said, going back into the kitchen and calling out to me over the sound of running water. "Even the sorriest bastard is right every once in a while."

She came back and handed me a glass of ice water. I took a long drink. "Thank you," I said, raising the glass to my forehead and resting its coolness against my skin. "This is exactly what I needed. How did you know?"

"I've thrown up enough to know that nothing tastes better afterward than plain old cold water. It's happened more lately. I guess I drink too much. Losing that job hit me hard. And the way it happened set me up as either an idiot or a con artist; no one will hire me now in the news field. They won't even let me fetch them their coffee and donuts. And you've seen the kind of waitress I make."

"I'm sorry."

"No need for you to be. You had nothing to do with it. The word came down from Max and that was that."

I sat back down in the folding chair. "When you slipped me the note in that restaurant, you mentioned revenge. What exactly do you propose to do?"

"I'm not sure. He's in a position of power now. He has all the Others' holdings as well as the Cadre's at his disposal. All nice and legal, I'm afraid, Bob once got a look at some papers on Eduard's desk, designating Max Hunter, aka Steven DeRouchard, as his heir."

"Who is Bob?"

"Bob Smith, my partner on the show? He at least found a job, doing used car commercials on late night cable. He's a natural." She sneered a bit. "Bob Smith was the one who brought prestige to the show. I was there to be a little pretty thing. You really don't remember any of this, do you?"

"No," I admitted. "Feeding brought back a lot of memories for me, but that wasn't one of them."

"Oh. Speaking of feeding, I'm going to want some lunch soon. Is that going to bother you?"

"No. Unless the food is heavily spiced with something like garlic."

Terri looked at me in disbelief, then burst out laughing. "Garlic?" she asked when she caught her breath. "That part of the myth is true? You're kidding me, right?"

"Not at all. However, I've always had the aversion, even before I became what I am." I stopped for a second. "Yes," I said, smiling with joy at being able to remember a fact so simple, "that's correct. In fact, when we were in Whitby, and I was giving an interview to . . ." I stopped and jumped up from the chair, looking around the apartment frantically. "Where's my bag? Do you have a tape player?"

"Over by the door where you dropped it. And yeah, there's a cassette player in the boom box, it's one of the few things that didn't sell. What's up?"

"I just realized what the tape I found in the pocket of my jeans is all about." I walked across the room and pulled out the cassette. " 'Voilà!' as Vivienne would say, here it is. Can we play this?"

"Sure, why not?"

If the earlier part of the day spent with Terri Hamilton seemed surreal, it was nothing compared to hearing the sound of my voice talking with George Montgomery, telling details of my life unremembered until now. For instance, I now recalled the bar Pete and I had owned in London and also

The Black Rose in Whitby, the cosy little flat Mitch and I occupied above the bar. Then there was the cabin in Maine I burned down when I thought Mitch had left me for another woman and the confrontation with Eduard DeRouchard in New Orleans and his eventual defeat by Victor. And I remembered Victor, the man I once thought was Max's Renfield. Victor, I smiled as I thought his name. He always made me feel dirty and unkempt. I wondered where he was now, what he was doing. Did he know what had happened to me and the others? Did he care? Or was he really the true power behind the events?

At one point as I told my story on the tape, I'd excused myself and gone to the bathroom while George Montgomery and Mitch carried on a hurried and muffled conversation regarding my health. "Are you sure she's not pregnant?"

"Positive, George. There's no way."

Hearing Mitch's voice on the tape shocked me, thrilled me down to my very soul. Until this very moment, I hadn't been sure that Max wasn't telling the truth and that Terri, who I now knew had no reason on earth to befriend me, wasn't the one who was lying. The tape, however, was solid and undeniable proof. When I'd finished telling my story, the machine clicked off and tears streamed down my face. Putting a hand up to wipe them away, I saw that they were clear, no longer blood-tinged, no longer an oddity to be hidden from the rest of the world. "Look," I said to Terri, holding out my hand so that she could see the tears on my fingertips. "They're tears. Regular, normal, everyday tears."

"So?" She'd grown remarkably quiet while we'd listened to the tape. The fact didn't surprise me; both Mitch and I said some very uncomplimentary things about her and her show. If someone had said those things about me, I would not want to have to hear them played back in my own living room.

"Nothing," I said. "It means nothing." I glanced over at her, but she kept her head down and wouldn't meet my eyes. "Terri, what I said on that tape, well, I did not know you then and . . ."

"Goddamn it, Deirdre." Terri's voice sounded muffled. "What is wrong with you? Didn't you listen?" She turned her face to me then and I saw that she was crying also. "After all the grief I caused you, why the hell should you care about my feelings? All that hardship and pain, and the deaths of vampires you knew—they can be laid right at my doorstep. I'm ashamed of myself for not seeing that what I was doing was wrong. More than wrong, actually. It was criminal. An incitement to murder."

"But you did not know."

"The hell I didn't. Do you remember that segment we showed, the one supposedly filmed in London?"

"Ah, yes, I do. Now."

"That wasn't real, it wasn't even good for God's sake. But I sat at that desk and pretended it was the truth."

I stared at her for a while, then started to laugh. "Terri, everyone knew it was fake. How on earth did your producers expect people to think it was for real?"

She shrugged. "Eduard wanted it. And I, we, always went along with Eduard. He signed the checks. We did everything he asked us to, as long as the money kept coming in. His death didn't even stop any of it. We had scripts and shows planned for two or three more seasons. And we kept cranking them out, one after another."

"The true fault lies with Eduard. And he has paid with his life. What you've done for me today, giving me shelter and offering me your blood, more than makes up for your sins."

"I guess so."

"It does." My voice held a tone of finality. "Not only that, but you've given me hope, you've given Mitch back to me. I didn't mention it before, but I saw him last night. Max brought him in to cure me. This man looked exactly like him, spoke like him, but it couldn't have been him." I paused a second, feeling a slow smile cross my face as the heaviness slipped from my heart. "Of course. Max must've had one of his flunkies impersonate Mitch. Apparently my kind can take the shape of anyone if they concentrate hard enough. I should know, that's how I escaped from the Ballroom. And now I can remember Larry Martin exhibiting that power."

Terri stood looking at me in confusion. I shook my head. "It doesn't matter. I was just thinking out loud. Now, tell me, does your phone still work? I need to make a call or two if you don't mind. And weren't you going to have some lunch?"

Terri nodded, then pointed to the phone sitting on the floor in the hallway. "Call anyone you want." All the bounce and the perkiness she'd exhibited earlier seem to drain out of her as she turned and walked slowly into the kitchen.

I tried not to worry about her, though. At this point I needed to focus on what I needed to get out of this city and back to Mitch. First step: calling The Black Rose—perhaps Mitch was still there, waiting for me, searching for me. After all, not that much time had passed. The number I wanted to call came to my mind and fingers easily. *Amazing*, I thought as I dialed the phone, *an hour ago I didn't even know he existed and now I know him and his phone number.*

The phone only rang once. "Black Rose Pub," Pete said.

"Hello, Pete. It's me. Dottie."

"Dottie, darlin'! Where are you, my dear? And where's everyone else? A fine welcome you were giving me, to come home after that long trip to find the pub dark and locked. Only a little note, no trace of a living creature. Not even the dogs to greet me. And the bar is buzzing with tales of you running off with another man."

I gave a short laugh. "I'm in New York, Pete. And I didn't run off with another man, I was drugged and kidnapped."

"No! You don't say. Here in Whitby? Why, I don't believe it."

"Believe it."

"Well, and there'd not be a need for you to lie about it. And if you were kidnapped, then I'd expect nothing less of Mitch than to go looking for you. But what happened to Maggie? And the little one?"

Pete still insisted on thinking of Maggie's son, Phoenix, as a small child. He'd actually been twelve or thirteen when we first saw him. "Maggie and Phoenix? They're not there either? None of them are there?"

"Sure, Dottie, and that's what I'm saying. I hoped when I heard your voice, you'd be able to tell me what was happening."

"Not enough time, Pete. But when everything gets taken care of, I'm sure you'll be hearing from someone. How was the cruise, by the way?"

"Lovely, it was lovely. Too bad the missus is dead. She'd have loved every minute of it."

"Yes, I'm sure she would have."

"Are you all right, darlin'? This kidnapper, he didn't hurt you, did he? I'm assuming you escaped, seeing as how you're calling me. Did you call the police?"

"I am fine. He didn't hurt me. Please don't worry about me, Pete. Everything will work out. And tell the story tellers in the pub that I didn't run off with another man. I hope no one told Mitch that story."

"Ah, well, it was Jim saying it. None of the rest of them paid him any mind. But yeah, he told it to Mitch."

I sighed, remembering how I'd reacted when I thought he'd gone off with someone else. At least he hadn't burned down the pub. "I have to go now, Pete. I don't want to run up the phone bill here; it's not my place. But I'll speak with you again soon."

The rest of the afternoon went by slowly. Terri seemed wrapped up in her own little private hell of guilt and nothing I said could convince her she was wrong. Finally, I quit trying to calm her and stretched out on the floor to rest before sundown.

When I woke up, Terri was gone. Before she left, she'd covered me with a blanket and left a note.

"Hi, Deirdre. You sleep like the dead. Ha! I'm going out for a while, but I'm okay. I hope to see you again when I get back. Thanks for everything. Sometimes one needs to have their eyes forced open."

I folded the note and put it into my pocket. Just as I got to the bathroom to splash water on my face, the front doorbell rang.

"I'm on my way," I called, smiling. Terri must've forgotten her key. But when I opened the door Victor was standing there. Dressed impeccably as always, he greeted me with a kiss on the cheek. "Deirdre," he nodded, "I see you recognize me. This is good. Your memory is returning."

"Victor?" I gestured for him to come in and he did, shutting the door behind him. "How did you know I was here?"

"I had a little talk with an old friend, my dear, and put two and two together. Shall we go?"

CHAPTER TWENTY-FOUR

"Wait a minute." I said, suspicion growing in my mind. "How do I know you're really Victor? You could be anyone."

He laughed. "You're learning, Deirdre. I've always thought you were entirely too trusting. However, we don't have time for this right now. Come with me."

Shaking my head, I crossed my arms in front of me. "I don't think so. Not until you prove to me you are who you say you are."

"And how am I to do that? Is your memory completely restored? If I dredge up something out of our mutual past, and you can't remember the incident, what proof is that?"

"You know about what's happened to me?"

"You offend me, young one. There's very little I don't know, especially when it involves my blood. And you carry my blood in you. You all do. Now, are you going to come with me, or not?"

I sighed, bit my lip, and shook my head.

"I can force you if you'd rather play the game that way."

Without any warning, my temper rose and I reached out and slapped him. "How dare you? This is not a game, Victor. Or have you been pulling our strings and feeding us our lines from backstage?"

He gave an elegant quirk of an eyebrow. At that moment, I made up my mind that this had to be Victor. No one else could have perfected that look: a combination of innocence, scorn, and superiority. And I realized where Max had learned the gesture.

"You still don't understand, do you? Everything is a game, Deirdre. You win, you lose, you come out even. You start over again. When you stand on the other end of eternity like I do, with aeons stretched between birth and now, you'll know that I'm telling you the truth." He laughed again. "But I fear I don't have aeons to spare right now. Nor, young lady, do you. If I surmised where you were, what makes you think Max will be far behind? And I'd rather not confront him. Not here. And not yet."

"You're afraid of him." I was shocked to discover it wasn't a question. Victor was afraid of Max.

Victor cleared his throat. "Let's say instead I'm wary of him and I'd rather have more of us around when our confrontation occurs. And it will occur. It's a certainty, the same certainty that led to the defeat of my brother, Eduard."

"Your brother?"

"A figure of speech, Deirdre. As you are my grandchild in vampiric reckoning, Eduard was my brother. Remember how it took all of our combined energy to kill Eduard?"

"No, I remember only that you killed him. On your own. None of us could approach him, he had us all petrified."

"But you see, I was drawing strength from each of you. Your inability to move wasn't just an effect of Eduard's powers, it was also partly my doing."

"But Max is not like Eduard." I paused, searching Victor's eyes and began to doubt my statement. "Is he?"

"More's the pity, my dear, I believe that he is. And that he is more powerful than any of us suspect. As well as being less concerned with consequences than even our delightful Vivienne."

I still hesitated.

"Deirdre," he reached his hand out and gently touched my cheek. With his touch, I felt the truth of his being. He really was Victor. No one could possibly impersonate him this well.

He put his other hand on the other side of my face and pulled me closer to him, so that I could see deep into his eyes. A flood of memories washed over me, their images flashing so quickly that I could barely take them all in. The final flash was of Victor and me, standing alone in the Cadre council room. We spoke of Max and his reasons for allowing me to kill him. For, we thought, he had made it possible for me to do so.

I moved back from Victor, dizzy and nauseated. "We thought that we'd communicated with his soul or his ghost, didn't we?"

Victor nodded. "Yes, he seemed so peaceful in your visions, and I very much wanted to believe he was content to let his life go, to let the striving end. I myself have felt that way so many times before that his rationale seemed conceivable. I'd venture

a guess that even you, as young as you are, have
also felt that way."

I nodded.

"Max set us up to believe what he wanted us to
believe, that he was dead and at rest. Instead, what
he truly wanted was a continuation of the game
he'd started with you decades before. Even sleeping safely in the body of the baby born as Steven
DeRouchard, suckling at the breast of his mother,
he was undoubtedly already plotting his return,
filling your mind and mine with lies."

"If he has this much power, and this much influ-
ence over all of us, what does he want with it? What
does he want with me?

"Deirdre," he said, touching my cheek again,
"you are more important than you think. Do you
even realize what you are? What you could be? Max
planned to poison you, to steal your memories and
turn you against your vampiric nature. He thought
to make you human enough so that you could be
utilized as his Breeder." Victor laughed unpleasantly. "I must admit that it's nice to know that even
Max is not all-knowing; his plans have backfired.
He didn't transform you into a docile mate. Instead,
he managed to do what none of us have ever managed to do. It has been countless centuries since
something new evolved. There have been humans
and vampires and Others. And now you, you are
something else. Something new. Not really human,
nor vampire, nor Other, but a hybrid of all three.
I'm not sure I understand entirely. But I do know
that I want you kept safe."

I shook my head. "It doesn't matter what I am. I
don't care, Victor. I'm goddamned tired being used
and being manipulated. I just want to go home."

"And where is home, Deirdre?"

I answered without hesitation. "Wherever Mitch is."

He smiled at me. For the first time since I'd met Victor, it seemed a genuine smile, lacking in his usual condescension and scorn. "That is quite fortunate. Because that's where we're going. But first, you must feed. Even at a distance, I can feel the hunger gnawing at you, soon it will become a consuming desire and in satisfying that desire, you may overreach yourself. I know that you and I have never been close, but I don't want to lose you. Not now."

I licked my dry lips. He was right, I ached with hunger every waking minute and it had been getting worse. "I have tried to feed, Victor," I said, "but it doesn't do any good. I can't keep the blood in my system long enough to sate the hunger. It's as if my body rejects it."

"Human blood will do that to you now, yes, that's true. But I wasn't speaking of human blood."

"Animal blood? But it doesn't really satisfy—"

"Not animal blood," he said, interrupting me. "My blood. It will stay with you and fortify you. And the very taking of the blood will tie the two of us closer together; a bond we both may need in order to deal with Max."

I hesitated, not sure I really wanted to be bound to Victor. I didn't trust him, even after all he said. The history between us was too full of betrayals.

"Deirdre, I will make this offer only once. And we must act quickly. We've already wasted too much time."

"I thought you had aeons at your disposal."

"It's not my time I'm concerned about, it's

yours. When Max finds you again, he'll use all of his powers to draw you back to him. And that must not happen."

"But we're talking about Max, and well, I'm sorry, Victor, but he cannot be as powerful as you say."

"And there's your second problem. You have always underestimated the man. Think, Deirdre. Use your brain for once instead of your heart."

I did as he asked, for once I shut off all the emotional ties I shared with Max and saw him clearly for what he was. I shivered. "Of course, Victor. You're right."

He nodded. "Now you must feed." Taking off his suit jacket and draping it carefully over his left arm, he rolled up the right sleeve of his immaculate white shirt and held his wrist out to me. "You can get more blood this way."

My hands shook as I pulled his wrist to my mouth. The smell of his skin alone intoxicated me, making me feel strong and impervious. And the taste of his blood went straight to my head, straight to my heart, carrying with it the heat of the flames that had disintegrated the seemingly infinite body of Eduard DeRouchard. It was as if I had never tasted blood before this moment, for human blood resembled Victor's blood only in the way water might resemble a fine aged wine. Human blood quenched the thirst but not the passion. Ah, but Victor's blood tasted of endless life and I glimpsed the distant shores of his beginnings, felt him enfold me in silken wings and lift me high to stare at the sun. From this time on, nothing would ever compare to this moment, to this taste. Even as I felt the nourishment heal my weakened body, even as I felt stronger and healthier than ever before, this

shared intimacy filled me with an ecstasy higher
and a despair deeper than any I'd ever experienced,
than any I'd ever want to experience again.

After what seemed like hours, he finally pried
my mouth away from his wrist. I couldn't decide if
it was a blessing or a curse. Perhaps it was both.
But I knew with certainty that I would never feed
like this again. Somehow, I also knew that I'd never
take another drop of blood from any living creature. Victor's blood would be the last.

The sound of my own sobbing drew me back
into Terri's apartment. Victor patted my back and
made little hushing sounds until I stopped crying.

"Feel better?" he asked, crooking that eyebrow
again.

I smiled at him through the last of the tears.
"Yes. Thank you."

"Good. Do you trust me now?"

I gave a rueful chuckle. "Implicitly. But you didn't
have to ask, did you?"

He shrugged. "I like reinforcement as much as
the next creature. Lily knew that instinctively. She's
a good woman, your daughter. And part of the reason I'm here."

"Lily." I grinned. "She's so vibrant, so angry. And
I'm thrilled that I can remember that."

"Your memory shouldn't give you any more trouble. I daresay my blood will neutralize all of the poisons. And it should keep you and the little one
going for quite some time until your system reaches
a balance."

"Little one?"

"You're pregnant, Deirdre. That's why I said
that Max had done what none of us had ever been
able to do. He reversed the vampiric clock with you,

so that even though you aren't quite human and may never be, you are still able to conceive."

"Little one?" The tears started again as I cradled my abdomen, searching for signs of life. "A baby? My baby? Mitch's baby? But Mitch hasn't changed, has he? How is that possible?"

"Remember the blood Sam gave you while you were in Whitby? It contained small amounts of the same poison that you carried. But it didn't have the same effect without the catalyst of Maggie's blood. Plus, Mitch is still relatively young in vampire terms. It's possible that his reproductive organs had not yet stagnated."

I blushed and Victor laughed. "I forget that you are still a product of your times, Deirdre, and I apologize for speaking so bluntly. But it's necessary that you know these things. Now, are you ready to go?"

I glanced at the curtained window, the sun was low in the sky but not close enough to setting to be safe.

"Don't we need to wait until sundown?"

Victor shook his head. "Not if you travel with me. You never even asked how I managed to get here during the day."

"I didn't think about it until now. How *did* you manage it?"

"I move quickly." He laughed and scooped me up in his arms as if I weighed nothing. "Part of the reason we shrivel in sunlight is that we have the expectation that we will." He covered me with his coat. "Now you are safe. And as for me, I'm so old, I've lost all expectations of anything. The world of the living is a constant wonder."

I couldn't even tell that we'd moved when he set

me down on my feet outside a different door. I smiled at him. "Mitch is here?"

Victor nodded, kissed me on the forehead and turned so fast his body became blurred and eventually disappeared halfway down the hallway.

I took a deep breath and knocked at the door.

CHAPTER TWENTY-FIVE

Mitch Greer: New York City

A policeman stopped me before I could get to the front desk to check in. "Sorry, sir, we're not allowing anyone in for a few minutes. We've asked everyone to wait outside."

I glanced over my shoulder. Already the sky was streaked with the oncoming dawn. "I'd much rather wait inside, if you don't mind. I won't get in your way."

"Move along, sir." I heard the impatience grow in his voice, but I stood my ground. I didn't dare wait outside.

At that moment a man in regular clothes walked up to the uniformed officer. They exchanged a few words concerning me and when the man turned to me his face almost immediately widened in a smile of welcome.

"Goddamn it all, Mitchell Greer! You old son of a bitch, you! How the hell are you? When did you get back in town?"

"Just this evening, Marty. And I'd really like to check in."

He nodded to the desk clerk. "He's okay," he said, "this is my former partner. Let him get some sleep, he looks like death warmed over."

"Thanks, Marty," I said, moving over to the desk and getting my key, "it's good to see you too. Give my regards to Barbara."

"Hey," he said, "I'm going up too, I'll ride on the elevator with you. This is a nasty one. Apparently there's some little French wildcat up there throwing a hissy fit. Guy who got stabbed was her boyfriend, I gather, and the other men have been trying to question her. Unfortunately none of us speak French, otherwise, I'd suspect we'd all be learning some new cuss words."

"Ah, fuck." I ran my fingers through my hair, not liking where this conversation was going. "You say she's French?" I asked. "Blond, good looking, about this tall?" I held my hand up to my shoulder. "Name of Vivienne Courbet?"

He nodded. "Damn, you're good, Mitch. How on earth did you know?"

The elevator door opened up and we both got off. "She's a friend of mine," I said, "as is her boyfriend."

"Was."

"What?"

"Her boyfriend," he checked his clipboard, "Dr. John Samuels. He's dead."

"Jesus."

"Yeah. He was pretty badly cut up. Whoever it was got him in vital areas he never even knew he had. I haven't seen that much blood in ages."

"Damn." None of this seemed real to me. How

could Sam be dead? What had happened? "Are you sure he's dead?"

Martin checked his clipboard again. "Yep. Pronounced dead on the scene. I'm sorry, Mitch."

"Me too. More than you know. Sam was a good man. But Vivienne didn't do it."

"To tell you the truth, I didn't think she did. No one could be that upset if they'd done it. But nevertheless, she's an eyewitness and we need to ask her some questions. The murder actually occurred in the adjoining room and there's a crew over there right now. So after we question her and get the whole story, we can close the door and pretty much leave her alone with her grief."

I nodded. "Let me come in with you. That will probably help."

"It certainly can't hurt. Thanks."

I opened the door and was greeted with the crash of a vase hitting the door frame right next to me. Vivienne, covered in blood, and nothing else, was pacing the room, ranting and raving. I didn't understand a word she said.

"Viv," I said, my voice shaking. "Don't throw anything else. It's Mitch."

"Oh." She flung herself across the room and into my arms. "*Mon Dieu*, Mitch, *il est mort.*"

I stroked the top of her head and made comforting sounds. "I know, Viv, I know. What happened?"

"That bitch. That Maggie. She did it. I was taking a shower and heard Sam call out."

"Maggie?" Martin asked.

"Margaret Richards." I said, not taking my attention from Vivienne, but holding her securely in my arms. "Black curly hair, green eyes, very tall, I'd say about six foot. A good-looking woman. And crazy as a loon. Sam brought her with us so that she could get treatment; he was a psychiatrist, you know."

"He's dead, Mitch." Vivienne started to sob hysterically. "I don't know where she got the knife. One minute she was out cold and the next she was slicing him up like a butcher. But I don't want her arrested. No, no, that is too good for her. I want her for myself. I'll tear her miserable Breeder body apart with my bare hands, slowly. I'll tear her goddamned black heart out of her body and cram it down her miserable throat."

"Viv," I said, taking her by the chin and pulling her face up so that I could look into her eyes. "We know you're upset. Can you think of anything else that might help the police find her?"

"Look for a woman matching her description, covered in blood, carrying a butcher knife. I cannot believe she managed to get far, she had enough Valium in her to tranquilize a grizzly bear."

"Or a cow?"

"*Oui*, Mitch, *mon cher.*" She gave a small shaky laugh, "Exactly." Then she started crying again. "What will I do without my Sam? *Mon beau morsel?*"

"I don't know, Viv. We'll all miss him." I turned my head to look at Martin. "Do you need anything else from her?"

"I think I can work with what you've given me." He bowed his head to Vivienne. "Miss Courbet? I'm sorry for your loss."

"*Merci,*" she said softly. "No sorrier than I, I fear."

"No. But still . . ." His voice dropped away and he moved toward the door. "You'll be in town for a while, won't you? In case we need anything else?"

"Yeah," I said. "Thanks."

He shut the door and Viv and I were alone. "Where are the others, Viv? Claude and Chris?"

She sniffed. "They had rooms on different floors, so they may not even know what happened. Perhaps you should call them." She looked down at herself. *"Pardon,"* she said, "I think I need another shower. Lock the door. And"—she glanced around the room nervously—"keep it locked."

I'm not sure how long Vivienne stayed in the shower, but I did know that no one in the surrounding rooms would get any rest. The echoes of her sobbing rang clearly through the running water. Then again, it was daytime by now, so most of the hotel clientele should be out and about. And complaining to the hotel desk about the crying of a woman who just saw her boyfriend stabbed to death seemed too callous, even by tough New York standards.

I did make a call to Chris's room, but there was no answer. I hoped that he hadn't heard about his mother's actions and hoped even more if he had that he hadn't tried to find her or calm her. He'd died in my arms once; two times was more than anyone should have to handle.

Vivienne's crying seemed to subside for a bit, then start up again, fiercer than before. I knew how she felt, but the luxury of tears was not allowed to me. What would we do without Sam? I relied on him, we all did, much more than I ever knew prior to this moment. And I couldn't help but wonder, if somewhere, deep inside him, there hadn't been a guilt reaction that caused him to be less cautious than normal in his treatment of Maggie. At that moment, the phone rang, thankfully pulling me out of that mire of thought.

"Mitch?" Claude's voice was less than steady. "I'm so glad you're there. What's happening? I'm on the floor below you. Earlier I heard screaming and a lot of activity. And now all I hear is water running and a woman crying. Is that Vivienne?"

"Yes." I hesitated, not quite wanting to break the bad news.

"Good lord," he said, "I didn't know she was capable of crying. I don't believe she's ever been sad for more than a few minutes in her entire life. Just the sound of it is enough to break my heart. What the hell happened?"

"Sam is dead."

"How? Why?"

I gave him the reason in a single word. "Maggie."

"Oh. I knew we should have left her behind, kept her locked up in that cage. She couldn't have hurt anyone there. But Sam wanted to help her. And Vivienne . . . well, she knew not to trust Maggie. That's why she brought me along. Some guard I proved to be, huh? I should have been there, maybe I could have done something."

"No, Claude, don't go there. It won't do any good for you to start feeling guilty."

"Yeah, I know. Do you want me to come up? I could make the elevator without too much damage, I guess."

The sound of crying stopped. "No, I think we'll be okay. Get some rest and I'll see that Vivienne does the same."

"And you? When will you rest?"

I sighed. How could I rest? Ever again? "At some point, Claude. Don't worry about me. And lock your door. They've not managed to catch Maggie and she may come back to score a few more."

"Yeah." His voice sounded grim. "But if she screws with me, I suspect she'll find her match." He snickered in his typical self-depreciating way. "She'd need a damn long knife to hit anything vital on me."

Viv came out of the bathroom, wrapped in a short velvet robe, her eyes and her skin glowing bright red. "Vivienne is here now, Claude. I need to go."

He paused. "Yeah. Um, give her my condolences, won't you? And tell her," his voice grew warmer, "tell her that she needn't fear for her own life. I'd do anything in my power to keep her well and safe."

Vivienne held her hand out for the phone. "Claude, *mon petit chou?* You are not to worry, I am safe with Mitch. And we shall find that *chienne foutue,* Maggie, and she will pay with her blood. Sleep well, *mon ami,* with dreams of revenge." She hung up the phone and stood for a while, staring at the bed.

"I have no more tears, Mitch, but I do not think I will be able to sleep without him. Could you stay?"

"Of course," I said, sitting down on the edge of the bed and patting the other side. "Slide in here and I'll keep you safe."

Vivienne slipped out of her robe and under the covers. I lay on the outside of the covers, fully dressed. I didn't dare do anything else. She had always been an entrancing woman and the desire to comfort her and myself, to lose our sorrow in each other was too tempting. And would have been wrong even had my heart and my love not belonged to someone else, most especially wrong when the very air reeked of the odor of Sam's blood. She snuggled up against me and even through the covers and my clothes I could feel the exciting tingle of her naked skin next to mine. I sighed. It was going to be a long day.

Eventually I relaxed and leaned into her, cradling her head against my arm, brushing her fine, soft blond hair away from her face. She whimpered in her sleep and whispered words of despair in a language I couldn't understand. It didn't matter, I knew what she was feeling. I felt it too. "Hush," I said, rocking her gently in my arms, "hush. He will live on in our hearts."

A sad smile crossed her face in sleep and she whispered his name back to me. When she finally lay quietly I knew that she'd fallen into the deep daytime sleep of the vampire. I did not allow myself the luxury, choosing instead to lie on my back and stare at the ceiling, unable to shut off my mind which raced here and there and back again, unearthing unthinkable events and worrying over them like a dog with a bone.

I called to the Wolf from the back of my mind, and he arrived, panting and impatient, tongue lolling with the delight of running. He had no words for sorrow, no need for regret. The remaining hours of the day I spent retreating into his consciousness, if not his shape, and once again ran the wilds of the moors outside Whitby, the Cat by my side.

Sunset came and a soft, tentative knock on the door jolted me back to the present and the hard hotel mattress. I shot out of bed and put a hand on the doorknob, muscles flexed and ready to throttle her should she attempt to enter. And this time I wouldn't let my feelings of pity for her stop me, I would stand strong and do what needed to be done. Taking a deep breath, I poised myself for attack, hesitating only one second to look out the peep hole to ascertain the identity of my prey.

Instead of flinging the door open and lunging, I began to laugh, waking Vivienne from her sleep of the undead. "What is it, *mon gars?*"

My hands fumbled with the lock. I couldn't get the door opened fast enough.

The next thing I knew Deirdre was in my arms again, and I breathed a sigh of relief and joy, kissing her so long and hard it stole my breath away. And hers as well.

She reached up and softly touched my cheek, her eyes welling up with tears. "Hi, honey," she said, softly. "I'm home."

"So I see," I said. "What took you so long?"

CHAPTER TWENTY-SIX

Vivienne squealed with delight and I stood away from Deirdre so that they could greet each other.

"Are you cured?" Vivienne asked. "And how did you get here? The sun is just now setting. Were you here in the hotel all along?"

"Victor brought me here," she said, "and yes, I'm cured. Or at least I've been given my memories back. Apparently the poisons have some far-reaching effects. But we don't need to speak of that now. Where's Sam? And Claude and Chris and all the rest of them. I have some news."

"Sit down, love," I said. She looked so fragile, so pale, seeming to have lost some of her spark. *No wonder*, I thought, *she's been through a lot. As we all have.* I stole a glance at Vivienne and caught a glimpse of my face in the mirror. To say which of us looked worse would be difficult. She gave me a questioning look. "Sit down," I said again, "we have news, too. And I think we'd better tell ours first."

Deirdre's eyes darted from me to Viv and back again to me. Biting her lower lip, she pulled one of the upholstered chairs out from under the desk and sat down. "Fine," she said. "I'm sitting. Now what's wrong?"

"Sam is dead."

"Oh." I wouldn't have thought it possible but her face turned even paler. She reached over and took Vivienne's hand and held it up to her face where her tears had started to flow. "Viv, I'm so very sorry. What happened?"

"Maggie got him." For the first time since I met her, Vivienne's face no longer looked youthful and innocent. Sam's death had changed her, aged her. Would she ever laugh again? I didn't know for sure, but knew the world would be a darker place if it were true.

"What was Maggie doing here? Why didn't you leave her back in Whitby? In fact, why aren't you all back there?"

I smiled at her. "It's a long story, love. But I'll make it short. The night you disappeared, Maggie left Whitby, taking Chris with her. We had to follow. She killed the other two dogs and threatened to do the same to him. I had no choice."

"Of course," she said. "I wasn't threatened. Not physically anyway. You made the right decision."

I continued with the rest of the story, up until my arrival at the Ballroom of Romance when she interrupted me with an excited exclamation.

"Then that was you, at the door, demanding to talk to Max?"

"Yeah."

She shook her head and gave a little smile. "If only I'd known. Derek didn't say who it was, just that it was someone Max would need to deal with himself. While you were arguing with Max, I slipped out the back door. If I'd known it was you, I'd have stayed around." A strange, haunted look crossed her face. "Or perhaps I would not have. Max brought you in earlier that evening, to address my delusions and you didn't claim me."

"It wasn't me, Deirdre, I swear it wasn't."

"I know that now, but at the time the evidence seemed overwhelming."

"Oh, love, I'm sorry . . ."

"Forget it, Mitch. I want to hear the rest of your story."

"There's not much more to tell. I searched the streets all night, going to places we used to go to, looking for you. I knew you'd been in that room off of Max's office."

She chuckled. "You may have passed me, actually. But you wouldn't have known me, I was disguised." She bowed her head for a minute and when she picked her face back up, it wasn't her. And yet, as I looked into her eyes, her heart and soul were staring back at me.

"Deirdre, I'd have known you regardless."

She shrugged and the false facial features seemed to slide off of her. "Maybe. I tried very hard not to be noticeable. But that doesn't matter. When you didn't find me, what did you do?"

"What could I do? I came back here almost at dawn. That's when I found out about Sam."

"She stabbed him, *ma soeur*, in so many places and so deep that it would make the hardest person weep in sorrow." Viv's voice sounded brittle. "He died instantly, I believe. But, God forgive me, I tried to bring him back. I ripped open my wrist with my nails and tried to force the blood down his throat. I called his name. I pleaded and begged for him to return. But he was gone and could not swallow my blood, could not hear my voice. Sam. Dead. How can this be? I still cannot believe."

Tears streamed down Deirdre's face again and she put her hands up to her eyes to hide them. Vivienne got up from where she sat on the bed and knelt in front of her, grasping her hands. "Don't cry, *ma soeur,* Sam always used to say there was nothing that made him feel more uncomfortable than a woman's tears." Viv drew in a short, sharp breath. "*Mon Dieu,* Deirdre. Your tears. They are clear. Sam was right." She sniffled. "If only he were here to know that."

Deirdre calmed with Vivienne's attentions. "What did Sam say? How is he right?"

"He said that you were changing, that you were no longer a vampire, nor a human. And he said something else." Viv smiled then, a sad vestige of her former mischievous grins, but a true smile anyway. "And he also said that you were with child. Is it true? Will you make this old tired monster kneeling in front of you an auntie?"

"Victor says so."

"Ah," Vivienne said, "then it must be true. And some good will come of this after all."

"Deirdre?" I'd stood back and let Vivienne comfort her, thinking that it would be good for both of them. I'd even thought about slipping out of the room and allow them to really talk. But this news was too wonderful to walk away from. "Is it true? Are you pregnant?"

She turned to me and smiled. "It seems so, Mitch. Are you happy?"

"Happy? Bloody hell, Deirdre, how could I not be happy? If it's a boy, we'll name him John Samuel Greer. What do you think, Viv?"

"Sam would have liked that, Mitch. But," Viv waved a hand at me, "I know that it cannot possibly be a boy. Lily and I have already decided it must be a girl."

I laughed. "Viv, who must be obeyed, has spoken."

"For now, though," Deirdre said, "I think that's enough talk about the baby. It will be what it will be. Right now we've got more important things to worry about. Maggie's in custody, right?"

I shook my head.

"No one caught her? She walked out of here with a bloody knife the size of a machete and no one stopped her?"

Vivienne flinched and I threw Deirdre a warning glance. "There wasn't time, *ma cher*," Viv said, "She was gone and I was tending to Sam."

"Yes, of course. I'm sorry, Vivienne, I didn't mean to imply you had done something wrong. I know you loved Sam, you must've gone crazy at first. I think I can assume where she went: she went to find Max. Or Steven. She got her orders from him on the phone. But why kill Sam, I wonder? Max would want to keep Sam alive, I'd think, just in case something went wrong with his little potions."

"Potions?" I asked. Deirdre surprised me with her take-charge attitude. She really had changed. What had he done to her?

"He gave me something to drink," she continued, almost as if in answer to my question. "A hideous concoction. But it calmed me, kept the memories submerged and made me more docile." She laughed bitterly, "I quit taking it after three or four days. But I still doubt he ordered Maggie to kill him. I'd think, rather, that his orders were to kill you, my love. You were the one who stood most in his way."

"But," I reminded her, "Sam stood in *her* way. She had to know that as long as he was alive, he would keep her sedated."

"Ah," she said, "of course."

I thought for a minute. "I don't think, though, that Maggie would run to Max. He terrified her, especially since she failed to kill me the first time she tried. My guess is that she's hiding out somewhere, biding her time, waiting to kill me or all of us. Then she can return to Max."

"Sounds very likely. So her time is limited. He'll kill her either way, but I doubt she knows that. Max doesn't like loose ends. We could just let him clean up his own problem."

"No," Viv stood up. "I want her. I will make her pay for what she did to Sam."

"Then what do we do?"

"To be honest, Deirdre, I don't have a bloody clue. Too much has happened, I can't even think straight right now."

Vivienne looked at me. "You did not sleep, did you, Mitch? How long do you think you can continue this?" Turning to Deirdre, she continued. "The man hasn't had a decent day or night's sleep since you disappeared. I will call Claude to come up and pass some time with me. You two should go to your room. Immediately." She smiled at both of us. "You've been away for too long."

Deirdre nodded, a shy smile lighting her face. "If you're sure you'll be okay, Vivienne, that's a good suggestion. I could use some sleep myself."

"Go," she waved her hands at us. "Do not worry about me, *mon amis*. I need some time alone anyway. Perhaps I will take a walk."

"Whatever you do, Viv," I reached over and ruffled her hair, "be safe. And be good."

She let out an exasperated breath. "Oh, foo, Mitch. I am always the former and never the latter. But if it makes you feel better"—she picked up the phone—"I will get Claude to accompany me."

"Perfect," I said, gave her a kiss on the cheek, and took Deirdre's arm.

We heard her making arrangements with Claude as we headed out the door. Deirdre hugged my arm to her. "We do have a room, don't we?"

I pulled the key out of my pocket. "Indeed we do, Mrs. Greer, although I've not been there yet." I looked at the number on the key envelope, consulted the room number sign on the wall and compared the nearby numbers. "It must be around the corner here." We turned to the right to follow the corridor and I looked at the room numbers again. "Yeah, and then all the way at the end of the hall."

"You spent the day with Vivienne?"

"Yes. Are you jealous?" I know that I would have been had our situations been reversed and Deirdre had spent the day with Sam, comforting him. I scowled at the thought.

"No, Mitch, I'm grateful that you were there to offer her some sort of comfort. I can't even begin to imagine what she must be feeling."

We nearly reached our room when we heard an angry screech from the direction we'd come. "Damn," I pushed the key into Deirdre's hands. "I'll go see what's wrong. You stay here."

"The hell I will. We'll go together or not at all."

We rushed back to Vivienne's room in time to see Maggie make a vicious swipe at Claude, who stood blocking Vivienne from harm. Blood spurted out of the slash, staining his white shirt and spilling over onto the floor. He didn't blink an eye, instead he laughed. "You'll have to do better than that,

Maggie." His huge hand encircled her wrist, forcing her to drop the knife and cry out in pain. I thought I heard the crack of breaking bones as Claude spun her around and held both of her arms behind her back with one hand. His other arm snaked around her neck. "Not so tough now, are you?" He said, then craned his head around to talk to Viv. "Get Sam's bag, will you? He must have something in there we can use to restrain her. And hurry. I feel sort of funny."

"No need for that," Victor's voice echoed from the doorway and Maggie winced. "She'll come along with me without a fight, won't you, Maggie."

She whimpered slightly but nodded. "Yes, Victor. You have to protect me. They all want to kill me. Even Steven wants to kill me. But I had no choice, you know that, don't you?"

Victor reached over and took her head in his hands. "Poor girl," he said, his voice surprisingly gentle, "I know what your choices have been as well as you. I will find a place where you can be alone and safe, where you won't harm yourself or others. Maybe we can salvage the girl you used to be."

"But Victor," Vivienne began to say, "she killed—"

"Don't overstep your bounds, Vivienne." His voice changed, the gentleness replaced by cold steel. "Direct your revenge at me, or not at all."

She took a step forward, stared up into his eyes, and backed away.

"Good," he said. "You've done the right thing. Anyone else care to dispute my claim on this woman? Mitch? Deirdre? Claude?"

I wanted to challenge him, not because I wanted to kill Maggie myself, that was the furthest thing from my mind. I wanted to take him on simply because of his superior attitude, because of his arrogant nature. And I wanted to test my powers against his. I had for years. I wanted to see if I could win. Almost stepping forward, I felt Deirdre's soft hand on my arm. The heat of her skin and the glow in her eyes changed my mind. Let Victor take care of Maggie if he could; I had better things to do.

CHAPTER
TWENTY-SEVEN

Deirdre Griffin: New York City

I held my breath, not believing that Mitch actually intended to challenge Victor. There was a time when I might have supported him in this effort; the qualities that annoyed Mitch about Victor had also annoyed me. But the blood I had taken from him gave me a deeper understanding of the man and what he was capable of. Placing a hand on Mitch's arm, I looked into his eyes and sighed my relief as I felt the tension slowly pass out of his body.

"Good," Victor said again. "Claude, are you all right?"

"Yeah, I think so." Claude pulled his hand away from his chest, unbuttoned what was left of his shredded shirt, and studied the wound. "It seems to be healing up just fine, thanks."

Victor placed a hand on Maggie's forehead. "Was there poison on the knife, Maggie?"

She shook her head and answered him with a whispered "No."

"Then sleep now," he passed his hand over her eyes and her body drooped. Victor picked her up as he had picked me up the previous evening. "I'll be back as soon as I can." He glared at Mitch. "Under no circumstances are you to play the hero and confront Max without me. Or it will be your funeral." He nodded to me and to Vivienne and walked out the door, carrying Maggie as if she were a sleeping child. To him, I suppose, she was. As were we all.

"Well," Vivienne said, with a trace of her former vivaciousness, "Victor has certainly changed from the doddering old man we saw last time he came around."

I laughed. "Did you ever think that he was that senile?"

She gave a little toss of her head. "I never thought it at all. I think perhaps he would be horrified to know how little he is able to trick us."

"Oh, I don't know," I said, "he seems to be doing just fine."

Claude gave a rumbling chuckle. "You all forget that I was set the chore of watching him, back in the Cadre days. I knew there was nothing wrong with him then, but never saw the need to mention it to anyone else."

Mitch nodded. "And with that, I think Deirdre and I will try to get to our room. Maybe we'll actually make it this time."

Vivienne looked away from us, thinking, I knew, of Sam. "And I think I shall still have that walk. Do you feel up to coming with me, Claude?"

"Absolutely." He reminded me of Moe at that

minute, eager and happy to go with his mistress. Mitch winked at me and mouthed the words, "I'll tell you about it later."

Claude, however, was oblivious to our exchange and I smiled. Yes, he was exactly like Moe. "Just let me stop by my room and change my clothes," he said to Vivienne. "I'll meet you in the lobby."

The three of us exited the room, with Claude going on his way toward the elevators and Mitch and I heading to our room. When we stopped at the door, Mitch ran the key through the electronic lock and held the door open for me. He laughed, "I was beginning to doubt this room even existed."

He moved the Do Not Disturb sign from the inside doorknob to the outer one. Then he locked the door and the deadbolt and turned to me where I stood.

"God, Deirdre, do you have any idea of how much I missed you?"

I smiled and reached a hand up to stroke his cheek. "About as much as I missed you."

"Damn straight. Now"—he picked me up and carried me over to the bed—"let's get reacquainted."

He lay me down on the bed and was starting to kiss me when the phone rang.

"Damn it," he said, picking it up. "What the hell do you want?"

"Dad?" I could hear Chris's voice clearly. "What's going on?"

Mitch sighed and ran his fingers through his hair—a gesture I remembered and loved. "Oh, Chris, I'm sorry. I didn't mean to yell at you. But it's been a horrendous day. Sam is dead, Chris."

"Dead? How?"

He hesitated. "I don't exactly know how to tell

you this. There's really no way to soften it. Your mother killed him."

"Mum?"

"Yes."

There was a long pause. "Mum killed Sam?"

"Yes."

"Oh, God. What happened? Where is she? Is she under arrest?"

"No," Mitch said. "Victor has her."

"Victor has her? What the hell business is it of his? I'd rather she were in jail."

I reached my hand out for the phone. "Chris?"

"Deirdre? You're back?"

I gave a sad laugh. "Yes. As your father said, it's been quite a day. But as for Victor, he's keeping her safe from herself and from any of us wishing to seek revenge."

"But why would he do that?"

"He told me Eduard was his brother. I'm not sure he meant it literally. Then again, I'm not entirely sure he didn't. One can never tell with Victor. In any event, she's safe and the rest of us are all right. Shaken and sad, but all right."

"Thanks." He paused. "I'm glad you're back."

"As am I, Chris. Did you want to talk to Mitch again?"

"No, tell him I'll catch up with him later. You two probably have better things to do."

I hung up the phone. "He says he'll talk to you later. Now I believe you said something about getting reacquainted?"

"I did indeed."

We made love, frantic at first, as if we were starved for the taste and feel of each other. Although in actual physical time we'd hardly been separated for that long, emotionally it felt as if we'd been apart for centuries. I feared at first that perhaps my changed nature would detract from the experience, but instead it was as if my senses were newborn. Each touch, each kiss, each sound he made as he loved me with his whole being was intensified, until they culminated in a thundering climax, one which seemed to encompass and surpass at the same time all of our previous lovemaking. As if this were our first time together and our only time together. I etched each and every sensation on my soul and my heart.

When we had finished, we lay as if glued together, panting and satiated, but each of us still striving to touch the other. And when we could speak again, we rolled apart but kept our hands joined. We talked for the rest of the night and spoke of our future together and the future of our child.

Mitch fell asleep shortly before dawn. I lay for a while next to him, listening to the rhythm of his breathing, put a hand on his chest to feel the steady beating of his heart. He slept soundly and didn't notice that I kissed his lips softly and got out of bed. I picked up my discarded clothes from the floor and dressed. "And now," I whispered to myself, as I quietly opened the door and shut it behind me, "now I will see if what Sam and Victor believed is actually true."

The night shift front desk clerk was filling in the day shift person on the recent hotel events when I got off the elevator in the lobby. "Earlier this evening, we had another scare from the same floor, but it turned out to be nothing. Watch out for the woman in 701, though, she's the one who lost her boyfriend yesterday. Miss Courbet is her name and she's quite distraught. As you might expect. Other than that," the clerk smiled at his replacement, "it was a fairly uneventful night."

"Yeah, right. You know damn well that's the most excitement you've ever had in your life."

"True," he said, and finally noticed me where I was standing in front of the counter. "Can I help you?"

"I'm sorry to bother you, but could you possibly tell me what time sunrise is?"

"Not a bother, ma'am. Give me just a second." He turned to his computer, called up the information and glanced back to me. "About fifteen minutes according to the weather site. And it's going to be a beautiful day, sunny and clear, if a little on the cold side."

"Thank you so much," I said and moved through the revolving doors to the street outside. The sky was tinged with the oncoming dawn and I felt the instinctive warnings of danger from deep within. But I didn't care, it had been so long since I'd felt the sun on my upturned face, and the aching had plagued me for most of my life. To satiate that desire, I'd risk a burn. Or even death.

I looked up and down the street until I found a building facing east with a wide entrance and a set of steps leading up to it. I settled in there, huddled against the railing, wishing I'd brought one of the coats Max bought me, watching the darkness of the night sky lighten.

Everything around me grew quiet, almost as if the city itself waited in as much anticipation as I for this moment. For it, however, dawn was an ordinary occurrence. For me it was at once both profound and fateful, a test of my very being.

My heart beat wildly, my palms felt sweaty. I hadn't

realized that I'd been holding my breath until the breath rushed out of me in a exhalation of surprise. The very first rays of the sun appeared, far away, behind layers and layers of buildings. By human standards this sunrise was nothing special, nothing like it would have been in the cabin in Maine where I imagined the sun would burst through the trees like a sudden flash of golden fire. But to me, it was a revelation. "Oh," I whispered, "I'd forgotten how beautiful the sun is."

The noise of the city rose up around me, but I paid it no attention. Instead, I got up from my perch on the stairs and stepped down to the sidewalk, my arms outstretched and my face turned up to catch the first rays. I closed my eyes and spun around, feeling the sun's warmth hit different parts of my face and body.

"Beautiful," I whispered again. "Just beautiful."

"Yes, it's quite something, isn't it?"

My eyes snapped open and I turned around. Victor slouched in a corner between the door and the entrance arch, not totally in the sun, but not avoiding it either.

I nodded. "Yes. It is. Quite something." I walked up a few steps and sat back down again, my back to the railing and my knees drawn up to my chest. "I'd forgotten."

"Yes, we all do. So that the first reappearance is one of life's special moments. And now, Deirdre, you are no longer a vampire. I don't know what your life expectancy will be, but I suspect it will be longer than a normal human life span. The vampiric elements of the blood that made you into that creature of the night have burrowed deep within your tissues and muscles, carrying the natural immunities of the vampire. You'll heal faster than a human, but not at the astonishing rate you once did. You should be immune still to normal human diseases. But you will also age. And you will eventually grow old and die."

As I sat there, drinking in his words on my new life, I felt the movement of the baby in my womb, only a gentle kick, a quiet reminder of its presence. Laughing out loud, I pressed my hands to my abdomen to feel again that small stirring of life. "And my baby? What will it be?"

Victor shook his head. "As for that, Deirdre, I have no idea. As I told you, you are something different. And your offspring? Well," he quirked his eyebrow, "your guess is as good as mine. Probably better."

I sat quietly for a while and wiped away a few tears. "It's frightening."

He laughed. "Of course it is. It's a new life. Now you have some difficult choices to make, while you are still dancing on the edge of that life. It is still possible for you to return to the vampiric ways right now, simply by drinking from any of your friends, or from your husband. I'm guessing that you'd have better than a fifty percent chance of surviving such an encounter. The baby, on the other hand, would die. Or rather, it would cease to age and live forever as an unborn fetus. You wouldn't give birth, you'd simply carry it with you throughout your years."

I shivered. "That's horrible."

He nodded. "It need not even be a deliberate taking of blood. One night during an especially impassioned lovemaking, you could accidently graze Mitch with your teeth. It would only take a drop to turn you back. And to kill your baby."

"But I'd be careful. I wouldn't want to do anything to jeopardize the baby. And I certainly wouldn't want to go back to what I was."

"Right now, of course, you wouldn't. Being closer to human, being free of the ties of your vampiric nature—oh, yes, no doubt it all seems very exciting right now. But what happens when you notice that your hair is turning gray, when you see those first wrinkles around your eyes, when you can no longer rise in the morning without pain in your legs or your back? When your lifelong partner ages not one day and people begin to mistake him for your son rather than your husband? And then your grandson? That the two of you love each other, I have no doubt now. But twenty years from now will it be the same? How about in forty years? Will you constantly regret the choice you made to see the sun rise one morning in New York City, growing more bitter with every passing year?"

I stared at him for a minute, then put my hands over my eyes.

"I'm sorry to say this to you, Deirdre, but you have a decision to make. And you need to make it soon, before you forget what I've told you."

I uncovered my face. "What is that decision, Victor?"

"To leave Mitch, to walk away from the vampire life you've led and go back to human ways."

"I can't leave Mitch."

"Not even for the sake of your baby?"

"Damn it, Victor, this isn't fair."

"No, it is not fair, Deirdre. But it's the way it is. Sam's funeral is scheduled for tomorrow morning. It makes an excellent excuse for you to be away from all of them."

"But where would I go?" I asked in a small voice I barely recognized as mine.

"I've had your cabin in Maine rebuilt. You were comfortable there, happy there. You even have a friend still living close by."

"Elly."

"Yes."

"I'll think about it, Victor. But that's all I can promise."

"That's all I ask. For your sake and for the sake of the baby."

I sighed and closed my eyes, raising my face again to pull in the warmth of the sun. When I turned back to where he'd stood, he was gone.

"Damn it, Victor," I said again as I got up and walked back to the hotel. "You're still pulling the strings, aren't you?"

CHAPTER
TWENTY-EIGHT

Mitch still slept when I crept back into the room. I sat in a chair next to the bed and watched him, thinking about what Victor had said. I didn't want to believe that what he said was true, that the decision facing me now involved my leaving the one person I'd ever completely loved for the sake of a child I never in my wildest dreams ever conceived would exist. On the other hand, I had not even a single reason to believe that Victor would lie to me. There was no sense in it, for one thing; removing me from the society of vampires would garner him nothing. Therefore, I had no choice but to believe that he offered this advice for my benefit and the benefit of the baby.

"But I don't want to go, my love," I said softly. "I thought we would spend eternity together."

Mitch rolled over and felt for me on the other side of the bed. "Deirdre?" he mumbled. "Where are you?"

"I'm here, Mitch. Sleep."

His mouth curved in a smile and my heart fell.
Victor had to be wrong.

Just then there was a soft knock at the door. Mitch
stirred, but didn't wake. I got up and opened the
door quietly. Chris stood there.

"Deirdre? You really are back! Is Dad sleeping?"

"Yes," I said, "he's exhausted. It's been a hard
time for all of us."

"Yeah," he said, not meeting my eyes. "I'm really
sorry about Sam."

"Yes, we will all miss him. Vivienne especially."

Chris shook his head. "Somehow I can't help but
feel partly responsible. I knew how bad she'd gotten, but I didn't ask for help from anyone. Instead
I just ran away."

"Do you want to talk about this?" I asked. "We
could go for a walk or something. I really don't
want to disturb Mitch."

"A walk? How can you . . ."

"I'll explain everything," I said, scribbling a note
for Mitch on the hotel message pad by the phone.
"But not in here."

We left the room and rode on the elevator. "It's
supposed to be a nice day out," I said with a smile.
"The sunrise was gorgeous."

"Then it's true? You've become human again?"

I gave a short laugh. "I'm not sure anyone knows
exactly what I am. At the very least it's been proven
that I can walk in the daylight again. It's probably
best to avoid labeling the phenomenon, at least
for now."

We exited the elevator and walked through the
lobby. "Have you had breakfast yet?" he asked, standing out of the way to allow me to go through the
revolving door first, then joining me on the street.
"Or can't you eat breakfast?"

"I have no idea, Chris. But coffee is always good."

"Coffee it is, then. And I might have a donut or something. I'm always hungry."

"Yes, I knew that about you. As Chris, anyway. Phoenix was a bit different. Do you remember much of all of that?"

"Some of it I remember clearly. The rest is pretty much a blur. And you? I take it your memory has been completely restored."

"So far so good," I said. We passed a small diner with tables outside. "Shall we stop here?"

"And sit outside? Isn't it a bit cold for that?"

"Is it? I was just thinking how wonderful it was to sit in the morning sun again."

Chris nodded. "Of course. Here is fine."

We sat outside for a while, until a man cracked open the door and called to us. "Outdoor tables are closed for the winter, folks, but there's plenty of room inside."

"See, Deirdre"—Chris said, getting up and holding the diner door open for me—"no one else cares at all about the sunshine."

"Silly people," I said.

I ordered coffee, Chris ordered a full breakfast. The smell of the food made me feel hungry and sick at the same time and the coffee, when it came, tasted odd. When the waiter brought Chris's breakfast, I asked for a glass of ice water and sipped it slowly while he devoured eggs, sausage, hash browns, and a double order of wheat toast.

"So," he said when he'd scraped the last of the egg yolk from the plate with the last piece of toast, "how are you feeling? Really?"

"I don't want to talk about me, Chris. Didn't you want to talk about your mother?"

"What's to say? She's a murderer and Victor's

taken her away. I would have liked to say good-bye, at least."

"It's better this way, Chris. Vivienne wanted to kill her, but he stepped in and intervened on Maggie's behalf. Victor will take good care of her."

"But Victor's senile. Isn't he?"

"No, Chris, not at all. And for what it's worth, I trust his promise to keep her safe. He knows what he's doing." I grew quiet, not much liking the place these thoughts were taking me. I didn't want Victor to be right.

"Well, I'd feel better if I knew where she was, you know? But if you say it's okay, I guess I'll not worry about it. I'm glad Vivienne didn't hurt her, at least. And maybe time away from all of this is exactly what Mum needs."

"I'll be seeing Victor tomorrow at Sam's funeral," I said, dreading the words, since it meant I was one step closer to the decision I didn't want to make. "I'll ask him if you can visit Maggie or something."

"Thanks." He paused, looking nervous. "Deirdre?"

"Yes?"

"Do you think Dad might consider becoming human again? I mean now that you are, it would make things a lot easier, wouldn't it? Otherwise, I just can't imagine you'd be able to handle it all after a while. It's not natural."

Would Mitch undergo the transformation process? If I asked him to, most likely. But did he really want to be human again? His vampiric instincts were dead on, his sheer delight in being able to transform shapes readily apparent. He loved being what he was. How could I take that away from him?

No, Victor was right. Staying was too much of a danger, for me, for the baby, and for Mitch. Separated, we'd be lonely for a while and my heart would always ache for him, but no one would need to deny their basic nature to please the other.

I sighed and wiped away a tear. "I'm not sure it's possible for him to change, Chris. Or that he'd want to. Why don't we just wait and see."

"And what happens to me?" He gestured at himself, "Inside I might be a full-grown man, but to the outside world, I'm still only twelve years old. I can't make it on my own."

"I don't believe anyone would dream of asking you to do that. You can always stay with Mitch and me, of course."

"Legally, though, I'm not even a blood relation. If my father was really Victor's brother, that makes him my uncle."

"I suppose it does. But I'm sure he won't mind if you stay with Mitch."

"Yeah, I guess not." He nodded and put some money on the table to pay the bill. "You look tired, Deirdre. Let me take you back to the hotel."

When I opened the door to the hotel room, Mitch propped himself up on one elbow and peered at me sleepily. "Were you out?"

"Yes, Chris and I had coffee."

"Ah, that's nice. What time is it?"

"It's early, Mitch, my love. Why don't you go back to sleep?"

"Don't mind if I do," he said, patting the side of the bed. "Join me?"

"I thought you'd never ask." I crawled in and snuggled up next to him.

"Mmmmmmm. You're so nice and warm, must've been the coffee."

Within seconds he slept again. I drifted in and

out of a light sleep, but mostly I just lay there next to him, breathing in his scent, enjoying the touch of his naked skin against mine. I considered waking him up so that we could make love one last time, but feared I would not be able to hide my intentions from him. Best that he didn't know. Victor could explain it to him and he'd see eventually that it was the right decision.

The baby moved inside me again, a stronger kick this time. I stroked my abdomen and smiled, laughing to myself about Vivienne's insistence that it was a girl. As for me, I wished for a boy, with Mitch's features and build.

With that thought, I fell into a deeper sleep and dreamt of Max. He was holding my hand, sitting with me in the maternity ward of the hospital as the baby was being born. He accepted the newborn wrapped in a blanket and laid it in my arms, kissing me on the forehead. "You know, Deirdre, this moment is only possible because of me. Everything you've ever wanted and you have only me to thank."

I woke shortly before sundown with the angry ringing of the phone.

I reached over and picked it up. "Hello?"

"It's time," Victor's voice sounded steady and calm. "Meet me in the lobby. I've called the rest of them. I wish they'd had the foresight to bring Lily along, but I think we'll manage without her."

Victor hung up without giving me a chance to respond. "Mitch?"

He sat up immediately and smiled at me. "Thank you."

"For what?"

"That was the best day's sleep I've had in over three years. And it was all because you were here. Safe and lying next to me."

"Victor wants us to meet him in the lobby as soon as possible."

"Good. It's about time we dealt with Hunter."

I shook my head. "I don't know, Mitch. What has he done to us?"

"What do you mean? He drugged you and kidnapped you, poisoned you and tried to brainwash you. And he's been sending Other assassins to kill us for years."

"Are we dead?"

He laughed. "Of course not. But think of all the heartache he's caused."

I shook my head. "Last time I checked there wasn't a law against being a bastard. None of us are dead, and as for all the manipulating he did of me, well, if not for that I'd not have what I have right now."

"And what is that?"

"A new life. A new beginning. And our child."

"Sam's dead, have you forgotten that? Maggie ripped him to shreds at his encouragement."

"No, he sent Maggie to kill you. And you are still alive. That Sam died is a tragedy, but laying that blame on Max is stretching it a bit."

Mitch pulled on his jeans and a black T-shirt. "I see your point, Deirdre. I don't want to see your point, but I can. Damn it. It would have been much better to just kick his ass. You can't convince me that he shouldn't be crushed. I'm sure he's committed enough atrocities in his lives to justify it."

"But, Mitch, there's no evidence, no proof of anything recent. No dead bodies, nothing but an attempt to hold me against my will. And I escaped."

"He might try it again."

I smiled sadly. "Yes, he might. Think back, my love, to when we met. Would you have arrested him then for his crimes?"

"Damn straight. Whose side are you on anyway, Deirdre? Maybe he really has brainwashed you."

"I don't think so, Mitch. I'm just not sure killing him will do any good. After all, it didn't work before."

"Good point, sweetheart. Let's just wait and see what happens, okay?"

"Fine. But remember what Victor said to you last night. There's no need for you to be a hero; I'd like to keep my white knight intact and alive. I'm going to go downstairs and talk to Victor now. I'll see you at sundown."

"Deirdre? Wait. You can't go down now. The sun is still up."

"And?"

"And well, you can't go."

I kissed him full on the lips. "I saw the sun rise this morning, Mitch. I have nothing to fear."

CHAPTER
TWENTY-NINE

Victor was lounging on one of the sofas in the lobby when I got off the elevator. He wore a different suit than he'd had on yesterday, a blue pinstripe with not one speck of visible lint. His shirt was perfectly pressed, bleached snowy white, and not one hair on his head was out of place. As always I felt slovenly in his presence, this time with good cause, since I was still wearing the flannel shirt and jeans I'd left the Ballroom in.

"Deirdre. You look lovely."

"Don't, Victor. It's not true and we both know it. But I seem to have lost everything I own somewhere along the way."

He laughed. "Yes, as have you all. We will see what we can do about that tonight. But I didn't mean your clothing. I meant you. For the first time since I've known you, you finally seem content and at peace. Have you thought about what you're going to do?"

"I'll take your advice, Victor."

He nodded. "Good. I've made all the necessary

arrangements for your trip. I'll hand it all over to
you tomorrow at Sam's funeral."

"There's one other thing."

"What's that?"

"It's Max. Mitch is thinking that we're going
over there to kill him. I'm sure the others are as
well. But I don't know . . ."

"You don't want revenge, Deirdre?"

"I had my revenge, Victor, when he died the first
time. I'm not sure he deserves to live, but I don't
want to be involved again in his death."

Victor smiled at me. "How human of you, Deirdre.
But you may put your mind to rest. I merely wish
to confront Max. My demands are simple. He is to
return things to the way they were before Eduard
DeRouchard took control. And he is to disband
the Others, and their arcane secrets are to be buried
and forgotten. That obscenity has gone on long
enough. If he refuses to meet my wishes, then he
will be held and tried by a council of my choosing."

I laughed. "He will agree, of course. And then
attempt to do what he wants anyway."

"Possibly. But he will also know that we will be
watching him. And that might keep him in line,
for a while, anyway. Eternal life is boring, my dear,
without conflict to keep it interesting."

The sun had set outside while we talked and the
elevator door opened. Mitch and the rest walked
toward us. "I'll take boring, Victor," I said softly.

He laughed. "I believe you, Deirdre. However, I
doubt that your life will ever be boring. I suppose
time will tell."

"So," Mitch said as he approached Victor, "what's
the plan?"

"We talk and negotiate. There will be no killing

unless it is initiated by Max. We are already too
few."

Mitch looked surprised. "Then why do we all
need to be there?"

"So that he knows we're serious."

"That is all well and good, Victor," Vivienne
said, "but what about Sam? He's dead because of
Max."

"If Max admits that he ordered Maggie to kill
Sam, then I will change my position. Otherwise,
Vivienne, Sam's death was an accident. Tragic and
senseless, yes, but an accident nonetheless. Anyone
who cannot accommodate my wishes in this matter need not come along."

Victor had hired a limousine for the night and
the ride to the Ballroom was remarkably silent.
Vivienne seemed to be sulking in her corner of the
car with Claude watching her every move. Once
again the similarity between him and Moe struck me
and I smiled at him from where Mitch and I sat,
holding hands. Victor stared out the window at the
city streets and seemed bored with the entire ex-
pedition.

The club hadn't opened yet when we arrived
but Victor tipped the doorman a hundred dollar
bill and he let us in. Vivienne looked around her
with a pouting expression. "He did put everything
back the way it was. It is too gauche for words."

Mitch put an arm around my waist. "I don't care
what Victor says. If Hunter touches you, even in
greeting, I'll kill the bastard."

"I will stay away from him, Mitch. Believe me,
I've no desire to see the man ever again." My statement seemed to placate him, but he kept his hold
on me.

We trouped down the hallway and Max came out

to greet us. "Welcome," he said, ushering us into his office. "And to what honor should I attribute such a visit?"

"We need to talk, old friend." Victor extended his hand and Max shook it.

"Looks more like a lynch party to me, Victor. How could it be otherwise with Greer in on it? But still, I'm thrilled to see you all. Vivienne, you're as enchanting as always." He took her hand and tried to kiss it. She pulled away from him quickly and his eyes gleamed. "And you"—he said, turning to the one person in our party he didn't know—"you must be Claude. I have heard about you. All good, of course." Then he moved in my direction. Mitch stepped forward with a snarl. "And of course, here is Deirdre. No party is complete without her and her own personal watchdog." His eyes were cold when he looked on me and I felt a chill climb up my spine. I might be willing to forgive and forget, but I feared that was something Max would never do. The good feeling I'd had toward him after my dream of this afternoon faded away into nothing and suddenly I was deathly afraid.

"Max." I nodded my head and said nothing else.

Obviously, he'd been expecting us, for in the place of the black leather couch, there stood a small conference table, with chairs gathered around it. "Sit," he said with a crooked smile. "We'll have some wine and we'll talk."

"No wine, Max." Victor said, motioning for us all to sit around the table. "This is hardly a social visit."

"Of course," he said, sitting down next to Vivienne. "But I am happy to see you all regardless." I heard the door to his office click shut and lock. "Deirdre and Mitch have met Derek, I know, but perhaps the rest of you haven't. I thought I might need a second pair of eyes and ears in the room."

I turned slightly in my chair to see Derek. He looked uncomfortable, but alert, standing at the door with his arms crossed, his gaze fastened on Max as if awaiting a signal. The side of his face sported a bruise from his chin to the corner of his eye. The message was clear: anyone leaving the room would have to get by him.

"Threats won't help you, Max. We only want to talk."

"So I heard, Victor. Talk then. Or read me my rights and take me away. If you can."

"There's no need for that," Victor continued. "Our demands are simple. Return all Cadre holdings. And disband the Other organization."

"And in return what do I get?"

"You get to live," Mitch growled at him from across the table.

"I've managed to live centuries without your permission, Greer, and I intend to keep doing so. You have your wife back, no harm, no foul. I barely laid a hand on her. To be honest, she's hardly worth the trouble she caused me."

Mitch pushed his chair back and rose halfway out of his seat, but I put a hand on his arm. "Don't," I said, "please, he's the one who's not worth it."

"Listen to her, Greer. Use your brain for once instead of your right hook."

Max looked to Victor. "I won't meet your demands, old man. I'm sitting on top of the world right now, so why would I give up any of it? Would you? Accept the fact that the power has moved out of your hands and into mine. You knew it would happen sooner or later. Bow out now while you still can." Max's voice rose ominously, echoing off the walls. "The only reason you all aren't still being hunted down like animals is because I ordered the killings to stop. It's certainly easy enough to countermand that order. All it takes is a nod in the right direction."

No, I thought wildly, *this is not the way it should go. He was supposed to give it all up.* I shot a concerned look at Victor, he sat at the table, studying his fingernails. When he felt my glance, he lay both of his hands flat on the table.

"Return the Cadre holdings," he said, "and disband the Others organization."

"I'll ask it again, Victor. Or what?"

"Or you will be held in custody until I can choose a council to render judgment. I could remind you that you were dangerously close to a similar judgment when Deirdre took matters into her own hands. I don't want to see that happen again."

"And I," Max laughed, "certainly wasn't looking forward to it then either. Why would I chose it now?"

"Because it is your only option."

"The hell it is." Something glimmered around Max as he stood up at the table and nodded to Derek. "I think the negotiations are over."

Victor stood, but before he could make a move, Max grabbed Vivienne by the waist and pulled her into the force field that was generating around him. "You forget, Victor. I had two teachers, you and Eduard. So I have twice the power."

"And none of the brains, Max. Let her go. You can't hurt her."

"Are you sure about that, Victor? I learned a few tips from Dr. Samuels's research that might surprise you. Pity that Maggie killed him too soon."

Max looked down at Vivienne with scorn. "I wasn't quite done with him."

She bared her teeth at him. He tightened his grip on her neck and reached into his pocket, producing a small vial of liquid. "One drop of this and our lovely little French whore here will shrivel away into nothing."

At that moment, Claude lunged up from the table to free Vivienne, accidently connecting with Derek, who apparently had been slowly moving toward us while our attention was riveted on Max. Claude's glancing blow hurled Derek across the room. He hit the wall groaning to the accompaniment of cracking bones.

"Let her go," Claude bellowed, "or by God, you'll die, you dirty son of a bitch." He reached into his coat and I caught a glimpse of a leather holster as he pulled out a revolver. "I can shoot you through her, if you like. She'll heal. Will you?"

Max looked up at Claude, an amused expression on his face. "I know now why you seem so familiar. You remind me of a dog I once killed."

Claude gave a laugh that was almost a growl. "Not a dog, Max. Never a dog." He tossed the gun to Mitch. "Cover him, and if he even attempts to open that bottle blow his brains out." He turned to Victor. "I'm sorry," Claude said, his voice growing deeper with each word, "I've never been good at following orders. You of all people should remember that."

Instantly the space where Claude had been standing was occupied by a huge bear, wearing the tattered remains of human clothing. He moved in on Max and Vivienne and enveloped them both in his enormous front paws. It looked almost as if the three of them were dancing and I suppressed the nervous urge to laugh. Then Max gave a horrible scream of pain and I heard the tearing of cloth and flesh. Claude moved away, gently holding Vivienne in paws coated with strips of flesh, gore and muscle.

Max looked down in fascination at his shirt front and the red stain that was slowly growing. A trickle of blood dripped from his mouth and he fell to the floor.

I turned away, holding my hand over my mouth, sickened by the bloody remains. The room was silent except for the soft moans coming from Derek.

Claude moved back into human form, his hands still coated with Max's blood. Stark naked, he looked enormous, ashamed and embarrassed. I ran to the room that had been my prison and returned with the spread from the bed and wrapped it around him. He gave me a grateful smile. "Thanks," he whispered. Then he turned to Vivienne. "Are you okay?"

She came over to him and gave him a hug. "I am fine, Claude. *Merci.* You did very well. I told you the animal form would come to you if you were patient enough."

"Or angry enough." He looked at Victor. "You might as well convene that council for me, Victor. I won't fight you."

"I hope not. But I don't think that will be necessary." He bent over Max where he lay on the floor. "He's not dead."

"What?"

Victor slipped out of his immaculate jacket and wrapped it around the gaping wounds on Max's back. "He's not dead. Did you think it would be that easy?"

Max groaned in agony and Victor clicked his tongue. "You should have taken the deal I offered you, Max. You will be a long time healing from this."

"What do we do with him then," Mitch asked, "if we can't kill him?"

"We've got the perfect place to incarcerate him. I'll take him to New Orleans when this is all over. For now, though, I still have some connections with the New York Police Department. They can hold him for me until it's time to go. He'll be too weakened to try to escape. For a few days, at least."

Victor heaved Max up off the floor and half-carried, half-dragged him to the door, pausing only a minute to lean over Derek on his way out. "I won't hold you responsible, young man. But see that you report to me as soon as your bones heal. You have a lot to learn."

CHAPTER THIRTY

All five of us ended up in Vivienne's room until dawn. Victor returned after a while and ordered a few bottles of wine from room service.

"Max isn't dead, Victor," I said, "but he might as well be, once you close the door to that tank. What's next? Will he stay in there forever?"

Victor sighed. "I don't know, Deirdre. I don't fully understand what happened to him. None of you would know it, but I saw great things in him when I chose him for the life. Unfortunately, the combination of eternal life and abnormal power does strange things to a man or a vampire." He made no attempt to hide the tears in his eyes. "It may not be true," he continued, with a nod at me, "but I choose to believe that he would have been content with death had Eduard not played God and given him rebirth. It may be that death really was what he wanted. I'm almost sorry I couldn't give it to him."

After that, none of us could say another word.

Dawn was approaching anyway and they all needed to seek shelter from the sun's rays. "Deirdre and I will be attending Sam's funeral tomorrow," Victor said to Mitch as we walked to the door, "so if she is not there when you wake up, do not worry. She'll be safe. And Deirdre? I took the liberty of sending more appropriate clothes to your room. It wouldn't do to have you appear at the grave site in jeans."

"Thank you, Victor." On impulse I gave him a hug. "I wish it had ended differently and that he'd taken your offer," I whispered to him. "I really wanted to believe that Max was not entirely evil."

He patted my cheek. "I know you did. And I love you for that, child. I'll be waiting for you outside in the limousine when you're ready. Take your time."

I showered and dressed while Mitch lay in bed, half-asleep. The dress Victor sent fit me perfectly and he'd even sent shoes, a purse, and a coat, along with makeup and a pearl necklace and earrings. "He thought of everything," I said to Mitch.

"Yeah. I'm sorry you have to do this alone, love. I wish I could be there, but . . ."

"I know, Mitch. And Sam would have understood. I'll make your good-byes for you." I leaned over the bed and kissed him.

"Hurry back," he said, giving me a playful slap on my backside.

"I'll try, Mitch. Until then, know that I love you."

"And I love you."

I almost relented and stayed, but as I straightened up, I felt the baby give me a kick. The vision Victor had planted in my head remained, haunting my thoughts with the horrifying idea of carrying an unborn child for all eternity. And if all it took was one drop of blood from Mitch? I shivered. *No,* I thought, *I can't allow that to happen.* The child deserved to live as normal a life as I could provide. No matter how much it tore me to pieces, how much my heart protested, there was really no other choice for me. And certainly no other acceptable choice for the child I carried. I had to leave.

I smiled to myself as I softly closed the door behind me, remembering something Mitch had once said. "Just because I know it's true, doesn't mean I have to like it."

Sam's funeral lasted over an hour, culminating in prayers at the grave side. Victor pulled me aside and handed me a folder of papers and a suitcase. "Here are your plane tickets," he said, "a key to the new cabin, and the clothes that you'd left behind at Max's place." He paused a bit and I shared the pain he felt. Max may not have been dead, but the life that spread before him was almost too hideous to contemplate. Death might have been kinder, but death would never claim Max.

Victor nodded. "Yes, death would have been kinder." Then he reached over and took my hand. "I've arranged to have someone pick you up at the airport and take you home."

"Are you sure I have to do this, Victor?"

"Trust me, Deirdre. It's for the best. I will explain it all to Mitch, I'm quite sure he'll understand."

I gave a sharp bitter laugh. "And I'm quite sure he won't. How could he? But thank you for everything you've done. I know you're only trying to protect me and the child. Will I see you again?"

"Absolutely, my dear."

"Give my love to Lily. I understand she's waiting for you to return to New Orleans. Keep her away from Max and keep her safe."

"I promise. She will be fine; I guarantee that. They will all be fine with time. Now go, and quickly, before you change your mind."

Victor had reserved me a window seat. Flying in the daylight proved to be a much more exciting experience than any of the night flights I'd ever taken. I sat glued to my seat, unable to take my eyes away from the window, totally enthralled with the view—the earth below when it was visible was breathtaking; to be able to see houses and fields and cars amazed me. When we flew high enough to get above the clouds, I gave a short exclamation of surprise at the pure clear blue depth of the sky and the seeming weight of the clouds piled up beneath. The man next to me smiled. "First flight?"

"You might say that. It's wonderful."

He shrugged, "I travel so much now I tend to forget how impressive it can be. Enjoy the flight." He turned back to his laptop calculator for the rest of the flight, apparently without giving me a second thought.

I laughed to myself. Ordinarily, he'd have been enthralled with me, my vampiric nature would call out to him and I would appear beautiful and exotic in his eyes. As for me, I would have been eyeing his skin and his blood, made hungry by his scent, tempted by his physical closeness and the clearly visible pulse of the veins in his neck. I'd wonder if there might be a way I could feed on him without being observed. And now? Now I was nothing more than a seat mate, a curiosity only. It would take me some time to become accustomed to being merely human, to get used to the fact that from now on, I'd have to get by on my own without relying on the charms I used to possess. Life was going to be interesting.

Elly waited for me at the airport, waving as I walked past the security gate. She smiled at me and held out her arms, holding me close. The scent of lavender and rosemary surrounded her like a cloud.

"How've you been?" she asked, looking me up and down. "You look different than I remember; there's a certain hunger your eyes used to hold that's gone now. And that's good, I guess." We started walking to the luggage claim area. "I had quite an interesting talk with the man who came to make arrangements to rebuild your house."

"Victor?"

"Yes, Victor Lange. He is, well, in a word, amazing. Is it true?"

"Is what true?"

We stood at the carousel now, waiting for the baggage to arrive and she pulled me away from the crowd so that we could talk in private. "That you are no longer a vampire? And that you are pregnant?"

"Ah. That. Yes, it's all true."

"Like I said. Amazing. Now, tell me. How do you feel?"

"Tired mostly. And a little bit nauseated." I did not wish to discuss the other emotions that flowed through me. The guilt and the sorrow of leaving were still too fresh for words. I brushed away a tear impatiently and Elly looked away from me.

"Well, then," she said, her voice seeming overly cheerful, "let's get your bag and get you home."

We settled into a routine, Elly and I. During the day she would show me her garden and explain the uses of the different plants. We would work in her kitchen, canning and preserving the food she grew. When the weather permitted, we would hike in the nearby woods. I had known the surrounding forest quite well as the Cat, but experiencing them as a human made it all seem new. Some days she would drive me into town in her run-down vehicle to see the doctor, for supplies, or for just a hot cup of coffee (decaffeinated for me) or tea at the diner. Since I still could not digest solid food, I subsisted entirely on dietary supplemental drinks. However, the smell of food no longer made me feel sick and I hoped that soon I could expand my diet.

In short, my days passed quickly but the nights were long and lonely and filled with dreams and nightmares of my former life. Of Max. Of Mitch.

Vivienne stopped to visit one night in the early spring, bearing a bottle of rich red wine. I declined to drink with her for the health of the baby but my refusal did nothing to dampen her spirits. She babbled for a bit about how she'd taken back the Ballroom of Romance and turned it into Dangerous Crossing Redux. *"Ma cher,* you wouldn't believe that no one calls it that, instead it's become Ducks." She giggled. "Imagine the swan owning a club called Ducks. It boggles the mind. Humans are very odd indeed."

"Are we?"

"Ah, I did not mean you. You can never be completely human." She grinned, a wicked smile that brought out her dimples. "You don't smell right, for one thing."

I laughed. "I suppose that's nice to know." I hesitated, wanting to ask the question that had haunted me since my departure. "How is, er, everyone doing? Do you hear much from Lily? Or Victor?"

Vivienne gave me a shrewd look, not fooled by my pause. "Everyone is fine. They miss you, of course. Chris is staying in New Orleans with Victor and Lily. They've all moved to a larger house."

"Why is Chris staying with them? I'd have thought he'd stay with Mitch."

"Victor, apparently, was designated as Chris's next of kin and legal guardian. Apparently his admission that Eduard was his brother was true. Unfortunately, I haven't heard any more of that story; he's still as close-lipped as he ever was. Lily is talking about making a visit to see the baby when it is born. Which reminds me"—she reached over and put her hand on my extended abdomen—"how is the little one doing?"

Her skin felt cold and the baby moved under her hand. She jumped in surprise, then pressed harder, and the baby kicked back. Vivienne giggled with delight. "See, the *petit chou* knows that her Auntie Viv is here. Do you know if it is a girl or a boy yet?"

"I had an ultrasound," I said, "and the doctor could have told me then, but I didn't want to spoil the surprise."

"You didn't want to know?"

I shook my head. "No. It doesn't seem important to me right now. A healthy baby will be miracle enough."

"*Oui.* I understand."

She finished the bottle of wine and the two of us

sat in front of the fire for a while, not speaking, until she reached over and took my hand. "I had a long talk with Victor. And I understand why you are here and how hard it must have been for you. I know how it feels to be apart from the one you love. That it was your choice may perhaps make it much worse."

"Are you doing all right?"

"All right?"

"Without Sam?"

"To be honest, Deirdre, as each day goes by, I miss him more. And yet I can live with the pain." She laughed, a sorrowful sound, deeper than her normal metallic high-pitched giggle. "I do not allow myself to think about it. For me, that works adequately. I was never much of a thinker."

"Ah. I'm sorry I mentioned it."

She gave a little flip of her hand. "It is what it is. We move forward, we have no choice in the matter. As you yourself know."

"Yes."

And still I couldn't ask about him. I didn't dare even say his name, the ache was too sharp.

Eventually, she got up from the chair. "Well, I must go, *ma cher*, before the dawn catches me napping."

"You could stay, Vivienne. We could make the loft safe from sunlight for you."

"Thank you for the offer, but no. I have a hotel room in town and Derek is waiting for me there. I thought it best not to bring him along on this visit."

"Derek? From the Ballroom of Romance? That Derek?"

"Victor has given him over to me for training," Vivienne said. "Max did a poor job of it."

"And I am not able to."

"You? Why would you be involved?"

"He's mine, isn't he? Max said that he was."

She laughed. "Max? Pah, he is hardly one to believe. Besides, if Derek were yours, you would have known it instantly. Rest easy, Derek is my responsibility now. And I will rule him with an iron hand."

"Or," I said with a smile, "a velvet glove."

Vivienne giggled. *"Oui.* Whatever it takes."

We sat again in silence. Finally she rose from her chair, came over to me and hugged me, kissing both cheeks in the process. "I am glad to see you are doing so well, sister. I wish . . ." Her voice trailed off.

"What do you wish, Viv? That things could go back to the way they were? I am alone, but content. Don't pity me."

She laughed. "No, that is not what I was going to say. I can feel your satisfaction with the life you have chosen, it shows on your face. I was, if you will pardon me for saying it, thinking that Mitch does not look as good as you do. It is, apparently, a difficult adjustment for him." She shot me a sideways glance and I could have sworn she smiled, for a split second. As if she had a secret she wanted to share.

"And?"

"And nothing. Just that he is not having an easy time. I thought you should know. *Bon soir,* Deirdre."

When Viv left, I felt lonelier than I had before. And her statement that Mitch found the adjustment to life without me difficult haunted my thoughts night and day. I, too, wished that it could be differ-

ent, that he would eventually find some happiness
for himself. I loved him too much to wish anything
else.

The days grew longer and the spring turned into
summer. After tending my own garden, I would
often sit on the steps of my front porch, my eyes
closed and my face upturned to the sun. As always
when I did this, a sad smile would cross my face
and I would drift away in thought to a time when
this little luxury would have been a death sentence.
And I knew, as the baby moved inside me, that I
had made the right choice.

"You might at least have said good-bye." I heard
Mitch's voice saying the same words I'd heard over
and over again. I didn't open my eyes, knowing that
I would be disappointed as I always had been when
I could hear him reproaching me, in the back of
my mind. He wasn't real.

"If I had, Mitch, I wouldn't have left."

"Bloody hell, Deirdre, it was a stupid thing to
do."

He'd never argued with me before in my mind,
nor did he swear. My eyes shot open and Mitch
stood in front of me. Smiling. The late afternoon
sun reflected against his gray hair.

"Mitch!"

"You'd damn well better not have been expecting anyone else."

I smiled, and struggled to my feet, embarrassed
and aware of the grace that I'd lost with the growth
of the child. He held out a hand, I took it and he
pulled me into a hard embrace.

I pushed away from him. "You shouldn't be here,"

I said, "Victor says that even one drop of your blood could stop the baby from growing, from being born. We don't want that to happen."

"Maybe," Mitch smiled, "Victor changed his mind."

"Did he?"

"No." He stopped for a minute, just smiling at me. Then he started to laugh. "Damn it, woman, have all of your powers of observation gone away?"

"No, I don't think so."

"Think again. Deirdre, my love, what time is it?"

I squinted up at the sun. "Probably around four or so. Why?" Even as I said it, I realized the significance. "You changed, Mitch? For me."

"Of course I did. Victor explained why you'd left and I understood. I wasn't happy about it, but there wasn't much to do. I wouldn't have wanted to jeopardize the baby either. Then one night, as the sun was setting, it hit me. I had a hard time finding Victor and had a hard time convincing him I wanted to take the poison. Poison, he called it, as if it wasn't the answer to my every prayer. It wasn't easy and I almost died, but I'm here and I'm as human as I'll ever manage to be. When it was all over and done with, I realized that Victor had planned it this way."

Mitch laughed and ran his fingers through his hair. "The old bastard knew both of us well enough to understand that the decision had to be one that each of us made without help or input. Any other way, and the two of us would torture ourselves for the rest of our lives over the assumed sacrifice of the other. But I still can't forgive the days and nights I waited for a word from you. So help me, Deirdre, if you ever run away from me again, I'll track you down and keep you prisoner."

I laughed and kissed him. "Since the night we met, I've always been your prisoner, Mitch. Come inside and I'll show you the new cabin."

EPILOGUE

"Do you miss it, Mitch?" The baby had awakened me in the middle of the night and I found him gone from our bed. When I had her changed and cleaned, I carried her down the stairs to the rocking chair in front of the fire. She nestled into me and began suckling and I kissed the top of her head. I said the words quietly so as not to startle her, poor little defenseless thing.

Mitch had been standing in front of the cabin's picture window when we came down the stairs, staring at the night sky. He turned and the light from the dying fire caught in his eyes, making them glow as they once did, before. "Miss it?" His voice was steady and firm. "Not really, no. But sometimes on nights like tonight, with the sky clear and the moon full, I feel the Wolf again. I miss him. And the Cat."

I smiled. "Yes, I never thought I would say it, but I miss the Cat, as well. And then there are times when all that has happened feels so far away, so distant, like a dream. All of the years and sorrows and deaths don't seem to matter much, not when compared to the smell of a clean baby and the touch of sunlight on my face."

"I'm going to make some coffee," he said. "I'm on morning shift at the station this week. No sense going back to sleep now."

The baby finished nursing and drowsed in my arms. I followed Mitch to the kitchen and sat down with her at the table, patting her back gently.

Mitch poured two mugs of coffee, added sugar and cream to his, and set mine in front of me. "How's that tooth coming in?"

"Fine. But it's sharp."

He laughed at me. "What else would you expect?"

When he went upstairs to put his uniform on, I trailed after him, lay the baby in her crib, and sat down on the bed.

"What's on the agenda today?" he asked, fastening his tie and settling his hat on his head.

"Elly's taking us into town for a doctor's appointment. And then I'm cooking you something special for dinner."

"Oh? What?"

"Fettuccine Alfredo."

"And life is good," he said, giving me a kiss on the top of the head. "See you tonight."

I watched him from the window, driving down the dirt road under the rising sun.

"So, after everything," I whispered to the baby, "life is good." I pulled a blanket over her, softly touching her cheek while she slept and dreamed. "And never forget, little one, life goes on."

Scare Up One of These
Pinnacle Horrors

BOOK YOUR PLACE ON OUR WEBSITE AND MAKE THE READING CONNECTION!

We've created a customized website just for our very special readers, where you can get the inside scoop on everything that's going on with Zebra, Pinnacle and Kensington books.

When you come online, you'll have the exciting opportunity to:

- View covers of upcoming books

- Read sample chapters

- Learn about our future publishing schedule (listed by publication month *and author*)

- Find out when your favorite authors will be visiting a city near you

- Search for and order backlist books from our online catalog

- Check out author bios and background information

- Send e-mail to your favorite authors

- Meet the Kensington staff online

- Join us in weekly chats with authors, readers and other guests

- Get writing guidelines

- AND MUCH MORE!

Visit our website at
http://www.kensingtonbooks.com